W9-BNS-129

THE
BURGLAR
WHO PAINTED LIKE
MONDRIAN

LAWRENCE BLOCK

THE
BURGLAR
WHO PAINTED LIKE
MONDRIAN

A BERNIE RHODENBARR MYSTERY

WHEELER
PUBLISHING, INC.
ROCKLAND, MA

★ AN AMERICAN COMPANY ★

Published in Large Print by arrangement with Dutton, an imprint of Dutton NAL, a member of Penguin Putnam Inc., in the United States and Canada.

Wheeler Large Print Book Series.

Set in 16 pt Plantin.

Library of Congress Cataloging-in-Publication Data

Block, Lawrence.
    The burglar who painted like Mondrian: a Bernie Rhodenbarr mystery / Lawrence Block.
        p. (large print) cm.(Wheeler large print book series)
    ISBN 1-56895-726-2 (hardcover)
    1. Rhodenbarr, Bernie (Fictitious character)—Fiction. 2. Thieves—New York (State)—New York—Fiction. 3. Detective and mystery stories. gsafd. 4. Large type books. I. Title. II. Series
[PS3552.L63B864 1999]
813'.54—dc21

99-022151
CIP

This is for
Lynne Wood
with special thanks to
Michael Trossman
who taught me how to prepare the canvas
and
Laurence Anne Coe
who helped me assemble the frame

ONE

IT WAS A SLOW day at Barnegat Books, but then most of them are. Antiquarian booksellers, after all, do not dream of retiring to the slow and simple life. They are already leading it.

This particular day had two high points, and as luck would have it they both came at once. A woman read me a poem and a man tried to sell me a book. The poem was "Smith, of the Third Oregon, Dies," by Mary Carolyn Davies, and the woman who read it was a slender and fresh-faced creature with large long-lashed brown eyes and a way of cocking her head that she must have learned from a feathered friend. Her hands—small and well formed, unringed fingers, unpolished nails—held a copy of Ms. Davies' first book, *Drums in Our Street*, which the Macmillan Company had seen fit to publish in 1918. And she read to me.

> "*Autumn in Oregon—I'll never see*
> *Those hills again, a blur of blue and rain*
> *Across the old Willamette. I'll not stir*
> *A pheasant as I walk, and hear it whirr*
> *Above my head, an indolent, trusting*
> * thing....*"

1

I'm rather an indolent, trusting thing myself, but all the same I cast a cold eye on the Philosophy & Religion section, where my most recent visitor had stationed himself. He was a hulking sort, late twenties or early thirties, wearing low Frye boots and button-fly Levi's and a brown wide-wale corduroy jacket over a darker brown flannel shirt. Horn-rimmed glasses. Leather elbow patches on the jacket. A beard that had been carefully trimmed. A headful of lank brown hair that had not.

"When all this silly dream is finished here,
The fellows will go home to where there fall
Rose petals over every street, and all
The year is like a friendly festival...."

Something made me keep my eyes on him. Perhaps it was an air about him, a sense that he might at any moment commence slouching toward Bethlehem. Maybe it was just his attaché case. At Brentano's and the Strand you have to check bags and briefcases, but my customers are allowed to keep them at hand, and sometimes their carryalls are heavier upon departure than arrival. The second-hand book trade is precarious at best and one hates to see one's stock walk out the door like that.

"But I shall never watch those hedges drip
Color, not see the tall spar of a ship
In our old harbor.—They say that I am
  dying,

*Perhaps that's why it all comes back
  again:
Autumn in Oregon and pheasants
  flying—"*

She let out a small appreciative sigh and closed the little book with a snap, then passed it to me and asked its price. I consulted the penciled notation on its flyleaf and the tax table that's taped to my counter. The last hike boosted the sales tax to 8¼ percent, and there are people who can figure out that sort of thing in their heads, but they probably can't pick locks. God gives us all different talents and we do what we can with them.

"Twelve dollars," I announced, "plus ninety-nine cents tax." She put a ten and three singles on the counter, and I put her book in a paper bag, fastened it with a bit of Scotch tape, and gave her a penny. Our hands touched for an instant when she took the coin from me, and there was a bit of a charge in the contact. Nothing overpowering, nothing to knock one off one's feet, but it was there, and she cocked her head and our eyes met for an instant. The author of a Regency romance would note that a silent understanding passed between us, but that's nonsense. All that passed between us was a penny.

My other customer was examining a buckram-bound quarto volume by Matthew Gilligan, S. J. *The Catogrammatic vs. the Syncogrammatic*, it was called, or was it the other way around? I'd had the book ever since

3

old Mr. Litzauer sold me the store, and if I'd never dusted the shelves it would never have been picked up at all. If this chap was going to steal something, I thought, let him hook that one.

But he returned Father Gilligan to his shelf even as Mary Carolyn Davies went out the door with my demure little poetry lover. I watched her until she crossed my threshold—she was wearing a suit and matching beret in plum or cranberry or whatever they're calling it this year, and it was a good color for her—and then I watched him as he approached my counter and rested one hand on it.

His expression, insofar as the beard showed it, was guarded. He asked me if I bought books, and his voice sounded rusty, as if he didn't get too many chances to use it.

I allowed that I did, if they were books I thought I could sell. He propped his attaché case on the counter, worked its clasps, and opened it to reveal a single large volume, which he took up and presented to me. *Lepidopterae* was its title, François Duchardin was its author, and Old World butterflies and moths were its subject matter, discussed exhaustively (I can only presume) in its French text and illustrated spectacularly upon its color plates.

"The frontispiece is missing," he told me, as I paged through the book. "The other fifty-three plates are intact."

I nodded, my eyes on a page of swallowtail butterflies. When I was a boy I used to pursue such creatures with a homemade net, killing them in a mason jar, then spreading their wings and pinning them in cigar boxes. I must have had a reason for such curious behavior, but I can't begin to imagine what it might have been.

"Print dealers break these up," he said, "but this is such a desirable volume and in such good condition I thought it really ought to go to an antiquarian book dealer."

I nodded again, this time looking at moths. One was a cecropia. That and the luna are the only moths I know by name. I used to know others.

I closed the book, asked him what he wanted for it.

"A hundred dollars," he said. "That's less than two dollars a plate. A print dealer would charge five or ten a plate, and he'd get that easily from decorators."

"Could be," I said. I ran my finger over the book's top edge, where a rectangle enclosed the stamped words *New York Public Library*. I opened the book again, looking for a *Withdrawn* stamp. Libraries do divest themselves of books, just as museums deaccession some of their holdings, though Duchardin's *Lepidopterae* hardly seemed a candidate for such treatment.

"Those overdue charges can mount up," I said sympathetically, "but they have these amnesty days now and then when you can return overdue books with no penalty. It seems unfair to those of us who pay our fines without protest, but I suppose it does get books back in circulation, and that's the important thing, isn't it?" I closed the book again, set it deliberately into his open attaché case. "I don't buy library books," I said.

"Somebody else will."

"I don't doubt it."

"I know one dealer who has his own *Withdrawn* stamp."

"I know a carpenter who drives screws with a hammer," I said. "There are tricks to every trade."

"This book didn't even circulate. It sat in a locked case in the reference section, available by special request only, and because of its value they found ways to avoid letting people have access to it. The library's supposed to serve the public, but they think they're a museum; they keep their best books *away* from people."

"It doesn't seem to have worked."

"How's that?"

"They couldn't keep this one away from you."

He grinned suddenly, showing clean if misaligned teeth. "I can get anything out of there," he said. "Anything."

"Really."

"You name a book and I'll lift it. I'll tell you, I could bring you one of the stone lions if the price was right."

"We're a little crowded around here just now."

He tapped *Lepidopterae*. "Sure you can't use this? I could probably ease up a little on the price."

"I don't do much volume in natural history. But that's beside the point. I honestly don't buy library books."

"That's a shame. It's the only kind I deal in."

"A specialist."

He nodded. "I'd never take anything from a dealer, an independent businessman struggling to make ends meet. And I'd never steal from a collector. But libraries—" He set his shoulders, and a muscle worked in his chest. "I was a graduate student for a long time," he said. "When I wasn't asleep I was in a library. Public libraries, university libraries. I spent ten months in London and never got out of the British Museum. I have a special relationship with libraries. A love-hate relationship, I guess you'd call it."

"I see."

He closed his attaché case, fastened its clasps. "They've got two Gutenberg Bibles in the library of the British Museum. If you ever read that one of them disappeared, you'll know who got it."

"Well," I said, "whatever you do, don't bring it here."

A couple of hours later I was sipping Perrier at the Bum Rap and telling Carolyn Kaiser all about it. "All I could think of," I said, "was that it looked like a job for Hal Johnson."

"Who?"

"Hal Johnson. An ex-cop now employed by the library to chase down overdue books."

"They've got an ex-cop doing that?"

"Not in real life," I said. "Hal Johnson's a character in a series of short stories by James Holding. He goes off on the trail of an overdue book and winds up involved in a more serious crime."

"Which I suppose he solves."

"Well, sure. He's no dope. I'll tell you, that book brought back memories. I used to collect butterflies when I was a kid."

"You told me."

"And sometimes we would find cocoons. I saw a picture of a cecropia moth and it reminded me. There were pussy willow bushes near the school I went to, and cecropia moths used to attach their cocoons to the branches. We would find the cocoons and put them in jars and try to let them hatch out."

"What happened?"

"Generally nothing. I don't think any of my cocoons ever hatched. Not every caterpillar gets to be a moth."

"Not every frog gets to be a prince, either."

"Isn't that the truth."

Carolyn finished her martini and caught the waitress's eye for a refill. I still had plenty of Perrier. We were in the Bum Rap, a comfortably tacky gin joint at the corner of East Eleventh Street and Broadway, which made it just half a block from both Barnegat Books and the Poodle Factory, where Carolyn earns her living washing dogs. While her trade provides relatively little in the way of ego gratification, it's more socially useful than looting libraries.

8

"Perrier," Carolyn said.

"I like Perrier."

"All it is, Bernie, is designer water. That's all."

"I guess."

"Got a busy night planned?"

"I'll go out for a run," I said, "and then I may bounce around a bit."

She started to say something but checked herself when the waitress approached with the fresh martini. The waitress was a dark-roots blonde in tight jeans and a hot-pink blouse, and Carolyn's eyes followed her back to the bar. "Not bad," she said.

"I thought you were in love."

"With the waitress?"

"With the tax planner."

"Oh, Alison."

"The last I heard," I said, "you were planning a tax together."

"I'm planning attacks and she's planning defenses. I went out with her last night. We went over to Jan Wallman's on Cornelia Street and ate some kind of fish with some kind of sauce on it."

"It must have been a memorable meal."

"Well, I've got a rotten mind for details. We drank a lot of white wine and listened to Stephen Pender sing one romantic ballad after another, and then we went back to my place and settled in with some Drambuie and WNCN on the radio. She admired my Chagall and petted my cats. One of them, anyway. Archie sat on her lap and purred. Ubi wasn't having any."

"What went wrong?"

"Well, see, she's a political and economic lesbian."

"What's that?"

"She believes it's politically essential to avoid sexual relations with men as part of her commitment to feminism, and all her career interaction is with women, but she doesn't sleep with women because she's not physically ready for that yet."

"What does that leave? Chickens?"

"What it leaves is me climbing the walls. I kept plying her with booze and putting the moves on her, and all I got for my trouble was nowhere fast."

"It's good she doesn't go out with men. They'd probably try to exploit her sexually."

"Yeah, men are rotten that way. She had a bad marriage and she's pretty steamed at men because of it. And she's stuck with her ex-husband's name because she's established professionally under it, and it's an easy name, too, Warren. Her own name is Armenian, which would be more useful if she were selling rugs instead of planning taxes. She doesn't exactly plan taxes, Congress plans taxes. I guess she plans avoiding them."

"I plan to avoid them myself."

"Me too. If she weren't so great looking I'd avoid her and say the hell with it, but I think I'll give it one more try. *Then* I'll say the hell with it."

"You're seeing her tonight?"

She shook her head. "Tonight I'll hit the bars.

A couple of drinks, a couple of laughs, and maybe I'll get lucky. It's been known to happen."

"Be careful."

She looked at me. "*You* be careful," she said.

A couple of subway trains whisked me home, where I changed to nylon shorts and running shoes and ducked out for a quick half hour in Riverside Park. It was mid September, with the New York Marathon a little over a month away, and the park was thick with runners. Some of them were of my stripe, the casual sort who knocked off three or four sluggish miles three or four times a week. Others were in marathon training, grinding out fifty or sixty or seventy miles a week, and for them it was Serious Business.

It was thus for Wally Hemphill, but he was following a program of alternate short and long runs, and the night's agenda called for four miles so we wound up keeping each other company. Wallace Riley Hemphill was a recently divorced lawyer in his early thirties who didn't look old enough to have been married in the first place. He'd grown up somewhere in eastern Long Island and was now living on Columbus Avenue and dating models and actresses and (*puff puff*) training for the Marathon. He had his own one-man practice with an office in the West Thirties, and as we ran he talked about a woman who'd asked him to represent her in a divorce action.

"And I went ahead and drew up papers," he

told me, "and it developed that this dizzy bitch wasn't married in the first place. She wasn't even living with anybody, didn't even have a boyfriend. But she has a history of this. Every once in a while something snaps inside her and she finds an attorney and institutes divorce proceedings."

I told him about my book thief who specialized in libraries. He was shocked. "Stealing from libraries? You mean there are people who would do that?"

"There are people to steal anything," I said. "From anyplace."

"Some world," he said.

I finished my run, stretched some, walked on home to my apartment building at the corner of Seventy-first and West End. I stripped and showered and did a little more stretching, and then I stretched out and closed my eyes for a while.

And got up and looked up two telephone numbers and dialed them in turn. No one answered my first call. My second was answered after two or three rings, and I chatted briefly with the person who answered it. Then I tried the first number again and let it ring an even dozen times. A dozen rings comes to one minute, but when you're calling it seems longer than that, and when someone else is calling and you let the phone go unanswered, it seems like an hour and a half.

So far so good.

I had to decide between the brown suit and the blue suit, and I wound up choosing the blue.

I almost always do, and at this rate the brown'll still be in good shape when its lapels come back into style again. I wore a blue oxford button-down shirt and selected a striped tie which would probably have indicated to an Englishman that I'd been cashiered from a good regiment. To an American it would be no more than a mark of sincerity and fiscal integrity. I got the knot right on the first try and chose to regard that as a favorable omen.

Navy socks. Scotch-grained black loafers, less comfortable than running shoes but rather more conventional. And comfy enough once I'd slipped in my custom-made orthotic arch supports.

I took up my attaché case, a slimmer and more stylish affair than my book thief's, covered with beige Ultrasuede and glowing with burnished brass fittings. I filled its several compartments with the tools of my trade—a pair of rubber gloves with their palms cut out, a ring of cunning steel implements, a roll of adhesive tape, a pencil-beam flashlight, a glass cutter, a flat strip of celluloid and another of spring steel, and, oh, a bit of this and a little of that. Were I to be lawfully seized and searched, the contents of that case would earn me an upstate vacation as a guest of the governor.

My stomach did a little buck-and-wing at the thought, and I was glad I'd skipped dinner. And yet, even as I was recoiling at the idea of stone walls and iron bars, there was a familiar tingle in my fingertips and a racy edge to the blood in my veins. Lord, let me outgrow such childish responses—but, uh, not yet, if you please.

I added a lined yellow legal pad to the attaché case and outfitted my inside breast pocket with a couple of pens and pencils and a slim leather-bound notebook. My outside breast pocket already held a hankie, which I took out, refolded, and tucked back into place.

A phone rang as I walked down the hall to the elevator. It may have been mine. I let it ring. Downstairs, my doorman eyed me with grudging respect. A cab pulled up even as I was lifting a hand to summon it.

I gave the balding driver an address on Fifth Avenue between Seventy-sixth and Seventy-seventh. He took the Sixty-fifth Street transverse across Central Park, and while he talked about baseball and Arab terrorists I watched other runners stepping out the miles. They were at play while I was on my way to work, and how frivolous their pastime seemed to me now.

I stopped the cab a half block from my destination, paid and tipped and got out and walked. I crossed Fifth Avenue and mingled with the crowd at the bus stop, letting myself have a good look at the Impregnable Fortress.

Because that's what it was. It was a massive, brawny apartment house, built between the wars and looming some twenty-two stories over the park. The Charlemagne, its builder had dubbed it, and its apartments turned up in the Real Estate section of the Sunday *Times* every once in a while. It had gone co-op some years back, and when its apartments changed hands now they did so for six-figure sums. *High* six-figure sums.

From time to time I would read or hear of someone, a coin collector, let us say, and I would file his name away for future reference. And then I would learn that he lived at the Charlemagne and I would drop him from my files, because it was akin to learning that he kept all his holdings in a bank vault. The Charlemagne had a doorman and a concierge and attended elevators with closed-circuit television cameras in them. Other closed-circuit devices monitored the service entrance and the fire escapes and God knows what else, and the concierge had a console at his desk where he could (and did) watch six or eight screens at once. The Charlemagne made a positive fetish of security, and while I could readily understand their attitude, you could hardly expect me to approve.

A bus came and went, taking with it most of my companions. The light changed from red to green. I hoisted my case full of burglar's tools and crossed the street.

The doorman at the Charlemagne made mine look like an usher in a Times Square peep show. He had more gold braid than an Ecuadorian admiral and at least as much self-assurance. He took me in from nose to toes and remained serenely unimpressed.

"Bernard Rhodenbarr," I told him. "Mr. Onderdonk is expecting me."

TWO

OF COURSE HE DIDN'T take my word for it. He passed me on to the concierge and stood by in case I should give that gentleman any trouble. The concierge rang Onderdonk on the intercom, confirmed that I was indeed expected, and turned me over to the elevator operator, who piloted me some fifty yards closer to heaven. There was indeed a camera in the elevator, and I tried not to look at it while trying not to look as though I was avoiding it, and I felt about as nonchalant as a girl on her first night as a topless waitress. The elevator was a plush affair, paneled in rosewood and fitted with polished brass, with burgundy carpeting underfoot. Whole families have lived in less comfortable quarters, but all the same I was glad to leave it.

Which I did on the sixteenth floor, where the operator pointed to a door and hung around until it opened to admit me. It opened just a couple of inches until the chainlock stopped it, but that was far enough for Onderdonk to get a look at me and smile in recognition. "Ah, Mr. Rhodenbarr," he said, fumbling with the lock. "Good of you to

16

come." Then he said, "Thank you, Eduardo," and only then did the elevator door close and the cage descend.

"I'm clumsy tonight," Onderdonk said. "There." And he unhooked the chainlock and drew the door open. "Come right in, Mr. Rhodenbarr. Right this way. Is it as pleasant outside as it was earlier? And tell me what you'll have to drink. Or I've a pot of coffee made, if you'd prefer that."

"Coffee would be fine."

"Cream and sugar?"

"Black, no sugar."

"Commendable."

He was a man in his sixties, with iron gray hair parted carefully on the side and a weathered complexion. He was on the short side and slightly built, and perhaps his military bearing was an attempt to compensate for this. Alternatively, perhaps he'd been in the military. I somehow didn't think he'd ever served as a doorman, or an Ecuadorian admiral.

We had our coffee at a marble-topped table in his living room. The carpet was an Aubusson and the furniture was mostly Louis Quinze. The several paintings, all twentieth-century abstracts in uncomplicated aluminum frames, were an effective contrast to the period furnishings. One of them, showing blue and beige amoeboid shapes on a cream field, looked like the work of Hans Arp, while the canvas mounted over the Adam fireplace was unmistakably a Mondrian. I don't have all that good an eye for paintings, and I can't always tell Rembrandt from

Hals or Picasso from Braque, but Mondrian is Mondrian. A black grid, a white field, a couple of squares of primary colors—the man had a style, all right.

Bookshelves ran from floor to ceiling on either side of the fireplace, and they accounted for my presence. A couple of days ago, Gordon Kyle Onderdonk had walked in off the street, dropping in at Barnegat Books as casually as someone looking to buy *Drums in Our Street* or sell *Lepidopterae*. He'd browsed for a spell, asked two or three reasonable questions, bought a Louis Auchincloss novel, and paused on his way to the door to ask me if I ever appraised libraries.

"I'm not interested in selling my books," he said. "At least I don't think I am, although I'm considering a move to the West Coast and I suppose I'd dispose of them rather than ship them. But I have things that have accumulated over the years, and perhaps I ought to have a floater policy to cover them in case of fire, and if I ever do want to sell, why, I ought to know whether my library's worth a few hundred or a few thousand, oughtn't I?"

I haven't done many appraisals, but it's work I enjoy. You can't charge all that much, but the hourly return is greater than I get sitting behind the counter at the store, and sometimes the chance to appraise a library turns into the opportunity to purchase it. "Well, if it's worth a thousand dollars," a client may say, "what'll you pay for it?" "I won't pay a thousand," I may counter, "so tell me what you'll take for it." Ah, the happy game of haggling.

I spent the next hour and a half with my legal pad and a pen, jotting numbers down and totting them up. I looked at all of the books on the open walnut shelves that flanked the fireplace, and in another room, a sort of study, I examined the contents of a bank of glassed-in mahogany shelves.

The library was an interesting one. Onderdonk had never specifically collected anything, simply allowing books to accumulate over the years, culling much of the chaff from time to time. There were some sets in leather— a nice Hawthorne, a Defoe, the inevitable Dickens. There were perhaps a dozen Limited Editions Club volumes, which command a nice price, and several dozen Heritage Press books, which retail for only eight or ten dollars but are very easy to turn over. He had some favorite authors in first editions—Evelyn Waugh, J. P. Marquand, John O'Hara, Wallace Stevens. Some Faulkner, some Hemingway, some early Sherwood Anderson. Fair history, including a nice set of Guizot's *France* and Oman's seven-volume history of the Peninsular War. Not much science. No *Lepidopterae*.

He had cost himself money. Like so many noncollectors, he'd disposed of the dust jackets of most of his books, unwittingly chucking out the greater portion of their value in the process. There are any number of modern firsts worth, say, a hundred dollars with a dust jacket and ten or fifteen dollars without it. Onderdonk was astonished to learn this. Most people are.

He brought more coffee as I sat adding up a column of figures, and this time he'd brought along a bottle of Irish Mist. "I like a drop in my coffee," he said. "Can I offer you some?"

It sounded yummy, but where would we be without standards? I sipped my coffee black and went on adding numbers. The figure I came up with was somewhere in excess of $5,400, and I read it off to him. "I was probably conservative," I added. "I'm doing this on the spot, without consulting references, and I shaded things on the low side. You'd be safe rounding that figure off at six thousand."

"And what would that figure represent?"

"Retail prices. Fair market value."

"And if you were buying the books as a dealer, presuming of course that this type of material was something you were interested in—"

"I would be interested," I allowed. "For this sort of material I could work on fifty percent."

"So you could pay three thousand dollars?"

I shook my head. "I'd be going with the first figure I quoted you," I said. "I could pay twenty-seven hundred. And that would include removal of the books at my expense, of course."

"I see." He sipped his own coffee, crossed one slim leg over the other. He was wearing well-cut gray flannel slacks and a houndstooth smoking jacket with leather buttons. His shoes might have been of sharkskin. They were certainly elegant, and showed off his small feet. "I wouldn't care to sell now," he said, "but if I do move, and it's a possibility if not a probability, I'll certainly give your offer consideration."

"Books go up and down in value. The price might be higher or lower in a few months or a year."

"I understand that. If I decide to dispose of the books the primary consideration would be convenience, not price. I suspect I'd find it simpler to accept your offer than to shop around."

I looked over his shoulder at the Mondrian and wondered what it was worth. Ten or twenty or thirty times the fair market value of his library, at a guess. And his apartment was probably worth three or four times as much as the Mondrian, so a thousand dollars more or less for some old books probably wouldn't weigh too heavily on his mind.

"I want to thank you," he said, getting to his feet. "You told me your fee. Did you say two hundred dollars?"

"That's right."

He drew out a wallet, paused. "I hope you don't object to cash," he said.

"I never object to cash."

"Some people don't like to carry cash. I can understand that; these are perilous times." He counted out four fifties, handed them to me. I took out my own wallet and gave them a home.

"If I could use your phone—"

"Certainly," he said, and pointed me to the study. I dialed a number I'd dialed earlier, and once again I let it ring a dozen times, but somewhere around the fourth ring I chatted into the mouthpiece, as if someone were on the other end. I don't know that Onderdonk was even within earshot of me, but if you're going to do something you might as well do it right, and why call attention to myself by holding a ringing phone to my ear for an unusually long time?

Caught up in my performance, I suppose I let the phone ring more than a dozen times, but what matter? No one answered it, and I hung up and returned to the living room. "Well, thanks again for the business," I told him, returning my legal pad to my attaché case. "If you do decide to add a floater to your insurance coverage, I can give you my appraisal in writing if they require it. And I can adjust the figure higher or lower for that purpose, as you prefer."

"I'll remember that."

"And do let me know if you ever decide to get rid of the books."

"I certainly will."

He led me to the door, opened it for me, walked into the hall with me. The indicator showed the elevator to be on the ground floor. I let my finger hover over the button but avoided pressing it.

"I don't want to keep you," I said to Onderdonk.

"It's no trouble," he said. "But wait, is that my phone? I think it is. I'll just say goodbye now, Mr. Rhodenbarr."

We shook hands quickly and he hurried back inside his apartment. The door drew shut. I counted to ten, darted across the hall, yanked open the fire door and scampered down four flights of stairs.

THREE

AT THE ELEVENTH-FLOOR landing, I paused long enough to catch my breath. This didn't take long, perhaps because of all those half-hour romps in Riverside Park. Had I known running would be such a help in my career I might have taken it up years ago.

(How did four flights of stairs get me from Sixteen to Eleven? No thirteenth floor. But *you* knew that, didn't you? Of course you did.)

The fire door was locked from the stairs side. Another security precaution; tenants (and anyone else) could go down and out in case of fire or elevator failure, but they could only leave the stairs at the lobby. They couldn't get off at another floor.

Well, that was nice enough in theory, but an inch-wide strip of flexible steel did its work in nothing flat, and then I was easing the door open, making sure that the coast (or at least the hallway) was clear.

I traversed the hallway to 11-B. No light showed under the door, and when I pressed my ear against it I couldn't hear a thing, not even the roar of the surf. I didn't expect to hear anything since I'd just let the phone in 11-B ring twelve or twenty times, but burglary is chancy enough even when you don't take chances. There was a bell, a flat mother-of-pearl button set flush against the doorjamb, and I rang it and heard it sound within. There was a knocker, an art nouveau affair in the shape of a coiled cobra, but I didn't want to make noise in the hallway. I didn't, indeed, want to spend an unnecessary extra second in that hallway, and with that in mind I bent to my task.

First the burglar alarm. You wouldn't think one was necessary at the Charlemagne, but then you probably don't have a houseful of objets d'art and a stamp collection on a par with King Farouk's, do you? If burglars don't take unnecessary chances, why should their victims?

You could tell there was a burglar alarm because there was a keyhole for it, set in the door at about shoulder height, a nickel-plated cylinder perhaps five-eighths of an inch in diameter. What man can lock, man can unlock, and that's just what I did. There is a handy little homemade key on my ring that fits most locks of that ilk, and with just the littlest bit of filing and fiddling it can make the tumblers tumble, and—oh, but you don't want to know all this technical stuff, do you? I thought not.

I turned the key in the lock and hoped that was all you had to do. Alarm systems are cunning devices with no end of fail-safe features built in. Some go off, for example, if you cut the household current. Others get twitchy if you turn the key in other than the prescribed fashion. This one seemed docile, but what if it was one of those silent alarms, ringing nastily away downstairs or in the offices of some home-protection agency?

Ah, well. The other lock, the one that was keeping the door shut, was a Poulard. According to the manufacturer's advertisements, no one has ever successfully picked the Poulard lock. I'd walk into his offices and dispute that claim, but where would it get me? The lock mechanism's a good one, I'll grant them that, and the key's complicated and impossible to duplicate, but I have more trouble on average with your basic Rabson. Either I picked the Poulard or I made myself very long and narrow and slithered in through the keyhole, because within three minutes I was inside that apartment.

I closed the door and played my pencil-beam flashlight over it. If I'd made some grave error knocking off the burglar alarm, and if it was the sort that was ringing in some agency's office, then I had plenty of time to get away before they came calling. So I examined the cylinder to see how it was wired in and if anything seemed to have gone awry, and after a moment or two of frowning and head-scratching I started to giggle.

Because there was no alarm system. All there was was a nickel-plated cylinder, attached to nothing at all, mounted in the door like a talisman. You've seen those decals on car windows warning of an alarm system? People buy the decals for a dollar, hoping they'll keep car thieves at bay, and perhaps they do. You've seen those signs on houses, BEWARE OF THE DOG, and they haven't got a dog? A sign's cheaper than rabies shots and Alpo, and you don't have to walk it twice a day.

Why install a burglar alarm at a cost of a thousand dollars or more when you could mount a cylinder for a couple of bucks and get the same protection? Why have a system you'd forget to set half the time, and forget to turn off the other half of the time, when the illusion of a system was every bit as effective?

My heart filled with admiration for John Charles Appling. It was going to be a pleasure to do business with him.

I'd been reasonably certain he wasn't home. He was at the Greenbrier in White Sulphur Springs, West-by-God-Virginia, playing golf and taking the sun and attending a tax-deductible convention of the Friends of the American Wild Turkey, a band of conservationists dedicated to improving wilderness conditions to create a more favorable habitat for the birds in question, thereby to increase their numbers to the point where the Friends can hie themselves off to the woods in autumn with shotgun and turkey lure in tow, there to slay the object of their affections. After all, what are friends for?

I locked the door now, just in case, and I drew my rubber gloves from my attaché case and pulled them on, then took a moment to wipe the surfaces I might have touched while checking the fake alarm cylinder. There still remained the outside of the door, but I'd smudge those prints on the way out. Then I took another moment to lean against the door and let my eyes accustom themselves to the darkness. And—let's admit it—to Enjoy the Feeling.

And what a feeling it was! I read once of a woman who spent every free moment at Coney Island, riding the big roller coaster over and over and over. Evidently she got the thrill from that curious pastime that I get whenever I let myself into another person's place of residence. That charged-up sensation, that fire-in-the-blood, every-cell-alive feeling. I've had it ever since I first broke into a neighbor's house in my early teens, and all the intervening years, all the crimes and all the punishments, have not dulled or dimmed it in the slightest. It's as much of a thrill as ever.

I'm not boasting. I take a workman's pride in my skills but no pride at all in the forces that drive me. God help me, I'm a born thief, the urge to burgle bred in my bones. How could they ever rehabilitate me? Can you teach a fish to leave off swimming, a bird to renounce flight?

By the time my eyes had grown accustomed to the darkness, the thrill of illegal entry had subsided to a less acute sense of profound well-being. Flashlight in hand, I took a quick tour of the apartment. Even if Appling and his wife were sequestered with the rest of the turkeys, there was always the chance that one of the rooms held some relative or friend or servant, sleeping peacefully or cowering in terror or putting in a quiet call to the local precinct. I went quickly in and out of each room and encountered nothing living but the house-plants. Then I returned to the living room and switched on a lamp.

I had plenty to choose from. The cobra door knocker was the first but hardly the last piece of art nouveau I encountered, and the living room was festooned with enough Tiffany lamps to cause a power failure. Large lamps, small lamps, table lamps, floor lamps—no one could want that much light. But then the collecting mania is by definition irrational and excessive. Appling had thousands upon thousands of postage stamps, and how many letters do you suppose he sent out?

Tiffany lamps are worth a fortune these days. I recognized some of them—the Dragonfly lamp, the Wisteria lamp—and you can pick up a nice suburban house for what a couple of those would bring at Parke-Bernet. You could also earn a very quick trip to Dannemora trying to walk out of the Charlemagne weighted down with leaded-glass lamps. I went around examining them—the place was as good as a museum—but I left them as I found them, along with any number of other gewgaws and pretties.

The Applings seemed to have separate bedrooms, and I found jewelry in hers, in a stunning tortoiseshell jewelry box in her top dresser drawer. The box was locked and the key was right there next to it in the drawer. Go figure some people. I unlocked the box with its little key—I could have opened it almost as quickly without the key, but why show off when there's no one around to ooh and ahh? I was going to leave the jewelry, although it did look awfully nice, but a pair of ruby earrings proved irresistible, and into my pocket they went. Would she miss one pair of earrings out of a whole box full of jewelry? And, if she did, wouldn't she think she'd misplaced them? What kind of burglar, after all, would take a couple of earrings and leave everything else?

A cagey one. A burglar whose presence in the Charlemagne that night was a matter of record, and who thus had to avoid stealing anything that would be conspicuous by its absence. I did take the ruby earrings—my profession, after all, can never be 100 percent risk-free—but when I came upon a sheaf of fifty- and hundred-dollar bills in J. C. Appling's dresser drawer, I left them there.

Not without effort, let me admit. There wasn't a fortune there, $2,800 at a rough count, but money is money and you just can't beat cash. When you steal things you have to fence them, but with cash you just keep it and spend the stuff at leisure.

But he might notice that it was gone. It might in fact be the first thing he checked upon returning to the apartment, and if it was missing he'd know immediately that he hadn't misplaced it, that it hadn't walked off of its own accord.

I thought of taking a couple of bills, figuring they wouldn't be missed, but how much is too much? It's more trouble making such nice distinctions than the cash warranted. Easier to leave the money where it was.

I hit paydirt in the den.

There was a bookcase there, but nothing like Onderdonk's library. Some reference works, a shelf full of stamp catalogs, a few books on guns, and a cheap set of reprint editions of the novels of Zane Grey. Bargain-table stuff at Barnegat Books, forty cents each, three for a buck.

A glassed-in wall case held two shotguns and a rifle, their stocks elaborately tooled, their barrels agleam with menace. I suppose they were for shooting turkeys but they'd do in a pinch for shooting burglars and I didn't like the looks of them.

Over the desk, an Audubon print of an American wild turkey hung in an antiqued frame. The real thing, stuffed and mounted and looking only a little forlorn, stood guard atop the bookcase. I suppose its friend J.C. shot it. First he'd have honked with one of the odd-looking wooden turkey lures he had on

30

display, and then he'd have triggered the shotgun, and now the creature had achieved a sort of taxidermal immortality. Oh, well. People who break into houses, glass or otherwise, probably shouldn't cast stones. Or aspersions, or whatever.

In any event, the turkeys and the guns and the books were beside the point. Along the back of the large desk, below the Audubon turkey, ranged a dozen dark green volumes a bit over a foot high and a couple of inches wide. They were Scott Specialty Stamp Albums, and they were just what the burglar ordered. British Asia, British Africa, British Europe, British America, British Oceania. France and French Colonies. Germany, German States and German Colonies. Benelux. South and Central America. Scandinavia. And, in an album which did not match its fellows, the United States.

I went through one album after another. Appling's stamps were not affixed to the page with hinges but were encased individually in little plastic mounts designed for the purpose. (Hinging a mint stamp is as economically unsound as discarding a book's dust jacket.) I could have removed the plastic mounts, and thought about it, but it was faster and simpler and subtler to tear whole pages from the loose-leaf binders, and that's what I did.

I know a little about stamps. There's a lot I don't know, but I can skim through an album and make good spot decisions as to what to take and what to leave. In the Benelux album, for example—that's Belgium, the Netherlands and Luxembourg, along with Belgian and Dutch colonies—I cleaned out all of the semi-postal issues (all complete, all mint, all readily salable) and most of the good nineteenth-century classics. I left the more highly specialized stuff, parcel post and postage due and such. In the British Empire albums I loaded up on the Victoria, Edward VII and George V issues. I didn't take very many pages from the Latin American albums, having less knowledge of the material.

By the time I was done my attaché case was packed solid with album pages and the albums they'd come from were all back in order on the desk top, their bulk not visibly reduced. I don't suppose I took one page in twenty, but the pages I took were the ones worth taking. I'm sure I missed the odd priceless rarity, and I'm sure I took the bad with the good, even as I do in life itself, but on balance I felt I'd done a first-rate job of winnowing.

I hadn't a clue what the lot was worth. One of the U.S. pages included the twenty-four-cent inverted airmail, a bicolor with the plane appearing upside-down, and I forget the most recent auction record for that issue but I know it ran well into five figures. On the other hand, it would have to be fenced, sold to someone who'd be aware he was buying stolen goods and who'd accordingly expect a bargain. Most of the other material was quite anonymous in comparison, and would bring a much higher proportion of its fair market value.

So what did I have in my attaché case? A hundred thousand? It wasn't impossible. And what could I net for it? Thirty, thirty-five thousand?

A fair ballpark figure. But it was no more than a guess and I might be miles off in either direction. In twenty-four hours' time I'd know a good deal more. By then all of the stamps would be off their pages and out of their mounts, sorted by sets and tucked into little glassine envelopes, their prices checked in last year's Scott catalog, which was the most recent copy to have turned up at the store. (I could buy the book new, but somehow it goes against the grain.) Then Appling's pages and mounts would go down the incinerator, along with any stamps that might have markings rendering them specifically identifiable. In a day's time, a box of stamps in glassine envelopes, all quite anonymous, would be my only link with the John Charles Appling collection. An indeterminate time after that, but surely not much more than a week, the stamps would have new owners and I'd have money in their stead.

And it might be months before Appling ever knew they were gone. It was likely that he'd detect their absence the first time he pulled out an album and paged through it, but it was by no means a sure thing. I'd left twenty times as much as I'd taken, in volume if not in value, and he might open a book, turn to a specific page, add a stamp, and never notice that other pages were missing.

It didn't really matter. He wouldn't notice the minute he walked into the house, and when he did notice he couldn't say when the theft had taken place—it might have occurred before or after his Greenbrier jaunt. His insurance company would pay, or it wouldn't, and he'd come out ahead or behind or dead even, and who cared? Not I. A batch of pieces of colored paper would have changed ownership, and so would a batch of pieces of green paper, and no one on God's earth was going to miss a meal as a result of my night's activities.

I'm not offering a moral defense of myself, you understand. Burglary is morally reprehensible and I'm aware of the fact. But I wasn't stealing the pennies off a dead man's eyes, or the bread from a child's mouth, or objects of deep sentimental value. I'll tell you, I love collectors. I can ransack their holdings with such little guilt.

The state, however, takes a sterner view of things. They draw no distinction between swiping a philatelist's stamps and lifting a widow's rent money. However good I get at rationalizing my pursuit, I still have to do what I can to stay out of jail.

Which meant getting the hell out of there. I turned off lights—there was a Tiffany lamp in the study, too, wouldn't you know—and I made my way to the apartment's front door. My stomach growled en route and I thought of checking the fridge and building myself a sandwich, figuring they'd no more miss a little food than a fortune in rare stamps. But Sing Sing and Attica are overflowing with chaps who stopped for a sandwich, and if I just got out of there I could buy myself a whole restaurant.

I squinted through the peephole, saw no one in the hallway, and put my ear to the door and heard no one in the hallway, either. I unlocked the door, eased it open, *saw* no one in the hallway, and let myself out. I picked the Poulard lock again, locking it this time so as to spare the manufacturer's feelings. I did not reset the spurious burglar alarm cylinder, just gave it a wink and went on my way, pausing only to smudge whatever prints I might have left on the outside of the door. Then, attaché case in hand, I crossed to the fire door, opened it, passed through it, and let out a long breath as it swung quietly shut behind me.

I climbed one flight, stopped long enough to strip off my rubber gloves and stuff them into my jacket pocket. (I didn't want to open the attaché case and chance spilling stamps all over the goddamn place.) I climbed three more flights of stairs, slipped the lock on the fire door, emerged in the hallway, and rang for the elevator. While it ascended from the lobby I checked my watch.

Twenty-five minutes to one. It had been close to eleven-thirty when I said good night to Onderdonk, so I'd spent just about an hour in the Appling apartment. It seemed to me that I should have been able to get in and out in half an hour, but I couldn't have shaved too many minutes off the time I spent going through the albums. I could have stayed out of the bedrooms, perhaps, and I didn't have to give as much attention as I did to the Tiffany lamps, but what is it they say about all work and no play? I was out of there safely and that was what counted.

A shame, though, that I couldn't have made my exit before midnight, when service shifts commonly change at apartment buildings. I'd be seen now by a second elevator operator, a second concierge, a second doorman. Otherwise I'd have been seen by the same set a second time, and which was riskier? Not that it mattered, since I'd already given my name, and—

The elevator arrived. As I stepped into the car I turned toward Onderdonk's closed door. "'Night now," I said. "I'll have those figures for you as soon as I can."

The door closed, the car descended. I leaned back against its wood paneling and crossed my legs at the ankle. "Long day," I said.

"Just starting for me," the operator said.

I tried to forget about the camera overhead. It was like trying to forget that you've got your left foot in a bucket of ice water. I couldn't look at it and I couldn't suppress the urge to look at it, and I did a lot of elaborate yawning. It was, actually, a rather quick ride, but it certainly didn't seem that way.

A brisk nod to the concierge. The doorman held the door for me, then hurried past me to the curb to summon a taxi. One turned up almost immediately. I gave the doorman a buck and told the driver to drop me at Madison and Seventy-second. I paid him, walked a block west to Fifth, and caught another cab back to my place. On the way I balanced the attaché case on my knees and relived some of the hour I'd spent in apartment 11-B. The moment when the Poulard lock, teased and tickled beyond endurance, threw up its tumblers and surrendered. The sight of that inverted airmail stamp, alone on a page, as if it had been waiting for me since the day they misprinted it.

I tipped the cabby a buck. My own doorman, a glassy-eyed young fellow who worked the midnight-to-eight shift in a permanent muscatel haze, did not rush to open the door of the taxi. I suppose he'd have held the lobby door for me but he didn't have to. It was propped open. He stayed on his stool, greeting me with a sly conspiratorial smile. I wonder what secret he thought we shared.

Upstairs I fumbled my own key into my own lock, for a change, and opened the door. The light was on. Considerate of them, I thought, to leave a light for the burglar. Wait a minute, I thought. What was this *them* stuff. I was the one who'd left the light on, except I hadn't, I never did.

What was going on?

I put a foot inside, then drew it warily back, as if trying to get the hang of a new dance step. I went on in and turned toward the couch and blinked, and there, blinking back at me like a slightly cockeyed owl, was Carolyn Kaiser.

"Well, Jesus," she said, "it's about time. Where the hell have you been, Bern?"

I pulled the door shut, turned the bolt. "You picked your way through my Rabson lock," I said. "I didn't think you knew how to do that."

"I don't."

"Don't tell me the doorman let you in. He's not supposed to, and anyway he doesn't have a key."

"*I* have a key, Bern. You gave me keys to your place. Remember?"

"Oh, right."

"So I stuck the key in the lock and turned it, and damned if the thing didn't pop open. You ought to try it yourself sometime. Works like a charm."

"Carolyn—"

"Have you got anything to drink? I know you're supposed to wait until it's offered, but who's got the patience?"

"There's two bottles of beer in the fridge," I said. "One's going to wash down the sandwich I'm about to make, but you're welcome to the other one."

"Dark Mexican beer, right? Dos Equis?"

"Right."

"They're gone. What else have you got?"

I thought for a moment. "There's a little Scotch left."

"A single malt? Glen Islay, something like that?"

"You found it and it's gone, too."

"'Fraid so, Bern."

"Then we're fresh out," I said, "unless you want to knock off the Lavoris. I think it's about sixty proof."

"Child of a dog."

"Carolyn—"

"You know something? I think I'm gonna go back to saying 'son of a bitch.' It may be sexist but it's a lot more satisfying than 'child of a dog.' You go around saying 'child of a dog' and people don't even know you're cursing."

"Carolyn, what are you doing here?"

"I'm dying of thirst, that's what I'm doing."

"You're drunk."

"No shit, Bernie."

"You are. You drank two beers and a pint of Scotch and you're shitfaced."

She braced an elbow on her knee, rested her head in the palm of her hand and gave me a look. "In the first place," she said, "it wasn't a pint, it was maybe six ounces, which isn't even half a pint. We're talking about three drinks in a good bar or two drinks in a terrific bar. In the second place, it's not nice to tell your best friend that she's shitfaced. Pie-eyed, maybe. Half in the bag, three sheets to the wind, a little under the weather, all acceptable. But shitfaced, that's not a nice thing to say to someone you love. And in the third place—"

"In the third place, you're still drunk."

"In the third place, I was drunk *before* I drank your booze in the first place." She beamed triumphantly, then frowned. "Or should that be the fourth place, Bernie? I don't know. It's hell keeping track of all these places. In the fifth place I was drunk when I got back to my place, and then I had a drink before I came up to your place, so that makes me—"

"Out of place," I suggested.

"I don't know what it makes me." She waved an impatient hand. "That's not the important thing."

"It's not?"

"No."

"What is?"

She looked furtively around. "I'm not supposed to tell anybody," she said.

"'To tell anybody what?"

"There aren't any bugs in this place, are there, Bern?"

"Just the usual roaches and silverfish. What's the problem, Carolyn?"

"The problem is my pussy's been snatched."

"Huh?"

"Oh, God," she said. "My kid's been catnapped."

"Your kid's been— Carolyn, you don't have any kids. How much did you have to drink, anyway? Before you got here?"

"Shit on toast," she said, loud. "Will you just listen to me? Please? It's Archie."

"Archie?"

She nodded. "Archie," she said. "They've kidnapped Archie Goodwin."

FOUR

"THE CAT," I said.

"Right."

"Archie the cat. Your Burmese cat. *That* Archie."

"Of course, Bern. Who else?"

"You said Archie Goodwin, and the first thing I thought—"

"That's his full name, Bern."

"I know that."

"I didn't mean Archie Goodwin the person, Bern, because he's a character in the Nero Wolfe stories, and the only way he could have been kidnapped would be in a book, and if that happened I wouldn't run up here in the middle of the night and carry on about it. You want to know the truth, Bern, I think you need a drink more than I do, which is saying something."

"I think you're right," I said. "I'll be back in a minute."

It was more like five. I walked down the hall past my friend Mrs. Hesch's apartment to Mrs. Seidel's. Mrs. Seidel was visiting family in Shaker Heights, according to Mrs. Hesch. I rang her bell for safety's sake, then let myself into her apartment. (She'd gone off without double-locking her door, so all I had to do was loid the springlock with a strip of plastic. Someone, I thought, would have to talk to Mrs. Seidel about that.)

I came back from there with a mostly full bottle of Canadian Club. I poured drinks for both of us. Carolyn had hers swallowed before I had the cap back on the bottle.

"That's better," she said.

I took a drink myself, and as it hit bottom I remembered that I was pouring it into a very empty stomach. It would be a lot easier to get me drunk than to get Carolyn sober, but I wasn't sure it was a good idea. I opened the fridge and built a sandwich of thin-sliced Polish ham and Monterey jack cheese on one of those dark musky rye breads that comes in little square loaves. I took a big bite and chewed thoughtfully and could have killed for a bottle of Dos Equis.

"What about Archie?" I said.

"He doesn't drink."

"Carolyn—"

"Sorry. I don't mean to be drunk, Bern." She tilted the bottle and helped herself to a few more cc's of the CC, as it were. "I went home and fed the cats and had something to eat, and then I got restless and went out. I kept bopping around. I think I had a touch of moon madness. Did you happen to notice the moon?"

"No."

"Neither did I, but I'll bet it's full or close to it. I kept feeling as though the problem was that I just wasn't in the right place. So I'd go somewhere else and I'd feel the same way. I went to Paula's and the Duchess and Kelly's West and a couple of straight bars on Bleecker Street, and then I went back to Paula's and played a little pool, and then I hit this pigpen on Nineteenth Street, I forget the name, and then I hit the Duchess again—"

"I get the picture."

"I was bouncing is what I was doing, and of course you have to have a drink when you go to a place, and I went to a lot of places."

"And had a lot of drinks."

"What else? But I wasn't looking to get drunk, see. I was looking to get lucky. Will true love ever come to Carolyn Kaiser? And, failing that, how about true lust?"

"Not tonight, I gather."

"I'll tell you, I couldn't get arrested. I called Alison a couple of times, which I swore I wasn't gonna do, but it's all right because she didn't answer. Then I went home. I figured I'd make it a reasonably early night, maybe have a brandy before I turned in, and I opened the door and the cat was missing. Archie, I mean. Ubi was fine."

Archie, full name Archie Goodwin, was a sleek Burmese given to eloquent yowling. Ubi, full name Ubiquity or Ubiquitous, I forget which, was a plump Russian Blue, more affectionate and a good deal less assertive than his Burmese buddy. Both had started life as males, and each had received at a tender age the sort of surgical attention which leaves one purring in soprano.

"He was hiding somewhere," I suggested.

"No way. I looked in all his hiding places. In things, under things, behind things. Besides, I ran the electric can opener. That's like a fire alarm to a dalmatian."

"Maybe he snuck out."

"How? The window was shut and the door was locked. John Dickson Carr couldn't have slipped him out of there."

"The door was locked?"

"Locked up tight. I always double-lock my dead bolt locks when I go out. You made me a believer in that department. And I locked the Fox police lock. I know I locked all those locks because I had to unlock them to get in."

"So he went out when you left. Or maybe he snuck out while you were letting yourself in."

"I would have noticed."

"Well, you said yourself that you'd had a few drinks more than usual to celebrate the full moon. Maybe—"

"I wasn't that bad, Bern."

"Okay."

"And he never does that anyway. Neither of the cats ever tries to get out. Look, you could say this and I could say that and we'd be going around Robin Hood's barn because I know for a fact the cat was snatched. I got a phone call."

"When?"

"I don't know. I don't know what time I got home and I don't know how much time I

44

spent looking for the cat and running the electric can opener. There was a little brandy and I finally poured some for myself and sat down with it and the phone rang."

"And?"

She poured another drink, a short one, and paused with the glass halfway to her lips. She said, "Bern? It wasn't you, was it?"

"Huh?"

"I mean I could see how it could be a joke that got out of hand, but if it was, tell me now, huh? If you tell me now there won't be any hard feelings, but if you don't tell me now all bets are off."

"You think I took your cat."

"No I don't. I don't think you've got that kind of an asshole sense of humor. But people do wacky things, and who else could unlock all those locks and lock 'em up again on the way out? So all I want you to do is say, 'Yes, Carolyn, I took your cat,' or 'No, you little idiot, I didn't take your cat,' and then we can get on with it."

"No, you little idiot, I didn't take your cat."

"Thank God. Except if you had I'd know the cat was safe." She looked at the glass in her hand as if seeing it for the first time. "Did I just pour this?"

"Uh-huh."

"Well, I must have known what I was doing," she said, and drank it. "The phone call."

"Right. Tell me about it."

"I'm not sure if it was a man or a woman. It was either a man making his voice high or

45

a woman making her voice husky, and I couldn't tell you which. Whoever it was had an accent like Peter Lorre except really phony. 'Ve haff ze poosycat.' That kind of accent."

"Is that what he said? 'Ve haff ze poosycat'?"

"Or words to that effect. If I want to see him again, di dah di dah di dah di dah."

"What are all the di dahs about?"

"You're not gonna believe this, Bern."

"He asked for money?"

"A quarter of a million dollars or I'll never see my cat again."

"A quarter of a—"

"Million dollars. Right."

"Two hundred and fifty thousand."

"Dollars. Right."

"For—"

"A cat. Right."

"I'll be a—"

"Child of a dog. Right. So will I."

"Well, it's nuts," I said. "In the first place the cat's not worth any real money. Is he show quality?"

"Probably, but so what? You can't breed him."

"And he's not a television star like Morris. He's just a cat."

"Just my cat," she said. "Just an animal I happen to love."

"You want a hankie?"

"What I want is to stop being an idiot. Shit, I can't help it. Gimme the hankie. Where am I gonna get a quarter of a million bucks, Bern?"

"You could start by taking all your old deposit bottles back to the deli."

"They add up, huh?"

"Little grains of water, little drops of sand. That's another thing that's crazy. Who would figure you could come up with that kind of money? Your apartment's cozy, but Twenty-two Arbor Court isn't the Charlemagne. Anyone bright enough to get in and out and lock up after himself—he really locked up after himself?"

"Swear to God."

"Who has keys to your place?"

"Just you."

"What about Randy Messinger?"

"She wouldn't pull this kind of shit. And anyway the Fox lock is new since she and I were lovers. Remember when you installed it for me?"

"And you locked it when you left, and unlocked it when you came back."

"Definitely."

"You didn't just turn the cylinder. The bar moved and everything."

"Bernie, trust me. It was locked and I had to unlock it."

"That rules out Randy."

"She wouldn't have done it."

"No, but somebody could have copied her keys. Do I still have my set?" I went and checked, and I still had them. I turned, saw my attaché case propped up against the sofa. If I sold its contents for their full market value, I might have two-fifths of the price of a secondhand Burmese cat.

Oh, I thought.

"Take a couple of aspirin," I said. "And if you want another drink, have it with hot water and sugar. You'll sleep better."

"Sleep?"

"Uh-huh, and the sooner the better. You take the bed, I'll take the couch."

"Don't be ridiculous," she said. "I'll take the couch. Except I won't because I don't want to go to sleep and I can't stay here anyway. They said they would call me in the morning."

"That's why I want you to get to sleep. So you'll be clearheaded when they call."

"Bernie, I got news for you. I'm not gonna be clearheaded in the morning. I'm gonna have a head like a soccer ball that Pelé got pissed at."

"Well, I'll be clearheaded," I said, "and one head is better than none. The aspirin's in the medicine cabinet."

"What a clever place for it. I bet you're the kind of guy who keeps milk in the fridge and soap in the soap dish."

"I'll fix you a hot toddy."

"Didn't you hear what I said? I have to be at my place for when they call."

"They'll call here."

"Why would they do that?"

"Because you don't have a quarter of a million dollars," I said, "and who could mistake you for David Rockefeller? So if they want a hefty ransom for Archie they must expect you to steal it, and that means they must know you've got a friend in the stealing business, and that means they'll call here. Drink this and take your aspirin and get ready for bed."

"I didn't bring pajamas. Have you got a shirt or something that I can sleep in?"

"Sure."

"And I'm not sleepy. I'll just toss and turn, but I guess that's all right."

Five minutes later she was snoring.

FIVE

A SIGN ON the counter said the suggested contribution was $2.50. "Contribute more or less if you prefer," it counseled, "but you must contribute *something*." The chap immediately in front of us plunked down a dime. The attendant started to tell him about the suggested contribution, but our lad wasn't open to suggestion.

"Read your own sign, sonny," he said sourly. "How many times do I have to go through this with you vermin? You'd think it was coming out of your own pockets. They haven't got you on commission, have they?"

"Not yet."

"Well, I'm an artist. The dime's my widow's

mite. Take it in good grace or in the future I'll reduce my contribution to a penny."

"Oh, you can't do that, Mr. Turnquist," the attendant said archly. "It would throw our whole budget out of whack."

"You know me, eh?"

"Everybody knows you, Mr. Turnquist." A heavy sigh. "Everybody."

He took Turnquist's dime and gave him a little yellow lapel pin for it. Turnquist faced us as he fastened the pin to the breast pocket of his thrift shop suit jacket. It was a sort of gray, and came reasonably close to matching his thrift shop trousers. He smiled, showing misaligned tobacco-stained teeth. He had a beard, a ragged goatee a little redder than his rusty brown hair and a little more infiltrated with gray, and the rest of his face was two or three days away from a shave.

"Little tin gods on wheels," he advised us. "That's all these people are. Don't take any crap from them. If Art can be intimidated, it ain't Art."

He moved on and I laid a five-dollar bill on the counter and accepted two lapel pins in return. "An artist," the attendant said meaningfully. He tapped another sign, which announced that children under the age of sixteen were not admitted, whether or not accompanied by an adult. "We ought to amend our policy," he said. "No children, no dogs, and no artists."

I'd awakened before Carolyn and went

directly to a liquor store on West Seventy-second, where I bought a replacement bottle of Canadian Club. I took it home and knocked on Mrs. Seidel's door, and when my knock went unanswered I let myself in and cracked the seal on the bottle, poured an ounce or so down the sink drain, capped the bottle and put it back where I'd found its fellow the night before. I let myself out and met Mrs. Hesch in the hallway, the inevitable cigarette burning unattended in the corner of her mouth. I stopped at her apartment for a cup of coffee—she makes terrific coffee—and we talked, not for the first time, about the coin-operated laundry in the basement. She was exercised about the driers, which, their dials notwithstanding, had two temperatures—On and Off. I was vexed with the washers, which were as voracious as Pac-Man when it came to socks. Neither of us said anything about the fact that I'd just let myself out of Mrs. Seidel's place.

I went back to my apartment and listened to Carolyn being sick in the bathroom while I put a pot of coffee on. She came out looking a little green and sat in the corner of the couch holding her head. I showered and shaved and came back to find her staring unhappily at a cup of coffee. I asked her if she wanted aspirin. She said she wouldn't mind some Extra-Strength Tylenol, but I didn't have any. I ate and she didn't and we both drank coffee and the phone rang.

A woman's voice, unaccented, said, "Mr.

Rhodenbarr? Have you spoken to your friend?"

I thought of pointing out that the question was implicitly insulting, presuming that I only had one friend, that I was the sort of person who couldn't possibly have more than a single friend, that I was lucky to have one and could probably expect to be deserted by her when she wised up.

I said, "Yes."

"Are you prepared to pay the ransom? A quarter of a million dollars?"

"Doesn't that strike you as a shade high? I know inflation's murder these days, and I understand it's a seller's market for Burmese cats, but—"

"Do you have the money?"

"I try not to keep that much cash around the house."

"You can raise it?"

Carolyn had come over to my side when the phone rang. I laid a reassuring hand on her arm. To my caller I said, "Let's cut the comedy, huh? Bring the cat back and we'll forget the whole thing. Otherwise—"

Otherwise what? I'm damned if I know what kind of a threat I was prepared to make. But Carolyn didn't give me the chance. She clutched my arm. She said, "*Bernie*—"

"Ve vill kill ze cat," the woman said, her voice much louder and suddenly accented. The effect was somewhere between an ad for Viennese pastry *mit schlag* and that guy in the World War II movies who reminds you that you've got relatives in Chermany.

"Now let's be calm," I said, to both of them. "No need to talk about violence."

"If you do not pay ze ransom—"

"Neither of us has that kind of money. You must know that. Now why don't you tell me what you want?"

There was a pause. "Tell your vriend to go home."

"I beg your pardon?"

"Zere is somesing in her mailbox."

"All right. I'll go with her, and—"

"No."

"No?"

"Stay vere you are. You vill get a phone call."

"But—"

There was a click. I sat looking at the receiver for a few seconds before I hung it up. I asked Carolyn if she'd heard any of it.

"I caught a few words here and there," she said. "It was the same person I talked to last night. At least I think it was. Same accent, anyway."

"She switched it on in midstream. I guess she forgot it at the beginning, and then she remembered she was supposed to sound threatening. Or else she slips into it when she gets excited. I don't like the idea of splitting up. She wants you to go to your apartment and me to stay here and I don't like it."

"Why?"

"Well, who knows what she's going to try to pull?"

"I have to go downtown anyway. Somebody's bringing me a schnauzer at eleven.

Shit, I don't have much time, do I? I can't face a schnauzer with a head like I've got. Thank God it's a miniature schnauzer. I don't know what I'd do if I had to wash a giant schnauzer on a day like this."

"Stop at your apartment on the way. If you've got time."

"I'll make time. I have to feed Ubi, anyway. You don't think—"

"What?"

"That they took him too? Maybe that's why they want me to go to my apartment."

"They said to check your mailbox."

"Oh, God," she said.

When she left I went to work on Appling's stamp collection. I suppose it was a cold-blooded thing to do, what with Archie's life hanging in the balance, but that still left him with eight and I wanted to render the Appling stamps unidentifiable as soon as possible. I sat under a good light at my kitchen table with a pair of stamp tongs and a box of glassine envelopes and a Scott catalog, and I transferred the stamps a set at a time from their mounts to the envelopes, making the appropriate notation on each envelope. I didn't bother figuring out the value. That would be another operation, and it could wait.

I was laboring over George V high values from Trinidad & Tobago when the phone rang. "What's this crap about my mailbox?" Carolyn demanded. "There's nothing in it but the Con Ed bill."

"How's Ubi?"

"Ubi's fine. He looks lost and lonely and his heart is probably breaking, but aside from that he's fine. Did that Nazi call back?"

"Not yet. Maybe she meant the mailbox at your shop."

"There's no box there. There's just a slot in the door."

"Well, maybe she got a wire crossed. Go wash the saluki anyway and see what happens."

"It's not a saluki, it's a schnauzer, and I know what'll happen. I'll wind up smelling of wet dog for a change. Call me when you hear from them, okay?"

"Okay," I said, and fifteen minutes later the phone rang again and it was the mystery woman. No accent this time, and no elaborate runaround, either. She talked and I listened, and when she was done I sat for a minute and thought and scratched my head and thought some more. Then I put Appling's stamps away and called Carolyn.

And now we were in a small room on the second floor of the gallery. We'd followed my caller's directions to the letter, and we were accordingly standing in front of a painting that looked remarkably familiar.

A small bronze rectangle affixed to the wall beside it bore the following information: *Piet Mondrian. 1872–1944. Composition with Color, 1942. Oil on canvas, 86 × 94 cm. Gift of Mr. & Mrs. J. McLendon Barlow.*

I wrote the dimensions in my pocket notebook. In case you haven't caved in and learned to think

55

metric, they worked out in real measurement to something like 35 by 39 inches, with the height greater than the width. The background color was white, tinted a little toward gray by either time or the artist. Black lines crisscrossed the canvas, dividing it into squares and rectangles, several of which were painted in primary colors. There were two red areas, two blue ones, and a long narrow section of yellow.

I stepped closer and Carolyn laid a hand on my arm. "Don't straighten it," she urged. "It's fine the way it is."

"I was just having a closer look."

"Well, there's a guard by the door," she said, "and he's having a closer look at us. There's guards all over the place. This is crazy, Bern."

"We're just looking at pictures."

"And that's all we're gonna do, because this is impossible. You could no more get a painting out of this place than you could get a child into it."

"Relax," I said. "All we're doing is looking."

The building where we stood, like the painting in front of us, had once been in private hands. Years ago it had served as the Manhattan residence of Jacob Hewlett, a mining and transport baron who'd ground the faces of the poor with inordinate success around the turn of the century. He'd left his Murray Hill townhouse at the corner of Madison and Thirty-eighth to the city, with the stipulation that it be maintained as an art museum under the direction and control of a foundation established by Hewlett for that purpose. While his own holdings had served as the core of the collections, paintings had been bought and sold over the years, and the foundation's tax-exempt status had encouraged occasional gifts and bequests, such as the donation of the Mondrian oil by someone named Barlow.

"I checked the hours when we came in," Carolyn was saying. "They're open from nine-thirty to five-thirty during the week and on Saturdays. On Sunday they open at noon and close at five."

"And they're closed Monday?"

"Closed all day Monday and open until nine on Tuesdays."

"Most museums keep hours about like that. I always know when it's Monday because the impulse comes on me to go to a museum, and they're all closed."

"Uh-huh. If we're planning to break in, we could do it either after hours or on Monday."

"Either way's impossible. They'll have guards posted around the clock. And the alarm system's a beaut. You can't just cross a couple of wires and pat it on the head."

"So what do we do? Snatch it off the wall and make a break for it?"

"Wouldn't work. They'd bag us before we got to the first floor."

"What does that leave?"

"Prayer and fasting."

"Terrific. Who's this guy? What's it say, van Doesburg? He and Mondrian must have gone to two different schools together."

57

We had sidled around to our left and were standing in front of a canvas by Theo van Doesburg. Like Mondrian's work, his was all right angles and primary colors, but there was no mistaking one artist for the other. The van Doesburg canvas lacked the sense of space and balance that Mondrian had. How curious, I thought, that a man could go for months without standing in front of a single Mondrian canvas, and then he'd stand before two of them on successive days. All the more remarkable, it seemed to me, was the similarity of the Hewlett's Mondrian to the one I'd seen hanging over Gordon Onderdonk's fireplace. If memory served, they were about the same size and proportion, and must have been painted at about the same stage in the artist's career. I was willing to believe that they'd look very different if one saw them side by side, but such a simultaneous viewing didn't appear to be an option, and if someone had told me that the Onderdonk painting had been hustled downtown and stuck up on the Hewlett's wall, I couldn't have sworn he was wrong. Onderdonk's painting was framed, of course, while this canvas was left unframed so as to show how the artist had continued his geometric design around the sides of the canvas. For all I knew Onderdonk's painting had twice as many colored areas. It might be taller or shorter, wider or narrower. But—

But it still seemed oddly coincidental. Coincidences don't have to be significant, of course. I'd picked up Carolyn at the Poodle

Factory and we'd shared a cab to the Hewlett, and I hadn't bothered reading our driver's name on the posted hack license, but suppose I had and suppose it had been Turnquist? Then, when the attendant had greeted the ill-clad artist by name, we might have remarked on the coincidence of having met two Turnquists in half an hour. But so what?

Still—

We circled the room, pausing now and then in front of a painting, including several that left me cold and a Kandinsky I liked a lot. There was an Arp. Onderdonk had an Arp, too, but since we hadn't been ordered to steal an Arp there was nothing particularly coincidental about it, or nothing remarkable about the coincidence, or—

"Bern? Should I just plain forget about the cat?"

"How would you go about doing that?"

"Beats me. Do you really think they'll do anything to Archie if we don't steal the painting?"

"Why should they?"

"To prove they mean business. Isn't that what kidnappers do?"

"I don't know what kidnappers do. I think they kill the victim to prevent being identified, but how's a Burmese cat going to identify them? But—"

"But who knows with crazy people? The thing is, they're expecting us to do the impossible."

"It's not necessarily impossible," I said. "Paintings walk out of museums all the time. In Italy museum theft is a whole industry, and

59

even here you see something in the papers every couple of months. The Museum of Natural History seems to get hit every once in a while."

"Then you think we can take it?"

"I didn't say that."

"Then—"

"Beautiful, isn't it?"

I turned at the voice, and there was our artist friend, his ten cent lapel badge fastened to his thrift shop jacket, his yellow teeth bared in a fierce grin. We were once again standing in front of *Composition with Color,* and Turnquist's eyes gleamed as he looked at the painting. "You can't beat old Piet," he said. "Sonofabitch could paint. Something, huh?"

"Something," I agreed.

"Most of this is crap. Detritus, refuse. In a word, you should pardon the expression, shit. My apologies, madam."

"It's all right," Carolyn assured him.

"The museum is the dustbin of the history of Art. Sounds like a quotation, doesn't it? I made it up myself."

"It has a ring to it."

"Dustbin's English for garbage can. English English, I mean to say. But the rest of this stuff, this is worse than garbage. *Dreck,* as some of my best friends would say."

"Er."

"Just a handful of good painters this century. Mondrian, of course. Picasso, maybe five percent of the time, when he wasn't cocking around. But five percent of Picasso is plenty, huh?"

"Er."

"Who else? Pollock. Frank Roth. Trossman. Clyfford Still. Darragh Park. Rothko, before he got so far down he forgot to use color. And others, a handful of others. But most of this—"

"Well," I said.

"I know what you want to say. Who's this old fart running off at the mouth? His jacket don't even match his pants and he's making judgments left and right, telling what's Art and what's garbage. That's what you're thinking, ain't it?"

"I wouldn't say that."

"Of course you wouldn't say it, you or this young lady. She's a lady and you're a gentleman and you wouldn't say such a thing. Me, I'm an artist. An artist can say anything. It's an edge the artist has over the gentleman. I know what you're thinking."

"Uh."

"And you're right to think it. I'm nobody, that's who I am. Just a painter nobody ever heard of. All the same, I saw you looking at a real painter's work, I saw you keep coming back to this painting, and right off I knew you could tell the difference between chicken salad and chicken shit, if you'll pardon me once again, madam."

"It's all right," Carolyn said.

"But it puts my back up to see people give serious attention to most of this crap. You know how you'll read in the paper that a man takes a knife or a bottle of acid and attacks some

61

famous painting? And you probably say to yourself what everybody else says. 'How could anybody do such a thing? He'd have to be a madman.' The person who does it is always an artist, and in the papers they call him a 'self-styled' artist. Meaning *he* says he's an artist but you know and I know the poor fellow's got shit for brains. Once again, dear madam—"

"It's okay."

"I'll say this," he said, "and then I'll leave you good people alone. It is a mark not of madness but of sanity to destroy bad art when it is placed on display in the nation's temples. I'll say more than that. The destruction of bad art is in itself a work of art. Bakunin said the urge to destroy is a creative urge. To slash some of these canvases—" He took a deep breath, expelled it all in a sigh. "But I'm a talker, not a destroyer. I'm an artist, I paint my paintings and I live my life. I saw the interest you were taking in my favorite painting and it provoked this outburst. Am I forgiven?"

"There's nothing to forgive," Carolyn told him.

"You're kind people, gracious people. And if I've given you something to think about, why, then you haven't wasted the day and neither have I."

SIX

"THERE'S THE ANSWER," Carolyn said. "We'll destroy the painting. Then they couldn't expect us to steal it."

"And they'll destroy the cat."

"Don't even say that. Can we get out of here?"

"Good idea."

Outside, a young man in buckskin and a young woman in denim were sprawled on the Hewlett's steps, passing an herbal cigarette back and forth. A pair of uniformed guards at the top of the stairs ignored them, perhaps because they were over sixteen. Carolyn wrinkled her nose as she passed the two.

"Sick," she said. "Why can't they get drunk like civilized human beings?"

"You could try asking them."

"They'd say, 'Like, man, wow.' That's what they always say. Where are we going?"

"Your place."

"Okay. Any particular reason?"

"Somebody took a cat out of a locked apartment," I said, "and I'd like to try to figure out how."

We walked west, subwayed downtown, and walked from Sheridan Square to Carolyn's place on Arbor Court, one of those wobbly Village streets that slants off at an angle, bridging the gap between hither and yon. Most people couldn't find it, but then most people wouldn't have occasion to look for it in the first place. We walked through a lazy overcast September afternoon that made me want to dash uptown and lace up my running shoes. I told Carolyn it was a great day for running, and she told me there was no such thing.

When we got to her building I examined the lock out in front. It didn't look too challenging. Anyway, it's no mean trick to get in the front door of an unattended building. You ring the other tenants' bells until one of them irresponsibly buzzes you in, or you loiter outside and time your approach so that you reach the doorway just as someone else is going in or out. It's a rare tenant who'll challenge you if you have the right air of arrogant nonchalance.

I didn't have to do all that, however, because Carolyn had her key. She let us in and we went down the hall to her apartment, which is on the ground floor in the back. I knelt and studied keyholes.

"If you see an eye staring back at you," Carolyn said, "I don't want to know about it. What are you looking for?"

"A sign that somebody tampered with the locks. I don't see any fresh scratches. Have you got a match?"

"I don't smoke. Neither do you, remember?"

"I wanted better light. My penlight's home.

64

It doesn't matter." I got to my feet. "Let me have your keys."

I unlocked all the locks, and when we were inside I examined them, especially the Fox lock. While I was doing this, Carolyn walked around calling for Ubi. Her voice got increasingly panicky until the cat appeared in response to the whirr of the electric can opener. "Oh, Ubi," she said, and scooped him up and plopped herself down in a chair with him. "Poor baby, you miss your buddy, don't you?"

I went over to the little window and opened it. Cylindrical iron bars an inch thick extended the length of the window, anchored in the brick below and the concrete lintel above. All the window needed was a few similar bars running horizontally and a few squares of color and it could be a Mondrian. I took hold of a couple of bars and tugged them to and fro. They didn't budge.

Carolyn asked me what the hell I was doing. "Someone could have hacksawed the bars," I said, "and fitted them back into place afterward." I tugged on a couple more. They made the Rock of Gibraltar seem like a shaky proposition in comparison. "These aren't going anyplace," I said. "They're illegal, you know. If there's ever a fire inspection they'll make you take them out."

"I know."

"Because if there's ever a fire, that's the only window and you'd never get out it."

"I know. I also know I'm in a ground floor apartment facing out on an airshaft and the burglars would trip over each other if I didn't have bars on the window. I could get those window gates that you can unlock in case of fire but I know I'd never find the key if I had to, and I'm sure burglars can get through those gates. So I think I'll just leave well enough alone."

"I don't blame you. Nobody got in this way unless he's awfully goddamn skinny. People can get through narrower spaces than you'd think. When I was a kid I could crawl through a milk chute, and I could probably still crawl through a milk chute, come to think of it, because I'm about the same size I was then. And it looked impossible. It was about ten inches wide by maybe fourteen inches high, but I made it. If you can get your head through an opening, the rest of the body will follow."

"Really?"

"Ask any obstetrician. Oh, I don't suppose it works with really fat people."

"Or with pinheads."

"Well, yeah, right. But it's a good general rule. Nobody got in this window, though, because the bars are what? Three, four inches apart?"

"You can leave the window open, Bern. It's stuffy in here. They didn't get in through the window and they didn't pick the locks, so what does that leave? Black magic?"

"I don't suppose we can rule it out."

"The flue's blocked on my fireplace, in case you figured Santa Claus pulled the job. How else could they get in? Up from the basement through the floor? Down through the ceiling?"

"It doesn't seem likely. Carolyn, what did the place look like when you came in?"

"Same as it always looks."

"They didn't go through the drawers or anything?"

"They could have opened drawers and closed them again and I wouldn't have noticed. They didn't mess anything up, if that's what you mean. I didn't even know I'd had anybody here until I couldn't find the cat. I *still* didn't know somebody'd been in here, not until I got the phone call and realized somebody stole the cat. He didn't just disappear on his own, Bernie. What difference does it make?"

"I don't know."

"Maybe somebody hooked my keys out of my purse. It wouldn't be that hard to do. Somebody could have come in while I was at the Poodle Factory, got ahold of my key ring, had a locksmith copy everything, then dropped the keys back in my bag."

"All without your noticing?"

"Why not? Say they swipe the keys while they're inquiring about getting a dog groomed, and then they come back to make an appointment and return the keys. It's possible, isn't it?"

"You leave your bag where anybody can get at it?"

"Not as a general rule, but who knows? Anyway, what the hell difference does it make? We're not just locking the barn after the horse has been stolen. We're checking the locks and dusting the bolt for fingerprints." She frowned. "Maybe we should have done that."

"Dusted for prints? Even if there'd been any, what good would they have done us? We're not the cops, Carolyn."

"Couldn't you get Ray Kirschmann to run a check on a set of fingerprints?"

"Not out of the goodness of his heart, and you can't really run a check on a single print unless you've already got a suspect in hand. You need a whole set of prints, which we wouldn't have even if whoever it was left prints, which they probably didn't. And they'd have to have been fingerprinted anyway for a check to reveal them, and—"

"Forget I mentioned it, okay?"

"Forget you mentioned what?"

"Can't remember. Well, let's just—*shit*," she said, and moved to answer the phone. "Hello? Huh? Hold on, I just—shit, they hung up."

"Who?"

"The Nazi. I'm supposed to look in the mailbox. I looked, remember? All I got was my Con Ed bill and that was enough bad news for one day. And there was nothing in the slot at the Poodle Factory except a catalog of grooming supplies and a flier from one of the animal cruelty organizations. There won't be another delivery today, will there?"

"Maybe they put something in the box without sending it through the mail, Carolyn. I know it's a federal offense but I think we're dealing with people who'll stop at nothing."

She gave me a look, then went out to the hall. She came back with a small envelope. It had been folded lengthwise for insertion through the small slot in the mailbox. She unfolded it.

"No name," she said. "And no stamp."

"And no return address either, and isn't that a surprise? Why don't you open it?"

She held it to the light, squinted at it. "Empty," she said.

"Open it and make sure."

"Okay, but what's the point? For that matter, what's the point of stuffing an empty envelope into somebody's mailbox? Is it really a federal offense?"

"Yeah, but they'll be tough to prosecute. What's the matter?"

"Look!"

"Hairs," I said, picking one up. "Now why in—"

"Oh, God, Bernie. Don't you see what they are?" She gripped my elbows in her hands, stared up at me. "They're the cat's whiskers," she said.

"And you're the cat's pajamas. I'm sorry. That just came out. Are they really? Why would anybody do that?"

"To convince us that they mean business."

"Well, I'm convinced. I was convinced earlier when they managed to get the cat out of a locked room. They've got to be crazy, cutting off a cat's whiskers."

"That way they can prove they've actually got him."

I shrugged. "I don't know. One set of whiskers looks a lot like another one. I figure you've seen one set, you've seen 'em all. Jesus Christ."

"What's the matter?"

"We can't get the Mondrian out of the Hewlett."

"I know that."

"But I know where there's a Mondrian that I *could* steal."

"Where, the Museum of Modern Art? They've got a couple. And there are a few in the Guggenheim too, aren't there?"

"I know one in a private collection."

"The Hewlett's was in private hands, too. Now it's in public hands, and unless it gets to be in our hands soon—"

"Forget that one. The one I'm talking about is still in a private collection, because I saw it last night."

She looked at me. "I know you went out last night."

"Right."

"But you didn't tell me what you did."

"Well, you can probably guess. But what I did first, what got me into the building, is I appraised a man's library. A nice fellow named Onderdonk, he paid me two hundred dollars to tell him what his books were worth."

"Were they worth much?"

"Not compared to what he had hanging on his wall. He had a Mondrian, among other things."

"Like the one in the Hewlett?"

"Well, who knows? It was about the same size and shape and I think the colors were the same, but maybe they'd look completely different to an expert. The thing is, if I could get in there and steal his Mondrian—"

"They'll know it's not the right one because it'll still be on the wall at the Hewlett."

"Yeah, but will they want to argue the point? If we can hand them a genuine Mondrian worth whatever it is, a quarter of a million is the figure they came up with—"

"Is it really worth that much?"

"I have no idea. The art market's down these days but that's about as much as I know. If we can give them a Mondrian in exchange for a stolen cat, don't you think they'd go for it? They'd have to be crazy to turn it down."

"We already know they're crazy."

"Well, they'd also have to be stupid, and they couldn't be too stupid if they managed to swipe the cat." I grabbed her phone book, looked up Onderdonk's number, dialed it. I let it ring a dozen times and nobody answered it. "He's out," I said. "Now let's just hope he stays out for a while."

"What are you gonna do, Bern?"

"I'm going home," I said, "and I'm going to change my clothes and put some handy gadgets into my pockets—"

"Burglar's tools."

"And then I'm going to the Charlemagne, and I'd better get there before four or someone'll recognize me, the doorman or the concierge or the elevator operator. But maybe they won't. I was wearing a suit last night and I'll dress down this time around, but even so I'd rather get there before four."

"How are you going to get in, Bern? Isn't that one of those places that's tighter than Fort Knox?"

"Well, look," I said, "I never told you it was going to be easy."

I hurried uptown and changed into chinos and a short-sleeved shirt that would have been an Alligator except that the embroidered device on the breast was not that reptile but a bird in flight. I guess it was supposed to be a swallow, either winging its way back to Capistrano or not quite making a summer, because the brand name was Swallowtail. It had never quite caught on and I can understand why.

I added a pair of rundown running shoes, filled my pockets with burglar's tools—an attaché case wouldn't fit the image I was trying to project. I got out a clipboard and mounted a yellow pad on it, then set it aside.

I dialed Onderdonk's number again and let it ring. Nobody answered. I looked up another number and no one answered it, either. I tried a third number and a woman answered midway through the fourth ring. I asked if Mr. Hodpepper was in, and she said I had the wrong number, but that's what she thought.

I stopped at a florist on Seventy-second and picked up an assortment for $4.98. It struck me, as it has often struck me in the past, that flowers haven't gone up much in price over the years, to the point where they're one of the few things left that give you your money's worth.

I asked for a small blank card, wrote *Leona Tremaine* on the envelope, and inscribed the card *Fondly, Donald Brown.* (I thought of signing it Howard Hodpepper but sanity prevailed, as it now and then does.) I paid for the flowers, taped the card to the wrapping paper, and went outside to hail a cab.

It dropped me on Madison Avenue around the corner from the Charlemagne. A florist's delivery boy does not, after all, arrive by taxi. I walked to the building's front entrance and moved past the doorman to the concierge.

"Got a delivery," I said, and read from the card. "Leona Tremaine, it says."

"I'll see she gets them," he said, reaching for the bouquet. I drew it back.

"I'm supposed to deliver 'em in person."

"Don't worry, she'll get 'em."

"Case there's a reply," I said.

"He wants his tip," the doorman interposed. "That's all he wants."

"From Tremaine?" the concierge said, and he and the doorman exchanged smiles. "Suit yourself," he told me, and picked up the intercom phone. "Miz Tremaine? Delivery for you, looks like flowers. The delivery boy's bringing them up. Yes, ma'am." He hung up and shook his head. "Go on up," he said. "Elevator's over there. It's apartment 9-C."

73

I glanced at my watch in the elevator. The timing, I thought, could not have been better. It was three-thirty. The doorman, the concierge and the elevator operator were not the crew who'd seen me enter last night, nor had they been around when I left with Appling's stamps in my attaché case. And in half an hour they'd go off duty, before they'd had a chance to wonder why the kid with the flowers was spending so much time in Ms. Tremaine's apartment. The crew that relieved them wouldn't realize I'd come delivering flowers and would assume I'd had legitimate business with some other tenant. Anyway, they don't hassle you as much on the way out, assuming you must have been okay to get past their security the first time around. It's different if you try to carry out the furniture, of course, but generally speaking getting in's the hard part.

The elevator stopped on Nine and the operator pointed at the appropriate door. I thanked him and went and stood in front of it, waiting for the sound of the door closing. It didn't close. Of course it didn't. They waited until the tenant opened the door. Well, she was expecting the flowers anyway, so what was I waiting for?

I poked the doorbell. Chimes sounded within, and after a moment the door opened. The woman who answered it had improbable auburn hair and a face that had fallen one more time than it had been lifted. She was wearing a sort of dressing gown with an oriental motif and she had a look about her of someone

74

who had just smelled something unseemly.

"Flowers," she said. "Now are you quite sure those are for me?"

"Ms. Leona Tremaine?"

"That's correct."

"Then they're for you."

I was still listening for the sound of the elevator door, and I was beginning to realize I wasn't going to hear it. And why should I? He wasn't going anywhere, he'd wait right there until she'd taken the flowers and given me my tip, and then he'd whisk me downstairs again. Terrific. I'd found a way to get into the Charlemagne but I still needed a way to stay there.

"I can't think who'd send me flowers," she said, taking the wrapped bouquet from me. "Unless it might be my sister's boy Lewis, but why would he take a notion of sending me flowers? There must be some mistake."

"There's a card," I said.

"Oh, there's a card," she said, discovering it for herself. "Just wait a moment. Let me see if there hasn't been some mistake here. No, that's my name, Leona Tremaine. Now let me open this."

Didn't anyone else in the goddamned building want the elevator? Would nothing summon this putz out of his reverie and float him away to another floor?

"'Fondly, Donald Brown,'" she read aloud. "Donald Brown. Donald. Brown. Donald Brown. Now who could that be?"

"Uh."

"Well, they're perfectly lovely, aren't they?"

75

She sniffed industriously, as if determined to inhale not merely the bouquet but the petals as well. "And fragrant. Donald Brown. It's a familiar name, but—well, I'm sure there's been a mistake, but I'll just enjoy them all the same. I'll have to get down a vase, I'll have to put them in water—" She broke off suddenly, remembering that I was there. "Is there something else, young man?"

"Well, I just—"

"Oh, for heaven's sake, I'm forgetting you, aren't I? Just one moment, let me get my bag. I'll just put these down, here we are, here we are, and thank you very much, and my thanks to Donald Brown, whoever he may be."

The door closed.

I turned and there was the goddamned elevator, waiting for to carry me home. The attendant wasn't exactly smiling but he did look amused. I rode down and walked through the lobby. The doorman grinned when he saw me coming.

"Well," he said. "How'd you make out, fella?"

"Make out?"

"She give you a good tip?"

"She gave me a quarter," I said.

"Hey, cheer up, that's not bad for Tremaine. She doesn't part with a nickel all year round and then at Christmas she tips the building staff five bucks a man. That's ten cents a week. Can you believe it?"

"Sure," I said. "I can believe it."

SEVEN

I DIDN'T KEEP Leona Tremaine's quarter for very long. I walked around the corner, passed a watering hole called Big Charlie's, and had a cup of coffee at a lunch counter on Madison Avenue, where I left the quarter as a tip, hoping it would delight the waitress as much as it had delighted me. I got out of there and started walking uptown until I came to a florist.

It was past four. The shift would have changed by now, unless someone was late. Still, it would probably be easier getting past a crew who'd seen me last night than convincing the doorman and concierge I wanted to make another in-person delivery.

I went in and paid $7.98 for essentially the same assortment that had set me back $4.98 on the West Side. Ah, well. No doubt this chap had higher rent to pay. In any event, I might get another quarter from Ms. Tremaine, and that would offset some of my expenses.

Leona Tremaine, I wrote once more on the outside of the envelope. And, on the card, *Won't you say I'm forgiven? Donald Brown.*

★   ★   ★

The staff had turned over at the Charlemagne. I recognized the concierge and the doorman from the night before, but if my face was familiar they didn't remark on it. Last night I'd been a guest of a tenant, all decked out in suit and tie, while today I was a short-sleeved member of the working class. If either of them recognized me, he probably assumed he'd seen me delivering flowers another time.

Again the concierge offered to see that the flowers were delivered, and again I insisted on making the delivery in person, and again the doorman snickered, guessing that I wanted my tip. It was nice to see they all had their lines down pat. The concierge announced me on the intercom and Eduardo took me up to the ninth floor, where Ms. Tremaine was waiting in the doorway of her apartment.

"Why, it's you again," she said. "I can't understand this at all. Are you *sure* these flowers are for me?"

"The card says—"

"The card, the card, the card," she said, and opened its envelope. "'Won't you say I'm forgiven? Donald Brown.' What a curious sentiment. More specific than *fondly,* I daresay, but rather more baffling. Who is this Donald Brown and why am I to forgive him?"

The elevator had not gone away.

"I'm supposed to ask if there's a reply," I said.

"A reply? A reply? To whom am I supposed to address this reply? It's quite clear to me that I'm not the intended recipient of these flowers, and yet how could such a mistake have been

78

made? I no more know of another Leona Tremaine than I know any Donald Brown. Unless it's someone I knew years ago whose name has apparently slipped my recollection." Her hands, tipped with persimmon-colored nails, unwrapped the elusive Mr. Brown's offering. "Lovely," she said. "Lovelier than the last, but I don't understand why they've been given to me. I don't begin to understand it."

"I could call the store."

"I beg your pardon?"

"I could call the flower shop," I suggested. "Could I use your phone? If there's a mistake I'll get in trouble, and if there's no mistake maybe they can tell you something about the person who sent you the flowers."

"Oh," she said.

"I really better call," I said. "I don't know if I should leave the flowers without calling in."

"Well," she said. "Well, yes, perhaps you'd better call."

She led me inside, drew the door shut. I tried to hear the elevator going off on other business, but of course I couldn't hear anything. I followed Leona Tremaine into a thickly carpeted living room filled with more furniture than it needed, the bulk of it French Provincial. The chairs and sofa were mostly tufted and the colors ran to a lot of pink and white. A cat displayed himself on what looked to be the most comfortable of the chairs. He was a snow-white Persian and his whiskers were intact.

"There's a telephone," she said, pointing to one of those old French-style instruments trimmed out in gold and white enamel. I lifted the receiver to my ear and dialed Onderdonk's number. The line was busy.

"It's busy," I said. "People phone in orders all the time. You know how it is." Why was I running off at the mouth like this? "I'll try again in a minute."

"Well."

Why was Onderdonk's line busy? He'd been out earlier. Why couldn't he stay out, now that I'd finally gotten into his building? I couldn't leave now, for God's sake. I'd never get back in again.

I picked up the phone and called Carolyn Kaiser. When she answered I said, "Miz Kaiser, this is Jimmie. I'm up at Miz Tremaine's at the Charlemagne."

"You got the wrong number," my quick-witted henchperson said. "Wait a minute. Did you say— Bernie? Is that you?"

"Right, the delivery," I said. "Same as before. She says she don't know any Donald Brown and she don't think the flowers are for her. Right."

"You're calling from somebody's apartment."

"That's the idea," I said.

"Is she suspicious of you?"

"No, the thing is she doesn't know who this guy is."

"What's it all about, Bern? Are you just killing time?"

"Right."

"You want me to talk to her? I'll tell her What's-his-face paid cash and he gave her name and address. Gimme the names again."

"Donald Brown. And she's Leona Tremaine."

"Gotcha."

I handed the phone to Ms. Tremaine, who'd been hovering. She said, "Hello? to whom am I speaking, please?" and then she said things like "Yes" and "I see," and "But I don't—" and "It's so mysterious." And then she gave the phone back to me.

"Someday," said Carolyn, "all of this will be crystal clear to me."

"Sure thing, Miz Kaiser."

"Same to you, Mr. Rhodenbarr. I hope you know what you're doing."

"Yes, ma'am."

I hung up. Leona Tremaine said, "'Curiouser and curiouser, said Alice.' Your Donald Brown is a tall, gray-haired gentleman, elegantly dressed, who carried a cane and paid for both deliveries with a pair of crisp twenty-dollar bills. He did not give his address." Her face softened. "Perhaps it's someone I knew years ago," she said quietly. "Under another name, perhaps. And perhaps I'll hear further from him. I'm sure to hear further from him, wouldn't you say?"

"Well, if he went to all this trouble—"

"Exactly. He would scarcely go to such lengths merely to remain forever mysterious. Oh, dear," she said, and fluffed her auburn hair. "Such unaccustomed excitement."

I edged toward the door. "Well," I said. "I guess I'd better be going."

"Yes, well, you've been very kind, making that phone call." We walked together toward the door. "Oh," she said, remembering. "Just let me get my bag and I'll give you something for your trouble."

"Oh, that's all right," I said. "You took care of me before."

"That's right," she said. "I did, didn't I? It slipped my mind. It's good of you to remind me."

If the elevator's there, I thought, I'll just give up. But it wasn't. The floor indicator showed it on Three, and as I watched it moved to Four. Maybe Eduardo had forgotten about me. Then again, maybe he was on his way back.

I opened the fire door and went out onto the stairs.

Now what? Onderdonk's line was busy. I'd dialed the number from memory and I could have gotten it wrong, or it could have been busy because someone else had dialed the same number a few seconds before I did. Or he could be home.

I couldn't chance breaking in if anybody was home. And I couldn't knock on the door first, either. And I couldn't spend eternity on the stairs, because while it was possible the concierge and elevator operator and doorman would forget all about me, it was also possible they would not. A call on the intercom would establish that I'd left the Tremaine apartment, at which point they could either assume I'd left via the stairs (or even on the elevator) without anyone's noting the fact or else they'd figure I was still in the building.

In which case they might start looking for me.

Even if they didn't, the stairway was no place to be. I had to be able to establish via the telephone that Onderdonk's apartment was empty before I could enter it. And, once I'd entered it, I had to wait until midnight before I left with the painting in tow. Because the staff that was on duty now would certainly remember me, no matter what I did, and what kind of florist's delivery boy leaves a building an hour after he brings the flowers? I could perhaps get away with it, merely sullying Ms. Tremaine's reputation a bit, letting them assume we'd passed the time in amorous dalliance, but if they'd checked with her in the meanwhile and already *knew* I'd left—

I climbed two flights of stairs. I loided the fire door, checked the hallway, found it empty, and did the only sensible thing I could think of. Without bothering to put on my gloves, without even taking the obvious precaution of ringing the bell, and certainly without wasting a moment on the mock burglar alarm, I whipped out my ring of picks and probes and let myself into John Charles Appling's apartment.

EIGHT

FOR A MOMENT I thought I'd made a horrible mistake. The apartment was brighter by day than it had been on my last visit. Even with the drapes drawn a certain amount of daylight filtered in, and I thought there were lights on, indicating someone's presence. My heart stopped or raced or skipped a beat or whatever it does at such times, and then it calmed down and so did I. I put on my rubber gloves and locked the door and took a deep breath.

It felt very odd being back in the Appling place. There was once again the thrill of illicit entry, but it was diminished by the fact that I'd been here before. You can get as much pleasure the second or third or hundredth time you make love to a particular woman—you can get more, actually—but you can't get that triumphant sense of conquest more than once, and so it is too with the seduction of locks and the breaching of thresholds. On top of that, I hadn't broken in this time to steal anything. I was just looking for sanctuary.

And that was strange indeed. Less than twenty-four hours earlier I'd been in a state of high tension that didn't begin to dissipate until I left this apartment. Now I'd had to break into it all over again just to feel safe.

I went to the phone, picked it up. But why call Onderdonk now? I didn't want to leave the building until midnight, so why break into his place before then? I could go now, of course, if he was out. I could snatch the Mondrian and bring it back downstairs to the Appling apartment, and I could wait there until it was after midnight and safe to leave.

But I didn't want to. Better to stay where I was and call Onderdonk around midnight, and if he was out I could break and enter and leave in a hurry, and if he was in I could say, "Sorry, wrong number," and give him three or four or five hours to go to sleep, and then do my breaking and entering while he lay snug in his bed. I'd rather not hit a dwelling while its occupants are at home, intent as I am on avoiding human contact while I work, but the one advantage of visiting them when they're already at home is you don't have to worry about their coming home before you're done. In this case I wanted one thing and one thing only and I didn't have to search for it. It was right out there in the living room, and if he was asleep in the bedroom I wouldn't have to go anywhere near him.

I dialed the number anyway. It rang half a dozen times and I hung up. I'd have let it ring longer, but since I wasn't going in anyway, not for at least seven hours, why bother?

I crossed the living room, edged the drapery

aside with a rubber-tipped finger. The window looked out on Fifth Avenue, and from where I stood I had a fairly spectacular view of Central Park. I also had no need to worry about anyone looking in, unless someone was perched half a mile away on Central Park West with a pair of binoculars and a whole lot of patience, and that didn't seem too likely. I drew the drapes and pulled up a chair so that I could look out at the park. I picked out the zoo, the reservoir, the band shell, and other landmarks. I could see plenty of runners, on the circular drive and the bridle path and the running track around the reservoir. Watching them was like observing highway traffic from an airplane.

Too bad I couldn't be out there with them. It was a perfect day for it.

I got restless after a while and moved around the apartment. In Appling's study I took down a stamp album and paged idly through it. I saw a number of things I really should have taken on my last visit but I didn't even consider taking them now. Before I'd been a burglar, a predator on the prowl. This time around I was a guest, albeit uninvited, and I could hardly so abuse my host's hospitality.

I did enjoy looking at his stamps, though, without being under any obligation to make them my own. I sat back and let myself relax in the fantasy that this was my apartment and my stamp collection, that I had located and purchased all those little perforated rectangles of colored paper, that my fingers had delighted in fitting them with mounts and affixing them in their places. Most of the time I have trouble imagining why anyone would want to devote time and money to pasting postage stamps in a book, but now I sort of got into it, and I even felt a little guilt about having looted such a labor of love.

I'll tell you, it's a good thing I didn't have his stamps with me. I might have tried putting them back.

Time crawled on by. I didn't want to turn on the television set or play a radio, or even walk around too much, lest a neighbor wonder at sounds issuing from a supposedly empty apartment. I didn't have the concentration for reading, and there's something about holding a book in gloved hands that keeps one from getting caught up in the story. I went back to my chair by the window and watched the sun drop behind the buildings on the west side of the park, and that was about it, entertainment-wise.

I got hungry sometime around nine and rummaged around the kitchen. I filled a bowl with Grape-Nuts and added some suspicious milk. It probably would have curdled in a cup of coffee but it was all right in the cereal. Afterward I washed my bowl and spoon and put them where I'd found them. I went back to the living room and took off my shoes and stretched out on the rug with my eyes closed. My mind's eye gave itself over to a vast expanse of white, and while I was observing its pure perfection—virgin snow, I thought, or the fleeces of a million lambs—while I was thus waxing poetic, black ribbons uncurled and stretched themselves across the white expanse, extending from top to bottom, from left to right, forming a random rectangular grid. Then one of the enclosed spaces of white blushed and reddened, and another spontaneously took on a faint sky tint that deepened all the way to a rich cobalt blue, and another red square began to bleed in on the lower right, and—

By God, my mind was painting me a Mondrian.

I watched as the pattern changed and re-formed itself, working variations on a theme. I'm not sure just what consciousness is and is not, but at one point I was conscious and at another I wasn't, and then there came a moment when I caught hold of myself and shook myself loose of something. I sat up, looked at my watch.

Seven, eight minutes past twelve.

I took another few minutes making sure I left Appling's apartment as I'd found it. I'd slept in my rubber gloves and my fingers were damp and clammy. I stripped off the gloves, dried the insides of the fingers, washed and dried my hands, and put them back on again. I straightened this and tidied that, drew the drapes, put back the chair I'd moved. Then I picked up the phone, checked Onderdonk's number in the book to make sure I got it right, dialed it, and let it ring an even dozen times.

I turned off the one light I'd had on, let myself out, locked the door after me and wiped the knob and the surrounding area and the doorbell. I hurried through the fire door and up four flights to Sixteen, let myself into the hallway, crossed over to Onderdonk's door and rang his bell. I waited for a moment, just in case, said a fervent if hurried prayer to Saint Dismas, and knocked off a four-tumbler Segal drop-bolt lock in not much more time than I'd spent pouring the milk over the Grape-Nuts.

Darkness within. I slipped inside, drew the door shut, breathed slowly and deeply and let my eyes adjust. I put my ring of picks back in my pocket and fumbled around for my penlight. I already had my gloves on, not having bothered to remove them for the quick run upstairs. I oriented myself in the darkness, or tried to, and I raised my penlight, pointed it to where the fireplace ought to be, and switched it on.

The fireplace was there. Above it was an expanse of white, just what I'd envisioned on Appling's floor before the black lines insinuated themselves across its length and breadth. But where were the black lines now? Where were the rectangles of blue and red and yellow?

Where, for that matter, was the canvas? Where was the aluminum frame? And why was there nothing above Onderdonk's fireplace but a blank wall?

I flicked off my light, stood again in darkness. The familiar thrill of burglary took on the added element of panic. Was I, for heaven's sake, in the wrong apartment? Had I, for the love of God, climbed one too few or one too many flights of stairs? Leona Tremaine was on Nine, and I'd gone up two flights to Eleven, where I'd been a guest of the Applings. From Eleven to Sixteen was four flights, but had I counted flights as I went and included the nonexistent thirteenth?

I flicked the light on. It was likely that all of the apartments in the B line had the same essential layout, and each would have a fireplace in that particular spot. But would other apartments have bookcases flanking the fireplace? And these were familiar shelves, and I could even recognize some of the books. There was the leatherbound Defoe. There were the two volumes, boxed, of Stephen Vincent Benét's selected prose and selected poetry. And there, faintly discernible in that expanse of white, looking almost like the negative image of an Ad Reinhardt black-on-black canvas, was the slightly lighter rectangle where the Mondrian had lately hung. Time and New York air had darkened the surrounding wall, leaving a ghost image of the painting I'd come to steal.

I lowered the light to the floor, made my way into the room. The picture wasn't there and the picture should have been there and something didn't compute. Was I still asleep? Was I dozing on Appling's floor, and had I merely dreamed the part about waking up and going upstairs? I decided I had, and I gave a mental yank to pull myself out of it, and nothing happened.

Something felt wrong, and I was feeling more than the unexpected absence of the painting. I moved farther into the room and played my light here and there. If anything else was missing, I didn't notice it. The Arp painting still hung where I'd seen it on my first visit. Other paintings were where I remembered them. I turned and swung the flashlight around, and its beam showed me a bronze head, Cycladic in style, on a black lucite plinth. I remembered the head from before, though I'd paid it little attention then. I continued to move the light around in a slow circle, and I may have heard or sensed an intake of breath, and then the flashlight's beam was falling full upon a woman's face.

Not a painting, not a statue. A woman, positioned between me and the door, one small hand held at waist level, the other poised at shoulder height, palm out, as if to ward off something menacing.

"Oh, my God," she said. "You're a burglar, you're going to rape me, you're going to kill me. Oh, my God."

Be a dream, I prayed, but it wasn't and I knew it wasn't. I was caught in the act, I had a pocket full of burglar's tools and no right to be where I was, and a search of my apartment would turn up enough stolen stamps to start a branch post office. And she was between me and the door, and even if I got past her she could

91

call downstairs before I could get anywhere near the lobby, and her mouth was ajar and any second now she was going to scream.

All for the sake of some goddamn cat with a clever name and an assertive personality. Six days a week the ASPCA's busy putting surplus cats to sleep, and I was going to wind up in slam trying to ransom one. I stood there, holding the light in her eyes as if it might hypnotize her, like a deer in a car's headlights. But she didn't look hypnotized. She looked terrified, and sooner or later the terror would ease up enough for her to scream, and I thought about that and thought about stone walls.

Stone walls do not a prison make, according to Sir Richard Lovelace, and I'm here to tell you the man was whistling in the dark. Stone walls make a hell of a prison and iron bars make a perfectly adequate cage, and I've been there and I don't ever want to go back.

Just get me out of this and I'll—

And I'll what? And I'll probably do it again, I thought, because I'm evidently incorrigible. But just get me out of it and we'll see.

"Please," she said. "Please don't hurt me."

"I'm not going to hurt you."

"Don't kill me."

"Nobody's going to kill you."

She was about five-six and slender, with an oval face and eyes a spaniel would have won Best of Breed with. Her hair was dark and shoulder-length, drawn back from a sharp widow's peak and secured in unbraided pigtails. She was wearing oatmeal jeans and a lime polo shirt with a real alligator on it. Her brown suede slippers looked like something a Hobbit would wear.

"You're going to hurt me."

"I never hurt anyone," I told her. "I don't even kill cockroaches. Oh, I put boric acid around, and I guess that's the same thing from a moral standpoint, but as far as hauling off and swatting 'em, that's something I never do. And not just because it makes a spot. See, I'm basically nonviolent, and—"

And why was I running off at the mouth like this? Nerves, I suppose, and the premise that she'd be polite enough not to scream while I was talking.

"Oh, God," she said. "I'm so frightened."

"I didn't mean to frighten you."

"Look at me. I'm shaking."

"Don't be afraid."

"I can't help it. I'm scared."

"So am I."

"You are?"

"You bet."

"But you're a burglar," she said, frowning. "Aren't you?"

"Well—"

"Of course you are. You've got gloves on."

"I was doing the dishes."

She started to laugh, and the laughter slipped away from her and climbed toward hysteria. She said, "Oh, God, why am I laughing? I'm in danger."

"No, you're not."

"I am, I am. It happens all the time, a woman surprises a burglar and she gets raped and killed. Stabbed to death."

"I don't even have a penknife."

"Strangled."

"I don't have any strength in my hands."

"You're making jokes."

"You're sweet to say so."

"You're—you seem nice."

"That's exactly it," I said. "You hit it. What I am, I'm your basic nice guy."

"But look at me. I mean don't look at me. I mean—I don't know what I mean."

"Easy. Everything's going to be all right."

"I believe you."

"Of course you do."

"But I'm still frightened."

"I know you are."

"And I can't help it. I can't stop trembling. On the inside it feels like I'm going to shake myself to pieces."

"You'll be okay."

"Could you—"

"What?"

"This is crazy."

"It's all right."

"No, you're going to think, I'm crazy. I mean, you're the one I'm afraid of, but—"

"Go ahead."

"Could you just hold me? Please?"

"Hold you?"

"In your arms."

"Well, uh, if you think it'll help—"

"I just want to be held."

"Well, sure."

I took her in my arms and she buried her face in my chest. Our polo shirts pressed together and became as one. I felt the warmth and fullness of her breasts through the two layers of fabric. I stood there in the dark—my penlight was back in my pocket—and I held her close, stroking her silky hair with one hand, patting her back and shoulder with the other, and saying "There, there," in a tone that was meant to be reassuring.

The awful tension went out of her. I kept holding her and went on murmuring to her, breathing in her scent and absorbing her warmth, and—

"Oh," she said.

She lifted up her head and our eyes met. There was enough light for me to stare into them and they were deep enough to drown a man. I held her and looked at her and Something Happened.

"This is—"

"I know."

"Crazy."

"I know."

I let go of her. She took her shirt off. I took my shirt off. She came back into my arms. I was still wearing those idiot gloves, and I tore them off and felt her skin under my fingers and against my chest.

"Gosh," she said.

NINE

"GOSH," SHE SAID again some minutes later. Our clothing was on the floor in a heap and so, in another heap, were we. Given a choice, I suppose I'd have gone for, say, a platform bed with an innerspring mattress and Porthault sheets, but we'd done remarkably well on an Aubusson carpet. The sense of dreamlike unreality that had begun with the mysterious disappearance of the Mondrian was getting stronger every minute, but I'll tell you, I was beginning to like it.

I ran a lingering hand over an absolutely marvelous curved surface, then got to my feet and groped around in the dimness until I found a table lamp and switched it on. She instinctively covered herself, one hand at her loins, the other across her breasts, then caught herself and laughed.

She said, "What did I tell you? I knew you were going to rape me."

"Some rape."

"I'm just grateful you took those gloves off. I'd have felt as if I'd dropped in for a Pap smear."

"Speaking of which, why did you?"

"Why did I what?"

"Drop in."

She tilted her head to the side. "Shouldn't I be asking you that question?"

"You already know why I'm here," I said. "I'm a burglar. I came here to steal something. What about you?"

"I live here."

"Uh-uh. Onderdonk's been alone since his wife died."

"He's been alone," she said, "but he hasn't been *alone*."

"I see. You and he have been—"

"Are you shocked? I just did it with you on the living room rug so you must have figured out I wasn't a virgin. Why shouldn't Gordon and I be lovers?"

"Where is he?"

"He's out."

"And you were waiting for him to come back."

"That's right."

"Why didn't you answer the phone a few minutes ago?"

"Was that you? I didn't answer it because I never answer Gordon's phone. After all, I don't officially live here. I just stay over sometimes."

"Don't you answer the bell, either?"

"Gordon always uses his key."

"So when he used it this time you turned off the lights and stood with your back against the wall."

"I didn't turn off the lights. They were already off."

"You were just sitting here in the dark."

"I was lying on the couch, actually. I was reading and I dozed off."

"Reading in the dark and you dozed off."

"I felt drowsy so I switched off the light, and *then* I dozed off in the darkness. And because I was half asleep I reacted slowly and perhaps illogically when you rang the bell and then opened the door. Satisfied?"

"Deeply satisfied. Where's the book?"

"The book?"

"The one you were reading?"

"Maybe it dropped to the floor and wound up under the couch. Or maybe I put it back on the shelf when I turned the light off. What difference does it make, anyway?"

"No difference."

"I mean, you're a burglar, right? You're not Mr. District Attorney, asking me where I was on the night of March twenty-third. I should be asking the questions. How did you get past the front desk? There's a good question."

"It's a great one," I agreed. "I landed on the roof with a helicopter and let myself down by rope and got into a penthouse apartment through the door from the terrace. Then I walked down a few flights of stairs and here I am."

"Didn't you steal anything in the penthouse?"

"They didn't have anything. I guess they were house-poor, you know? Spent all their money on the apartment."

"I suppose that happens all the time."

"You'd be surprised. How did *you* get past the desk?"

"Me?"

"Uh-huh. You don't officially live here. Why would they let you up when Onderdonk was out?"

"He was here when I came. Then he went out."

"And left you here in the dark."

"I told you I—"

"Right. You turned the light off when you got drowsy."

"Didn't that ever happen to you?"

"I never get drowsy. What's the capital of New Jersey?"

"New Jersey? The capital of New Jersey?"

"Right."

"Is this some kind of a trick question? The capital of New Jersey. It's Trenton, isn't it?"

"That's right."

"What does that have to do with anything?"

"Not a thing," I admitted. "I just wanted to see if your face changed when you told the truth. The last honest thing you said was 'Gosh.' You cut the lights when you heard me coming and you tried to melt into the wall. You were scared to death when you saw me but you'd have been scared clear into the next world if it had been Onderdonk. Why don't you tell me what you came to steal and whether or not you found it yet? Maybe I can help you look."

She just looked at me for a moment and her

face went through some interesting changes. Then she sighed and rummaged around in the heap of clothing.

"I'd better get dressed," she said.

"If you feel you must."

"He'll be back soon. Or at least he might. Sometimes he stays the night but he'll probably be back around two. What time is it?"

"Almost one."

We sorted out our clothes and began getting into them. She said, "I haven't stolen anything. You're welcome to search me if you don't believe me."

"Good idea. Strip."

"But I just—for a second I thought you were serious."

"Just my little joke."

"Well, you had me going there." She thought for a moment. "Maybe I should just tell you why I'm here."

"Maybe you should."

"I'm married."

"Not to Onderdonk."

"God, no. But Gordon and I—let's say I was indiscreet."

"On this very rug?"

"No, this was a first for me. You were my first burglar and my first romp on a carpet." She grinned suddenly. "I always had fantasies of being taken passionately and abruptly by a stranger. Not of being raped, exactly, but of being, oh, carried away. Transported by desire."

"I hope I didn't ruin your fantasies for you."

"*Au contraire,* darling. You brought them to life."

"Shall we get back to Onderdonk? You were indiscreet."

"Very, I'm afraid. I wrote him some letters."

"Love letters?"

"Lust letters is more like it. 'I wish I had your this in my that. I'd like to verb your noun until you verb.' That sort of thing."

"I bet you write a terrific letter."

"Gordon thought so. After we stopped seeing each other—we broke it off weeks ago—I asked for my letters back."

"And he refused?"

" 'They were written to me,' he said. 'That makes them my property.' He wouldn't give them back."

"And he was using them to blackmail you?"

Her eyes widened. "Why would he do that? Gordon's rich, and I don't have any money of my own."

"He could have blackmailed you for something besides money."

"Oh, you mean sex? I suppose he could have but he didn't. The affair ended by mutual consent. No, he simply wanted to retain the letters as a way of keeping the affair's memory fresh. He said once that he intended to save them for his old age. Something to read when reading was the only thing left for him."

"I suppose it beats Louis Auchincloss."

"I beg your pardon?"

"Nothing. So he kept your letters."

"And the photographs."

"Photographs?"

"He took pictures a couple of times."

"Pictures of you?"

"Some of me and some of both of us. He has a Polaroid with a cable shutter release."

"So he could get some good shots of you verbing his noun."

"He could and did."

I straightened up. "Well, we've still got a few minutes," I said, "and I'm pretty good at search-and-destroy missions. If the letters and photos are in this apartment, I bet I can find them."

"I already found them."

"Oh?"

"They were in his dresser and it was almost the first place I looked."

"And where are they now?"

"Down the incinerator."

"Dust to dust, ashes to ashes."

"You have a way with words."

"Thank you. Mission accomplished, eh? You found the letters and pictures, sent them down to be burned or compacted or whatever they do at the Charlemagne, and then you were on your way."

"That's right."

"So how come you were still here when I let myself in?"

"I was on my way out," she said. "I was heading for the door. I had my hand on the knob when you rang the bell."

"Suppose it had been Onderdonk."

"I thought it was. Not when I heard the bell,

because why would he ring his own door? Unless he knew I was in his apartment."

"How'd you get in?"

"He never double-locks the door. I opened it with a credit card."

"You know how to do that?"

"Doesn't everybody? All you have to do is watch television and you see them doing it. It's educational."

"It must be. The door was double-locked when I tried it. I had to pick the tumblers."

"I turned the bolt from inside."

"Why?"

"I don't know. Reflex, I guess. I should have put the chain on while I was at it. Then you'd have known somebody was here and you wouldn't have come in, would you?"

"Probably not, and you wouldn't have had a chance to bring your fantasy to life."

"That's a point."

"But suppose instead of me it had been Onderdonk. Would you have verbed him on the carpet or hauled him off to the bedroom?"

She sighed. "I don't know. I guess I would have told him what I'd done. I think he probably would have laughed about it. As I said, we parted on good terms. But he was a big man and he had a temper, and that's why I was scrunched up against the wall hoping for a way to get out without being seen. And knowing it was impossible, but not knowing what else to do."

"What happened to the painting?"

She blinked at me. "Huh?"

"There. Over the fireplace."

She looked. "He had a painting hanging there, didn't he? Of course he did. You can see the outline."

"A Mondrian."

"Of course, what am I thinking of. His Mondrian. *Oh.* You came here to steal his Mondrian!"

"I just wanted to look at it. The museums all close around six and I had a sudden urge to bask in the inner glow of great art."

"And here I thought you just hit this apartment at random. But you were here for the Mondrian."

"I didn't say that."

"You didn't have to. You know, he said something about that painting. It was a while ago. I wonder if I can remember what it was."

"Take your time."

"Isn't there an exhibition forming of Mondrian's work? Either Mondrian or the whole De Stijl school of abstract painting. They wanted Gordon to lend them his Mondrian."

"And they picked it up this afternoon?"

"Why, is that when it left its spot on the wall? If you knew it was gone this afternoon, why did you come for it tonight?"

"I don't know when it left. I just know it was here yesterday."

"How do you know that? Never mind, I don't think you want to tell me that. I may not remember this correctly—I wasn't paying too much attention—but I think Gordon was having the painting reframed for the exhibition. He had it framed in aluminum like the rest of the ones here and he wanted some other kind of frame that would enclose the canvas without covering up its edges. Mondrian was one of those painters who continue the design of the painting right around the sides of the canvas, and Gordon wanted that part to show because it was technically part of the work, but he didn't want to display a completely unframed canvas. I don't know how he was going to have it done, but, well, I wouldn't be surprised if that's what happened to the painting. What time is it?"

"Ten minutes past one."

"I have to go. Whether he's coming back or not, I have to go. Are you going to steal anything else? Other paintings or anything else you can find?"

"No. Why?"

"I just wondered. Do you want to leave first?"

"Not particularly."

"Oh?"

"It's my chivalrous nature. Not just the old principle of ladies first, but I'd worry about you forever if I didn't know you got out safely. How are you going to get out, by the way?"

"I won't even need my credit card. Oh, you mean how'll I get out of the building? The same way I got in. I'll ride down in the elevator, smile sweetly, and let the doorman get me a cab."

"Where do you live?"

"A cab ride away."

"So do I, but I think we should take separate cabs. You don't want to tell me where you live."

"Not really, no. I don't think it's a good idea to tell burglars my home address. You might make off with the family silver."

"Not since the price drop. It's barely worth stealing these days. Suppose I wanted to see you again?"

"Just keep opening doors. You never know what you'll find on the other side."

"Isn't that the truth. Could be the lady, could be the tiger."

"Could be both."

"Uh-huh. You've got sharp claws, incidentally."

"You didn't seem to mind."

"I wasn't objecting, just commenting. I don't even know your name."

"Just think of me as the Dragon Lady."

"I didn't notice anything draggin'. My name is Bernie."

She cocked her head, gave the matter some thought. "Bernie the Burglar. I don't suppose there's any harm in your knowing my first name, is there?"

"Besides, you could always make one up."

"Is that what you just did? But I couldn't. I never lie."

"I understand that's the best policy."

"That's what I've always heard. My name is Andrea."

"Andrea. You know what I'd like to do,

Andrea? I'd like to throw you right back down on the old Aubusson and have my way with you."

"My, that doesn't sound bad at all. If we had world enough and time, but we really don't. *I* don't, anyway. I have to get out of here."

"It would be nice," I said, "if there were a way I could get in touch with you."

"The thing is I'm married."

"But occasionally indiscreet."

"Occasionally. But discreetly indiscreet, if you get my drift. Now if you were to tell *me* how to get in touch with *you*—"

"Uh."

"You see? You're a burglar and you don't want to run the risk that I'll get an attack of conscience or catch a bad case of the crazies and go to the police. And I don't want to run a similar sort of risk. Maybe we should just leave it as is, ships that pass in the night, all that romantic stuff. That way we're both safe."

"You could be right. But sometime down the line we might decide the risk's worth running, and then where would we be? You know what the saddest words of tongue or pen are."

" 'It might have been.' You're witty, but John Greenleaf was Whittier."

"My God, you read poetry and you're a smartass and you can verb like a mink. I can't let you get away altogether. I know."

"You know what?"

"Buy the *Village Voice* every week and read the personals in the 'Village Bulletin Board' section. Okay?"

"Okay. You do the same."

"Faithfully. Can a burglar and an adulteress find happiness in today's world? We'll just have to see, won't we? Go ahead, you ring for the elevator."

"You don't want to ride down with me?"

"I want to tidy up here a little. And I'll hang around so that we leave the building a few minutes apart. If I get in any trouble, you don't want to get hooked into it."

"Will you get in trouble?"

"Probably not, because I'm not stealing anything."

"That's what I was asking, really. I mean, I shouldn't care if you steal anything, including the carpet we verbed on, but evidently I do. Bernie, would you hold me?"

"Are you scared again?"

"Nope. I just like the way you hold me."

I put my gloves on and waited with the door a few inches ajar until I saw her ring for the elevator. Then I drew the door shut, turned the bolt, and gave the apartment a very quick look-see, just to make sure there was nothing I should know about in any of the other rooms. I didn't open a drawer or a closet, just ducked into each room and flicked the lights on long enough to establish that there were no signs of Andrea's presence. No drawers pulled out and dumped, no tables overturned, no signs that the apartment had been visited by a burglar or a cyclone or any comparable unwelcome phenomenon.

And no dead bodies in the bed or on the floor. Not that one goes around expecting that sort of thing, but I was once caught in the act of burgling the apartment of a man named Flaxford, and Mr. F. himself was dead in another room at the time, a fact which became known to the police before it joined my storehouse of information. So I gave a quick look-see here and there, and if I'd come across the Mondrian, leaning against the wall or perhaps wrapped in brown paper and waiting for the framer, I'd have been roundly delighted.

No such luck, nor did I spend much time looking. I did all of this reconnaissance rather more quickly than it takes to tell about it, as a matter of fact, and when I was out in the hallway the elevator was on its way up.

Was it swarming with boys in blue? Had I, like Samson and Lord Randall and the Bold Deceiver before me, been done in by a woman's treachery? No point, surely, in sticking around to find out. I ducked through the fire door and waited for the elevator to stop on Sixteen.

But it didn't. I peeked through the open fire door, and I listened carefully, and the cage went on past Sixteen, stopped, waited, and went on down, passing Sixteen in its descent. I returned to the hallway, picked the tumblers to lock Onderdonk's door, recalled that Andrea'd said he never double-locked it, picked it again to leave it on the springlock as he was said to have done, sighed heavily at all of this wasted time and effort, stripped off my silly rubber gloves, put them in a pocket, and rang for the elevator.

No cops in the elevator. No cops in the lobby or out on the street. No hassle from the elevator operator, the concierge or the doorman, even when I refused the last-named chap's offer to hail me a taxi. I said I felt like walking, and I walked three blocks before hailing a cab myself. That way I didn't have to switch to some other cab a few blocks away. I could just ride straight home, and that's what I did.

Once there, I would have liked to go straight to bed. But I had J. C. Appling's stamps to worry about and I was worried. I'd have taken a chance and left the job unfinished, but not after all I'd gone through at the Charlemagne in the past ten hours. I'd had far too many human contacts, enough so that I stood a chance of attracting police attention. I hadn't done anything in Onderdonk's apartment, hadn't stolen anything at all but Appling's stamps (and those earrings, mustn't forget those earrings) but I certainly didn't want those stamps sitting around if someone with a tin shield and a warrant came knocking on my door.

I was up all night with the damned stamps. I swear you never have that problem with cash; you just spend it at leisure. I got all the stamps into glassine envelopes and all of Appling's album pages into the incinerator, and then I fitted the envelopes into a hidey-hole I probably shouldn't tell you about, but what the hell. There's a baseboard electrical outlet that's a phony, with no BX cable feeding

110

into an aluminum box at its rear. It's just a plate and a couple of receptacles, mounted to the baseboard with a pair of screws, and if you undo the screws and remove the plate you can reach your hand into an opening about the size of a loaf of bread. (Not the puffy stuff but a nice dense loaf from the health food store.) I keep contraband there until I can unload it, and I also stow burglar tools there. (Not all of them because some of them are innocent enough out of context. You can keep a roll of adhesive tape in the medicine chest and a penlight in the hardware drawer and feel secure about it. Picks and probes and prybars, however, are another story, incriminating in or out of context.)

There's another hidey-hole, similar in nature, where I keep my mad money. I even have a radio plugged into one of its receptacles, and the radio even works, running on batteries since its dummy cord is plugged into thin air. I've got a few thousand dollars there in untraceable fifties and hundreds, and it'll do to bribe a cop or post a bond or, if things ever get that desperate, pay my way to Costa Rica. And I hope to God it never comes to that because I'd go nuts there. I mean who do I know in Costa Rica? What would I do if I got a craving for a bagel or a slice of pizza?

I never did get to sleep. I showered and shaved and put on clean clothes. I went out and had a bagel (but not a slice of pizza) and a plate of eggs and bacon and a lot of coffee at the Greek place a block from my door. I sipped the coffee and my mind, exhausted and overamped from too many hours awake and too much concentration on itty bitty squares of colored paper, slipped a few hours into the past. I remembered eager hands and smooth skin and a warm mouth, and I wondered if there was any truth mixed in with the lies she'd told me.

There was that sweet magic between us, the physical magic and the mental magic, and I was tired enough to drop my guard and let her in. It would be easy, I thought, to let go a little bit more and fall in love with her.

And it wouldn't be *that* dangerous, I decided. Not much worse than hang-gliding blindfolded. Safer on balance than swimming with an open wound in shark-infested waters, or playing catch with a bottle of nitroglycerine, or singing "Rule, Britannia" at Carney's Emerald Lounge in Woodside.

I paid the check and overtipped, as lovers are wont to do. Then I walked over to Broadway and caught a train heading downtown.

TEN

I UNLOCKED THE steel gates, opened the door, scooped up the mail and tossed it on the counter, shlepped the bargain table outside and turned the sign in the window from *Sorry...We're CLOSED* to *OPEN...Come in!* By the time I was perched on my stool behind the counter I had my first browser of the day. He was a round-shouldered gentleman in a Norfolk jacket and he was taking a mild interest in the shelves of General Fiction while I was taking about as much interest in the mail. There were a couple of bills, quite a few book catalogs, a postcard asking if I had the Derek Hudson biography of Lewis Carroll—I didn't— and a government-franked message from some clown who hoped he could continue representing me in Congress. An understandable desire. Otherwise he'd have to start paying his own postage.

While the chap in the Norfolk jacket was paging through something by Charles Reade, a sallow young woman with teeth like a beaver bought a couple of things from the bargain table. The phone rang and it was someone wanting to know if I had anything by Jeffery Farnol.

Now I've had thousands of phone calls and I swear no one ever asked me that before. I checked the shelves and was able to report that I had clean copies of *Peregrine's Progress* and *The Amateur Gentleman*. My caller wondered about *Beltane the Smith*.

"Not unless he's under the spreading chestnut tree," I said. "But I'll have a look."

I agreed to put the other two titles aside, not that anyone else was likely to snatch them up meanwhile. I took them from the shelves, ducked into my back room, placed them on my desk where they could bask in the illumination of the portrait hanging over the desk (St. John of God, patron saint of booksellers), and came back to confront a tall and well-fed man in a dark suit that looked to have been very meticulously tailored for someone else.

"Well, well, well," said Ray Kirschmann. "If it ain't Miz Rhodenbarr's son Bernard."

"You sound surprised, Ray," I said. "This is my store, this is where I work. I'm here all the time."

"Which is why I came here lookin' for you, Bern, but you were in back and it gave me a turn. I figured somebody snuck in and burgled you."

I looked over his shoulder at the fellow in the Norfolk jacket. He'd gone on from Charles Reade to something else, but I couldn't see what.

"Business pretty good, Bern?"

"I can't complain."

"It's holdin' up, huh? Except you were never a one for holdups, were you? Makin' ends meet?"

"Well, there are good weeks and bad weeks."

"But you get by."

"I get by."

"And you got the satisfaction of treadin' the straight an' narrow path between right an' wrong. That's gotta be worth somethin'."

"Ray—"

"Peace of mind, that's what you got. It's worth a lot, peace of mind is."

"Uh—"

I nodded in the direction of the browser, who had assumed the unmistakable stance of a dropper of eaves. Ray turned, regarded my customer, and pinched his own abundant chin between thumb and forefinger.

"Oh, I get your drift, Bern," he said. "You're worried this gentleman here'll be taken aback to learn about your criminal past. Is that it?"

"Jesus, Ray."

"Sir," Ray announced, "you may not realize this, but you're gonna have the privilege of buyin' a book from a former notorious criminal. Bernie here was once the sort'd burgle you outta house an' home, and now he's a walking testimony to criminal rehabilitation. Yessir, I'll tell you, all of us in the NYPD think the world of Bernie here. Say, mister, you're welcome to hang around an' browse. Last thing I want to do is chase you."

But my customer was on his way, with the door swinging shut behind him.

"Thanks," I said.

"Aw, he was a stiff anyway, Bern. Never woulda bought that book. Guys like him, treat the place like a library. How you gonna make a dime on a bum like that?"

"Ray—"

"'Sides, he looked shifty. Probably woulda stole the book if he had half the chance. An honest guy like yourself, you don't realize how many crooked people there are in the world."

I didn't say anything. Why encourage him?

"Say, Bern," he said, leaning a heavy forearm on my glass counter. "You're around books all the time, you're all the time readin'. What I want to do is read somethin' to you. You got a minute?"

"Well, I—"

"Sure you do," he said, and reached into his inside jacket pocket, and just then the door burst open and Carolyn exploded through it. "There you are," she cried. "I called and you didn't answer, and then I called and the line was busy, and then I— Oh, hi, Ray."

"'Oh, hi, Ray,'" he echoed. "Say it like you're glad to see me, Carolyn. I'm not some dog that you gotta give me a bath."

"I'm going to leave that line alone," she said.

"Thank God," I said.

"You called and he wasn't here," Ray said, "and then you called and the line was busy, and then you ran over here. So you got somethin' to say to him."

"So?"

"So say it."

"It'll keep," she said.

"Then maybe you oughta run along, Carolyn. Go get your vacuum cleaner and suck the ticks off a bloodhound."

"I could make you the same suggestion," she said sweetly, "but without the vacuum cleaner. Why don't you go solicit a bribe, Ray? I got business with Bernie."

"So do I, sweetie. I was just lookin' for a literary opinion from him. The hell, I don't guess it'd hurt you to hear what I gotta read to him."

He drew a little card from his pocket. "'You have the right to remain silent,'" he intoned. "'You have the right to consult an attorney. If you do not have legal counsel, you have the right to have counsel provided for you.'" There was more, and the wording wasn't exactly the way I remembered it, but I'm not going to look it up and reproduce the whole thing here. If you're interested, go throw a rock through a precinct house window. Somebody'll come out and read it to you word for word.

"I don't get it," I said. "Why are you reading me that?"

"Aw, Bernie. Lemme ask you a question, okay? You know an apartment building called the Charlemagne?"

"Sure. On Fifth Avenue in the Seventies. Why?"

"Ever been there?"

"As a matter of fact I was there the night before last."

"No kiddin'. Next you're gonna tell me you've heard of a man named Gordon Onderdonk."

I nodded. "We've met," I said. "Once here, in the store, and again two nights ago."

"At his apartment at the Charlemagne."

"That's right." Where was he going with all this? I hadn't stolen anything from Onderdonk, and the man would hardly have reported me to the police for lifting his letters from Andrea. Unless Ray was taking an elaborate windup before delivering the pitch, and all this Onderdonk stuff was prelude to some more incisive questions about J. C. Appling's stamp collection. But the Applings hadn't even returned to the city as of midnight, so how could they have discovered the loss and reported it, and how could Ray have already tied it to me?

"I went there at his invitation," I said. "He wanted an appraisal of his personal library, although he's not likely to be selling it. I spent some time going through his books and came up with a figure."

"Decent of you."

"I got paid for my time."

"Oh, yeah? Wrote you out a check, did he?"

"Paid me in cash. Two hundred dollars."

"Is that a fact. I suppose you'll report the income on your tax return, a good law-abidin' reformed citizen like yourself."

"What's all this sarcasm about?" Carolyn demanded. "Bernie didn't do anything."

"Nobody ever did. The prisons are full of

innocent guys who got railroaded by corrupt police."

"God knows there are enough corrupt police to go around," Carolyn said, "and if they're not railroading innocent people, what are they doing?"

"Anyway, Bern—"

"Besides eating in restaurants and not paying for their meals," she went on. "Besides swapping jokes on street corners while old ladies get mugged and raped. Besides—"

"Besides puttin' up with insults from some little dyke who needs a rabies shot an' a muzzle."

I said, "Get to the point, Ray. You just read me my rights and it says I don't have to answer questions, so you can stop asking them. I'll ask you one. What's this circus about?"

"What's it about? What the hell do you think it's about? You're under arrest, Bernie. Why else'd I read you your Miranda?"

"Under arrest for what?"

"Aw, Jesus, Bern." He sighed and shook his head, as if his pessimistic view of human nature had once again been confirmed. "This guy Onderdonk," he said. "They found him in his bedroom closet, bound and gagged with his head bashed in."

"He's dead?"

"Why, was he breathin' when you left him like that? Inconsiderate of the bastard to die, but that's what he did. He's dead, all right, and what I gotta bring you in for is murder."

119

He showed me a pair of handcuffs. "I gotta use these," he said. "Regulations which they're enforcin' again these days. But take your time first and close up, huh? And do a good job. Place might wind up stayin' closed for a while."

I don't think I said anything. I think I just stood there.

"Carolyn, whyntcha hold the door and me'n Bern'll bring in the table. You don't want to leave it out there. They'll steal it empty in an hour and then somebody'll walk off with the table. Aw shit, Bern, what's the matter with you, anyway? You were always a gentle guy. Stealin's stealin', but what'd you go an' kill him for?"

ELEVEN

"WHAT GIVES ME the most trouble," Wally Hemphill said, "is finding the time to fit in the miles. Of course what really helps is if I got a client who's a runner himself. You know how some people'll do their business over nine holes of golf? 'Suit up,' I'll say, 'and we'll lope around the reservoir and see where we stand on this.' You think we could pick up the pace a little, Bernie?"

"I don't know. This is pretty fast, isn't it?"

"I'd judge we're doing a 9:20 mile."

"That's funny. I could have sworn we were going faster than sound."

He laughed politely and picked up the pace and I sucked air and stayed with him. Gamely, you might say. It was still Thursday and I still hadn't been to bed, and it was now around six-thirty in the evening and Wally Hemphill and I were making a counterclockwise circuit of Central Park. The circular park drive was closed to cars throughout its six-mile loop, and runners beyond number were out taking the air and turning its oxygen into carbon dioxide.

"Call Klein," I'd told Carolyn when I left the store in handcuffs. "Tell him to come collect me. And pick up some cash from my place and bail me out."

"Anything else?"

"Have a nice day."

As Ray and I walked in one direction and Carolyn walked in the other, I thought how Norb Klein had represented me several times over the years. He was a nice little guy who looked sort of like a fat weasel. He had an office on Queens Boulevard and a small-time criminal practice that never got him any headlines. He wasn't very impressive in court but he handled himself nicely behind the scenes, knowing which judge would be sympathetic to the right approach. I was trying to remember when I'd seen Norb last when Ray said, conversationally, "You didn't hear, Bern? Norb Klein's dead."

"What?"

"You know what a skirt chaser he was, and he never had a hooker for a client that he didn't sample the merchandise, and how'd he wind up goin' out? He was bangin' his secretary on his office couch, same girl's been with him eight, ten years, and his ticker blows out on him. Massive whatchacallit, coronary, an' he's dead in the saddle. Girl said she tried everythin' to revive him, and I just bet she did."

"Jesus," I said. "Carolyn!"

So we'd had a hurried conference on the street, and the only name I could think of was Wally Hemphill's, who was ensuring himself against Norb Klein's fate by training for the upcoming Marathon. His was a general legal practice, running to divorces and wills and partnership agreements and such, and I had no reason to believe he knew his way around what people persist in calling the criminal justice system. But he'd come when called, God love him, and I was out on bail, and I'd declined on the advice of my attorney to answer any and all questions put to me by the police, and if I just survived the trek around the park I might live forever.

"It's funny," Wally said now, leading our charge up a hill as if he thought he was Teddy Roosevelt. "We'd see each other in Riverside Park, we'd do a few easy miles together, and I always thought of you as a runner."

122

"Well, I rarely go more than three miles, see, and I'm not used to hills."

"No, you didn't let me finish. I'm not knocking your running, Bernie. I thought of you as a runner and it never occurred to me that you might be a burglar. I mean you don't think of burglars as regular-type guys who talk about Morton's Foot and shin splints. You know what I mean?"

"Try to think of me as a guy who runs a secondhand book store."

"And that's why you were at Onderdonk's apartment."

"That's right."

"At his invitation. You went over the night before last, that was Tuesday night, and you appraised his library."

"Uh-huh."

"And he was alive when you left."

"Of course he was alive when I left. I never killed anybody in my life."

"You left him tied up?"

"No, I didn't leave him tied up. I left him hale and hearty and saying goodbye to me at the elevator. No, come to think of it, he ducked back into his apartment to answer the phone."

"So the elevator operator didn't actually see him there when he took you out of the building."

"No."

"What time was that? If he was talking to somebody on the phone, and if we can find out who—"

"It was probably around eleven. Something like that."

"But the elevator operator who took you down went on after midnight, didn't he? And the doorman and the whatchamacallit—"

"The concierge."

"Right. They changed shifts at midnight, and they identified you, said they let you out of the building around one. So if you left Onderdonk at eleven—"

"It could have been eleven-thirty."

"I guess you had a long wait for the elevator."

"They're like the subways, you miss one at that hour and you can wait forever for the next one."

"You had another engagement in the building."

I don't think Norb Klein would have figured it out any faster. "Something like that," I agreed.

"But then you went back again last night. Without using Onderdonk to get you into the building. The after-midnight staff said you left the building late two nights running, and both times the elevator operator swears he picked you up at Onderdonk's floor. Did he?"

"Uh-huh."

"And the other staff people say you managed to get in delivering sandwiches from the deli."

"It was flowers from the florist, which shows how reliable eyewitnesses are."

"I think they said flowers, as a matter of fact."

"From the deli?"

"I think they said flowers from the florist, and I think my memory changed it to sandwiches from the deli, and I think you're fooling yourself if you think those witnesses aren't going to be good ones. And the medical evidence isn't good."

"What do you mean?"

"According to what I managed to learn, Onderdonk was killed by a blow to the head. He was hit twice with something hard and heavy, and the second shot did it. Fractured skull, cerebral hematoma, and I forget the exact language but what it amounts to is he got hit and he died of it."

"Did they fix the time?"

"Roughly."

"And?"

"According to their figures, he died sometime between when you arrived at the Charlemagne and when you left."

"When I left the second time," I said.

"No."

"No?"

"You went up to Onderdonk's apartment Tuesday night, right? And left a little before one Wednesday morning, something like that."

"Something like that."

"Well, that's when he died. Now that's give or take a couple of hours, that's for sure, because they're just not that accurate when another twenty-four hours has gone by before the body's discovered. But he definitely got it that night. Bernie? Where are you going?"

Where I was going was over the 102nd Street cutoff, which trims a full mile off the six-mile circuit and avoids the worst hill. Wally wanted the extra mile and the hill training that went with it, but I just kept trotting doggedly west on the cutoff road and all he could do was run alongside arguing.

"Listen," he said, "in a couple of years you'll be begging for some hill training. Those prison yards, you get plenty of time to run but it's all around a flat tenth-of-a-mile track. Even so, I got a client up at Green Haven who's doing upwards of a hundred miles a week. He just goes out there and runs for hours. It's boring, but it has its advantages."

"He probably doesn't have too much trouble remembering the route."

"There's that, and he's averaging something like fifteen miles a day. You can imagine the kind of shape he'll be in when he gets out."

"When'll that be?"

"Oh, that's hard to say. But he should be coming up for parole in a couple of years, and he'll have a very good chance if he behaves himself between now and then."

"What did he do?"

"Well, he had a girlfriend and she had a boyfriend and he found out, and he sort of cut them a little."

"Socially?"

"With a knife. They, uh, died."

"Oh."

"These things happen."

126

"Like clockwork," I said. "Wally, ease up. These uphills cut the legs out from under me."

"You gotta charge the hills, Bernie. That's how you develop your quads."

"It's how I develop angina. How could he have been dead before I left the building?"

He didn't say anything for a moment, and we ran along in a companionable silence. Then he said, without looking my way, "Bernie, I could see how it could happen accidentally. He was a big, powerful guy and you had to knock him out and tie him up to rob him. You knocked him cold and tied him up and he was alive at that point, and then some leakage inside his head or something murky along those lines, it killed him and you didn't even know it. Because obviously you wouldn't go back to the building the next day if you knew he was dead. Except wait a minute. If you thought you left him tied up and alive, why would you go back to the building? You wouldn't want to show your face within a mile of that building, would you?"

"No."

"You didn't kill him."

"Of course not."

"Unless you killed him and you knew he was dead, and you went back—to what?"

"I didn't hit him or steal from him, let alone kill him, Wally, so that makes the question a hard one to answer."

"Forget Onderdonk for a minute. Why did you go back to the Charlemagne? You'd already committed a burglary there the night before. That's what you did, right? Stole something from somebody after you left his apartment?"

"Right."

"So why'd you go back? Don't tell me the building was such a soft touch because I won't believe it."

"No, it's worse than Fort Knox. Shit."

"It's easier if you level with me, Bernie. And anything you tell me is privileged. I can't reveal it."

"I know that."

"So?"

"I went back to Onderdonk's apartment."

"To Onderdonk's apartment."

"Right."

"You had another appointment with him? No, because you used the scam with the sandwiches to get in the door."

"Flowers."

"Did I say sandwiches again? I meant flowers. You went back there knowing he was dead?"

"I went back there knowing he was out because he didn't answer his goddamn phone."

"You called him? Why?"

"To establish that he was out so I could go back."

"What for?"

"To steal something."

Left foot, right foot, left foot, right foot. "Something caught your eye when you were appraising his library."

"That's right."

"So you thought you'd drop in and lift it."

"It's more complicated than that, but that's the idea, yes."

"It's getting harder to think of you as a bookseller and easier to think of you as a burglar. What the papers call an unrepentant career criminal, but this bit makes you sound like a kleptomaniac with foresight. You went back to an apartment that you'd already left your fingerprints all over the night before? And where you'd already given your right name to get into the building?"

"I'm not saying it was the smartest move I ever made."

"Good, because it wasn't. I don't know, Bernie. I'm not sure hiring me was the smartest move you ever made, either. I'm a pretty decent attorney but my criminal experience is limited, and I can't say I did a hell of a lot for the client who cut those two people, but then I didn't knock myself out because I figured we'd all sleep better with him running around the yard at Green Haven. But you need someone who can work a combination of bribery and plea bargaining, if you want my honest opinion, and I don't have the moves for that."

"I'm innocent, Wally."

"I just can't understand why you hit the building again yesterday."

"It seemed like a good idea at the time, okay? Wally, I didn't get any sleep last night and I never run more than four miles tops. I've got to stop."

"We can slow down a little."

"Good." I kept moving my feet. "What difference did the second visit make?" I asked him. "I'd be in the same trouble anyway, with my prints all over the apartment and the staff remembering me, and if they really figure the time of death the way you said, the second visit is redundant."

"Uh-huh. Except it makes it much harder in court to argue that you were never there in the first place."

"Oh."

"You were there for over eight hours yesterday, Bernie. That's another thing I don't understand. You spent eight hours in an apartment with a dead man and you say you didn't even know he was dead. Didn't he strike you as a little unresponsive?"

"I never saw him, Wally." Puff, puff. "Ray Kirschmann said the body was discovered in the bedroom closet. I checked all the rooms but I didn't go into the closets."

"What did you take from his apartment?"

"Nothing."

"Bernie, I'm your lawyer."

"And here I thought you were my coach. It doesn't matter. Even if you were my spiritual adviser the answer would be the same. I didn't take anything from Onderdonk's apartment."

"You went there to steal something."

"Right."

"And you left there without it."

"Right again."

"Why?"

"It was gone when I got there. Somebody'd already hooked it."

"So you turned around and went home."

"That's right."

"But not for eight hours or so. Something on television you didn't want to miss? Or were you reading your way through his library?"

"I didn't want to leave the building until the shift changed. And I didn't spend eight hours in Onderdonk's apartment. I stayed in another apartment, an empty one, until after midnight."

"There's things you're not telling me."

"Maybe a couple."

"Well, that's okay, I guess. But you haven't done much direct lying to me, have you?"

"No."

"You're sure about that?"

"Positive."

"And you didn't kill him."

"God, no."

"And you don't know who did. Bernie? *Do* you know who killed him?"

"No."

"Got an idea?"

"Not a clue."

"Once more around? We'll take the Seventy-second Street cutoff, do a nice easy four-mile loop. Okay?"

"No way, Wally."

"C'mon, take a shot at it."

"Not a chance."

"Well," he said, chest heaving, arms pumping, "I'll catch you later, then. I'm gonna go for it."

TWELVE

"SHE MUST HAVE killed him," Carolyn said. "Right?"

"You mean Andrea?"

"Who else? That'd be one reason why she was scared shitless when you walked in on her. She was afraid you'd discover the skeleton in her closet. Of course it wasn't her closet and he wasn't a skeleton yet, but—"

"You figure she overpowered him and tied him up and killed him? She's just a girl, Carolyn."

"That's a real pig remark, you know that?"

"I mean in terms of physical strength. Maybe she could hit him hard enough to knock him out, maybe even hard enough to kill him, and maybe she could even drag him into the closet when she was done, but somehow I can't believe she did any of those things. Maybe she went there to look for her letters, just as she said."

"Do you believe it?"

"Somehow I don't. But I'm willing to believe she went there looking for something."

"The Mondrian."

"And then what did she do, smuggle it past me secreted in her bodily cavities?"

"Not likely. You'd have found it."

I gave her a look. It was morning, Friday morning, and if I didn't feel like a new man, I at least felt like a secondhand one in excellent shape. I'd left Wally Hemphill in the park and went straight home to a shower and a hot toddy and a full ten hours of sleep with the door double-bolted and the blinds shut and the phone unplugged. I'd come downtown early and tried Carolyn at the Poodle Factory every ten minutes or so, and when she answered I hung the BACK IN TEN MINUTES sign in the window and went outside and pulled the door shut.

Across the street, a couple of shaggy guys lurking in a doorway shrank into the shadows when I glanced their way. They looked like a bottle gang without a bottle, and I had second thoughts about leaving my bargain table on the street, but what could they steal? My books on home winemaking were all safe inside the store. I left the table where it was and picked up two cups of coffee around the corner, then took them to Carolyn's canine beauty parlor.

She was clipping a Bichon Frise when I got there. I mistook it at first for a snow-white poodle, and Carolyn was quick to point out why it didn't look at all like a poodle, and after a couple of paragraphs of American Kennel Club lore I cut her off in midsentence and brought her up to date. The visit to the Charlemagne, the bit with the flowers, the incident in Onderdonk's apartment, the conversation with Wally Hemphill. Everything.

Now she said, "How bad is it, Bernie? Are you in deep shit or what?"

"Let's call it chest high and rising."

"It's my fault."

"What do you mean?"

"Well, it's my cat, isn't it?"

"They kidnapped Archie to get at me, Carolyn. If you hadn't had a cat they'd have found some other way to put pressure on me. All to get a picture off a museum wall, and that's as impossible as it ever was. You asked if Andrea killed him. That was my first thought, but the times are all wrong. Unless the Medical Examiner's crazy, Onderdonk was killed while I was stealing Appling's stamps."

"He was alone when you left him."

"As far as I know."

"And someone else dropped in on him, beat his head in, tied him up, and stuffed him in the closet. And stole the painting?"

"I suppose so."

"Isn't it interesting that someone just happens to kill a guy and steal a painting from him, and we're supposed to steal a painting by the same artist in order to get my cat back?"

"The coincidence struck me, too."

"Uh-huh. You get this coffee at the felafel joint?"

"Yeah. Not very good, is it?"

"It's not a question of good or bad. It's a matter of trying to figure out what they put in it."

"Chickpeas."

"Really?"

"Just a guess. They put chickpeas in everything. I must have lived the first twenty-five years of my life without knowing what a chickpea was, and all of a sudden they're inescapable."

"What do you figure caused it?"

"Probably nuclear testing."

"Makes sense. Bern, why tie Onderdonk up and stuff him in the closet? Let's say they killed him in order to get away with the painting."

"Which is crazy, because it didn't look as though anything else was taken. The other art was worth a fortune but the place didn't even look as though it had been searched, let alone stripped."

"Maybe somebody just needed the Mondrian for a specific purpose."

"Like what?"

"Like ransoming a cat."

"Didn't think of that."

"The point is—next time get the coffee at the coffee shop, okay?"

"Sure."

"The point is, why tie him up and why put him in the closet? To keep the body from being discovered? Makes no sense, does it?"

"I don't know."

"Did whatsername, Andrea, did she know he was in the closet?"

"Maybe. I don't know."

"She was pretty cool, wasn't she? She's in an apartment with a dead guy in the closet and a burglar walks in on her and what does she do? Rolls around on the oriental rug with him."

"It was an Aubusson."

"My mistake. What do we do now, Bern? Where do we go from here?"

"I don't know."

"You didn't tell the police about Andrea."

I shook my head. "I didn't tell them anything. It's not as if she could give me an alibi. I could try telling them that I was in the Appling apartment while somebody was killing Onderdonk, but where would that get me? Just charged with another burglary, and even if I showed them the stamps I couldn't prove I hadn't killed Onderdonk before or after I performed philately on Appling's collection. Anyway, I don't know her name or where she lives."

"You don't think her name's Andrea?"

"Maybe. Maybe not."

"You could run an ad in the *Voice*."

"I could."

"What's the matter?"

"Oh, I don't know," I said. "I, oh, I sort of liked her, that's all."

"Well, that's good. You wouldn't want to caper on the carpet with someone you hated."

"Yeah. The thing is, I sort of thought I might get together with her again. Of course she's a married woman and there's no future in that sort of thing, but I thought—"

"You had romantic feelings."

"Well, yeah, Carolyn, I guess I did."

"That's not a bad thing."

"It isn't?"

"Of course not. I have them myself. Alison came over last night. We met for a drink, and then I explained I didn't want to miss an important phone call so we went back to my place. The phone call I was talking about was about the cat, but it never came, and we just sat around and listened to music and talked."

"Did you get lucky?"

"Bern, I didn't even try. It was just sort of peaceful and cozy, you know what I mean? You know how standoffish Ubi can be, and he's especially whacko with Archie gone, but he came over and curled up in her lap. I told her about Archie."

"That he was missing?"

"That he'd been kidnapped. The whole thing. I couldn't help it, Bernie. I had to talk about it."

"It's okay."

"Romance," she said. "It's what makes the world go round, isn't it, Bern?"

"So they say."

"You and Andrea, me and Alison."

"Andrea's about five-foot-six," I said. "Slender, narrow at the waist. Dark hair to her shoulders, and she was wearing it in pigtails when I saw her."

"Alison's slim, too, but she's not that tall. I'd say five-four. And her hair's light brown and short, and she doesn't wear any lipstick or nail polish."

"She wouldn't, not if she's a political and

economic lesbian. Andrea wears nail polish. I can't remember about the lipstick."

"Why are we comparing descriptions of our obsessions, Bern?"

"I just had this dumb idea and I wanted to make sure it was a dumb idea."

"You thought they were the same girl."

"I said it was a dumb idea."

"You're just afraid to let yourself have romantic feelings, that's all. You haven't been involved with anybody that way in a long time."

"I guess."

"Years from now," she said, "when you and Andrea are old and gray, nodding off together before the fire, you'll look back on these days and laugh quietly together. And neither of you will have to ask the other why you're laughing, because you'll just know without a word's being spoken."

"Years from now," I said, "you and I will be having coffee somewhere, and one of us will puke, and without a word's being spoken the other'll immediately think of this conversation."

"And this lousy coffee," said Carolyn.

THIRTEEN

WHEN I GOT back to my shop the phone was ringing, but by the time I got inside it had stopped. I thought I'd just pulled the door shut, letting the springlock secure it, but evidently I'd taken the time to lock it with the key because now I had to unlock it with the key, and that gave my caller the extra few seconds needed to hang up before I could reach the phone. I said the things one says at such times, improbable observations on the ancestry, sexual practices and dietary habits of whoever it was, and then I bent down to pick a dollar bill off the floor. A scrap of paper beside it bore a penciled notation that the payment was for three books from the bargain table.

That happens sometimes. No one has yet been so honest as to include the extra pennies for sales tax, and if that ever happens I may find myself shamed out of crime altogether. I put the dollar in my pocket and settled in behind the counter.

The phone rang again. I said, "Barnegat Books, good morning," and a man's voice, gruff and unfamiliar, said, "I want the painting."

"This is a bookstore," I said.

"Let's not play games. You have the Mondrian and I want it. I'll pay you a fair price."

"I'm sure you will," I said, "because you sound like a fair guy, but there's something you're wrong about. I haven't got what you're looking for."

"Suit yourself. Do yourself a favor, eh? Don't sell it to anyone else without first offering it to me."

"That sounds reasonable," I said, "but I don't know how to reach you. I don't even know who you are."

"But I know who *you* are," he said. "And I know how to reach *you*."

Had I been threatened? I was pondering the point when the phone clicked in my ear. I hung up and reviewed the conversation, searching for some clue of my caller's identity. If there was one present, I couldn't spot it. I guess I got a little bit lost in thought, because a moment or two down the line I looked up to see a woman approaching the counter and I hadn't even heard the door open to let her into the store.

She was slender and birdlike, with large brown eyes and short brown hair, and I recognized her at once but couldn't place her right away. She had a book in one hand, an oversized art book, and she placed the other hand on my counter and said, "Mr. Rhodenbarr? 'Euclid alone has looked on Beauty bare.'"

I'd heard the voice before. When? Over the phone? No.

"Ms. Smith of the Third Oregon," I said.

"That's not Mary Carolyn Davies you're quoting."

"Indeed it's not. It's Edna St. Vincent Millay. The line came to mind when I looked at this."

She placed the book on the counter. It was a survey volume covering modern art from the Impressionists to the current anarchy, and it was open now to a color plate which showed a geometrical abstract painting. Vertical and horizontal black bands divided an off-white canvas into squares and rectangles, several of which were painted in primary colors.

"The absolute beauty of pure geometry," she said. "Or perhaps I mean the pure beauty of absolute geometry. Right angles and primary colors."

"Mondrian, isn't it?"

"Piet Mondrian. Do you know much about the man and his work, Mr. Rhodenbarr?"

"I know he was Dutch."

"Indeed he was. Born in 1872 in Amersfoort. He began, you may recall, as a painter of naturalistic landscapes. As he found his own style, as he grew artistically, his work became increasingly abstract. By 1917 he had joined with Theo van Doesburg and Bart van der Leck and others to found a movement called *De Stijl*. It was an article of faith for Mondrian that the right angle was everything, that vertical and horizontal lines intersected space in such a way as to make an important philosophical statement."

There was more. She gave me the four-dollar lecture, declaiming it as fervently as she'd read about poor Smith a couple of days earlier. "Piet Mondrian held his first exhibition in America in 1926," she told me. "Fourteen years later he moved here. He'd gone to Britain in 1939 to get away from the war. Then, when the Luftwaffe started bombing London, he came here. New York fascinated him, you know. The grid pattern of the streets, the right angles. That was the beginning of his boogie-woogie period. You look confused."

"I didn't know he was a musician."

"He wasn't. His painting style changed, you see. He was inspired by the traffic in the streets, the elevated railways, the yellow cabs, the red lights, the jazzy pulsebeat of Manhattan. You're probably familiar with *Broadway Boogie Woogie*—that's one of his most famous canvases. It's in the Museum of Modern Art. There's also *Victory Boogie Woogie* and, oh, several others."

In several other museums, I thought, where they were welcome to remain.

"I see," I said, which is something I very often say when I don't.

"He died on February 1, 1944, just six weeks before his seventy-second birthday. I believe he died of pneumonia."

"You certainly know a great deal about him."

Her hands moved to adjust her hat, which didn't really need adjusting. Her eyes aimed themselves at a spot just above and to the left of my shoulder. "When I was a little girl," she said evenly, "we went to my grandmother's and grandfather's every Sunday for dinner. I lived with my parents in a house in White Plains, and we came into the city where my grandparents had a huge apartment on Riverside Drive, with enormous windows overlooking the Hudson. Piet Mondrian had stayed at that apartment upon arriving in New York in 1940. A painting of his, a gift to my grandparents, hung over the sideboard in the dining room."

"I see."

"We always had the same seating arrangement," she said, and closed her big eyes. "I can picture that dinner table now. My grandfather at one end, my grandmother at the other near the door to the kitchen. My uncle and aunt and my younger cousin on one side of the table, and my mother and father and me on the other. All I had to do was gaze above my cousin's head and I could look at the Mondrian. I had it to stare at almost every Sunday night for all of my childhood."

"I see."

"You'd think I'd have tuned it out as children so often do. After all, I'd never met the artist. He died before I was born. Nor was I generally responsive to art as a child. But that painting, it evidently spoke to me in a particular way." She smiled at a memory. "When I was in art class, I always tried to produce geometrical abstracts. While the other children were drawing horses and trees, I was making black-

and-white grids with squares of red and blue and yellow. My teachers didn't know what to make of it, but I was trying to be another Mondrian."

"Actually," I said tentatively, "his paintings don't look all that hard to do."

"He thought of them first, Mr. Rhodenbarr."

"Well, there's that, of course, but—"

"And his simplicity is deceptive. His proportions are quite perfect, you see."

"I see."

"I myself had no artistic talent. I wasn't even a fair copyist. Nor did I have any true artistic ambitions." She cocked her head again, probed my eyes with hers. "The painting was to be mine, Mr. Rhodenbarr."

"Oh?"

"My grandfather promised it to me. He was never a wealthy man. He and my grandmother lived comfortably but he never piled up riches. I don't suppose he had much idea of the value of Mondrian's painting. He knew its artistic worth, but I doubt he would have guessed the price it would command. He never collected art, you see, and to him this painting was nothing more or less than the valued gift of a treasured friend. He said it would come to me when he died."

"And it didn't?"

"My grandmother was the first to die. She contracted some sort of viral infection which didn't respond to antibiotics, and within a month's time she was dead of kidney failure. My parents tried to get my grandfather to live with them after her death but he insisted on staying where he was. His one concession was to engage a live-in housekeeper. He never really recovered from my grandmother's death, and within a year he too was dead."

"And the painting—"

"Disappeared."

"The housekeeper took it?"

"That was one theory. My father thought my uncle might have taken it, and I suppose Uncle Billy thought the same of my father. And everyone suspected the housekeeper, and there was some talk of an investigation, but I don't think anything ever came of it. The family came to some sort of agreement that there'd been a burglary, because there were other things missing, some of the wedding silver, and it was easier to attribute it to some anonymous burglar than for us to make a thing of suspecting each other."

"And I suppose the loss was covered by insurance."

"Not the painting. My grandfather had never taken out a floater policy on it. I'm sure it never occurred to him. After all, it had cost him nothing, and I'm sure he never thought it might be stolen."

"It was never recovered?"

"No."

"I see."

"Time passed. My own father died. My mother remarried and moved across the country. Mondrian remained my favorite painter, Mr. Rhodenbarr, and whenever I looked at one of his works in the Modern or the Guggenheim I felt a strong primal response. And I felt a pang, too, for *my* painting, *my* Mondrian, the work that had been promised to me." She straightened up, set her shoulders. "Two years ago," she said, "there was a Mondrian retrospective at the Vermillion Galleries. Of course I went. I was walking from one painting to another, Mr. Rhodenbarr, and I was breathless as I always am in front of Mondrian's work, and then I stepped up to one painting and my heart stopped. Because it was my painting."

"Oh."

"I was shocked. I was stunned. It was my painting and I would have known it anywhere."

"Of course you hadn't seen it in ten years," I said thoughtfully, "and Mondrian's paintings do have a certain sameness to them. Not to take away anything from the artist's genius, but—"

"It was my painting."

"If you say so."

"I sat directly across from that painting every Sunday night for years. I stared at it while I stirred my green peas into my mashed potatoes. I—"

"Oh, did you do that, too? You know what else I used to do? I used to make a potato castle and then make a sort of moat of gravy around it, and then I'd have a piece of carrot for a cannon and I'd use the green peas for cannonballs. What I really wanted was some way to catapult them into the brisket, but that was where my mother drew the line. How did your painting get to the Vermillion Galleries?"

"It was on loan."

"From a museum?"

"From a private collection. Mr. Rhodenbarr, I don't care how the painting got into the private collection or how it got out of it. I just want the painting. It's rightfully mine, and at this point I wouldn't even care if it weren't rightfully mine. It's been an overwhelming obsession ever since I saw it at the retrospective. I have to have it."

What was it about Mondrian, I wondered, that appealed so strongly to crazy people? The catnapper, the man on the phone, Onderdonk, Onderdonk's killer, and now this ditsy little lady. And, come to think of it, who was she?

"Come to think of it," I said, "who are you?"

"Haven't you been listening? My grandfather—"

"You never told me your name."

"Oh, my name," she said, and hesitated for only a second. "It's Elspeth. Elspeth Peters."

"Lovely name."

"Thank you. I—"

"I suppose you think I stole the painting from your grandfather's house lo these many years ago. I can understand that, Ms. Peters. You bought a book in my shop and my name stuck in your mind. Then you read something or heard

147

something to the effect that I had a minor criminal career years ago before I became an antiquarian bookman. You made a mental connection, which I suppose is understandable, and—"

"I don't think you stole the painting from my grandfather."

"You don't?"

"Why, did you?"

"No, but—"

"Because I suppose it's possible, although you would have been a fairly young burglar yourself at the time, wouldn't you? Personally I've always thought that my father was right and Uncle Billy took it, but for all I know Uncle Billy was right and my father took it. Whoever took it sold it, and do you know who bought it?"

"I could take a wild guess."

"I'm sure you could."

"J. McLendon Barlow."

That was news to her. She stared at me. I repeated the name and it still didn't seem to mean anything to her. "That was the man who loaned it to the Vermillion Galleries," I said, "and later on he donated it to the Hewlett Collection. Remember?"

"I don't know what you're talking about," she said. "The painting—*my* painting—was on loan from the collection of a Mr. Gordon Kyle Onderdonk."

"Oh," I said.

"And I read newspapers, Mr. Rhodenbarr. That minor criminal career of yours doesn't seem to have ceased with your entry into the book business. If the papers are to be believed, you were arrested for Mr. Onderdonk's murder."

"I suppose that's technically true."

"And now you're out on bail?"

"More or less."

"And you stole the painting from his apartment. My painting, my Mondrian."

"Everyone seems to think that," I said, "but it's not true. The painting's gone, I'll admit that, but I never laid a glove on it. There's some sort of traveling exhibit coming up and Onderdonk was going to lend them his painting. He sent it out for reframing."

"He wouldn't do that."

"He wouldn't?"

"The sponsors of the show would attend to that, if they felt the work needed reframing. I'm positive you took the painting."

"It was gone when I got there."

"That's very difficult to believe."

"I had trouble believing it myself, Ms. Peters. I still have trouble, but I was there and saw for myself. Or didn't see for myself, since there was nothing to see except an empty space where a picture had been."

"And Onderdonk told you he'd sent the picture out for framing?"

"I didn't ask him. He was dead."

"You killed him before you noticed the painting was gone?"

"I didn't get a chance to kill him because somebody beat me to it. And I didn't know he was dead because I didn't look in the closet for his body, because I didn't know there was a body to look for."

"Someone else killed him."

"Well, I don't think it was suicide. If it was, it's the worst case of suicide I ever heard of."

She looked off into the middle distance and a couple of frown lines clouded her brow. "Whoever killed him," she said, "took the painting."

"Could be."

"Who killed him?"

"I don't know."

"The police think you did it."

"They probably know better," I said. "At least the arresting officer does. He's known me for years, he knows I don't kill people. But they can prove I was in the apartment, so I'll do for a suspect until they come up with a better one."

"And how will that come about?"

I'd already thought of this. "Well, if I can figure out who did it, I suppose I could pass the word."

"So you're trying to learn the identity of the killer."

"I'm just trying to get through the days one at a time," I said, "but I'll admit I'm keeping my eyes and ears open."

"When you find the killer, you'll find the painting."

"It's not when, it's if. And even so, I may or may not find the painting at the same time."

"When you do, I want it."

"Well—"

"It's rightfully mine. You must realize that. And I mean to have it."

"You just expect me to hand it over to you?"

"That would be the smartest thing you could do."

I stared at this delicate creature. "Good grief," I said. "Was that a threat?"

She didn't draw her eyes away, and what big eyes they were. "I would have killed Onderdonk," she said, "to get that painting."

"You're really obsessed."

"I'm aware of that."

"Listen, this may strike you as a wild idea, but have you ever thought about therapy? Obsessions just keep the focus off our real problems, you know, and if you could have the obsession lifted—"

"When I have my hands on my painting, the obsession will be lifted."

"I see."

"I could be a good friend to you, Mr. Rhodenbarr. Or I could be a dangerous enemy."

"Suppose I did get the painting," I said carefully.

"Does that mean you already have it?"

"No, it means what I just said. Suppose I get it. How do I get hold of you?"

She hesitated for a moment, then opened her bag and took out a fine-line felt tip pen and an envelope. She held the envelope upside-down and tore off a piece of its flap, returned the rest of the envelope to her purse, and wrote a telephone number on the scrap. Then she hesitated for another beat and wrote *E. Peters* beneath the number.

"There," she said, setting the slip on the counter beside the open art book. She capped her pen, put it back in her purse, and seemed about to say something when the door opened and the tinkling of bells announced a visitor.

The visitor in turn announced herself. It was Carolyn, and she said, "Hey, Bern, I got another phone call and I thought—" Then Elspeth Peters turned to face Carolyn, and the two women looked at each other for a moment, and then Elspeth Peters walked past her and on out the door.

FOURTEEN

"DON'T FALL IN love with her," I told Carolyn. "She's already in the grip of an obsession."

"What are you talking about?"

"The way you stared at her. I figured you were falling in love, or perhaps in lust. Which is understandable, but—"

"I thought I recognized her."

"Oh?"

"I thought for a minute she was Alison."

"Oh," I said. "Was she?"

"No, of course not. I'd have said hello if she was."

"Are you sure?"

"Of course I'm sure. Why, Bern?"

"Because she said her name was Elspeth Peters, and I don't believe her. And she's tied into the Mondrian business."

"So? Alison's not, remember? Alison's tied into me."

"Right."

"There's a strong resemblance, but that's all it is, a resemblance. How's she tied in?"

"She thinks she's the painting's rightful owner."

"Maybe she stole the cat."

"Not that painting. Onderdonk's painting."

"Oh," she said. "There's too many paintings, you know that?"

"There's too much of everything. You just had a phone call, you started to say. From the Nazi?"

"Right."

"Well, it couldn't have been Peters. She was here with me."

"Right."

"What did she want?"

"Well, she sort of put my mind at rest," Carolyn said. "She said the cat was alive and well and nothing bad would happen to him as long as I cooperated. She said I didn't have to worry about them cutting off an ear or a foot or anything, that the bit with the whiskers was to show they meant business but they wouldn't hurt him or anything. And she said she knew the painting was going to be difficult to get but she was sure we could do it if we put our minds to it."

"It sounds as though she was trying to comfort you."

"Well, it worked, Bern. I feel a lot better about the cat. I still don't know if I'm ever gonna see him again, but I'm not crazy the way I was. Talking with Alison about it last night helped a lot, and now the phone call. Just so I know nothing terrible's gonna happen to the cat—"

I barely heard the door, but I did look up and see him, and as he approached I sshhhed Carolyn, and she broke off in the middle of a sentence and turned to see why I was interrupting her.

"Shit," she said. "Hello, Ray."

"Hello, yourself," said the best cop money can buy. "You know, you find out who your friends are in this business. Here's a couple of people I know for years, and all I gotta do is walk in the room and one says sshhh and the other says shit. What's gonna happen to the cat, Carolyn?"

"Nothing," she said. Years ago she'd heard somewhere that the best defense is a good offense, and she'd never forgotten it. "The real question is what's gonna happen to Bernie if his so-called old friends keep arresting him every time he turns around. You ever hear of police harassment, Ray?"

"Just be grateful I never heard of police brutality, Carolyn. Whyntcha take a hike, huh? Stretch your legs. They could use it."

"If you're gonna do short jokes, Ray, I'll do asshole jokes, and where'll that leave you?"

"Jesus, Bern," he said. "Can't you get her to act like a lady?"

"I've been working at it. What do you want, Ray?"

"About three minutes of conversation. Private conversation. If she wants to stick around, I suppose we could go in your back room."

"No, I'll go," Carolyn said. "I gotta use the bathroom anyway."

"Now that you mention it, so do I. No, you go ahead, Carolyn. Bernie an' I'll talk, so you take your time in there." He waited until she had left the room, then laid a hand on the art book that Elspeth Peters had left on my counter. It was closed now, no longer open to the Mondrian reproduction. "Pictures," he said. "Right?"

"Very good, Ray."

"Like the one you lifted from Onderdonk's place?"

"What are you talking about?"

"A guy named Mondrian," he said, except he pronounced it *Moon-drain*. "Used to hang over the fireplace and covered by $350,000 insurance."

"That's a lot of money."

"It is, isn't it? Far as they can tell so far, that's the only thing that was stolen. Pretty good-sized paintin', white background, black lines

155

crisscrossin', a little color here an' there."

"I've seen it."

"Oh? No kiddin'."

"When I appraised his library. It was hanging over the fireplace." I thought for a moment. "I think he said something about sending it out for framing."

"Yeah, it needed a new frame."

"How's that?"

"I'll tell you how it is, Bernie. The picture frame from the Moondrain was in the closet with Onderdonk's body, all broken into pieces. There was the aluminum frame, pulled apart, and there was what they call the stretcher that the canvas is attached to, except it wasn't."

"It wasn't? It wasn't what?"

"Attached. Somebody cut the paintin' off the stretcher, but there was enough left so that a guy from the insurance company only had to take one look to know it was the Moondrain. To me it didn't look like much. Just about an inch-wide strip of canvas all the way around, white with black dashes here and there like Morse code, and I think one strip of red. My guess is you rolled it and wore it out of the buildin' under your clothes."

"I never touched it."

"Uh-huh. You musta been in some kind of rush to cut it out of the frame instead of takin' the time to unfasten the staples. That way you coulda got the whole canvas. I don't figure you killed him, Bern. I been thinkin' about that, and I don't think you did it."

"Thanks."

156

"But I know you were there and you musta got the paintin'. Maybe you heard somebody comin' and that's why you rushed and cut it outta the frame. Maybe you left the frame hangin' on the wall an' left Onderdonk tied up, and somebody else stuck the frame in the closet and killed him while they were at it."

"Why would anybody do that?"

"Who knows what people'll do? This is a crazy world with crazy people in it."

"Amen."

"The point is, I figure you got the Moondrain."

"Mondrian. Not Moondrain. Mondrian."

"What's the difference? I could call him Pablo Fuckin' Picasso and we'd still know who we were talkin' about. I figure you got it, Bern, and if you haven't got it I figure you can get it, and that's why I'm here on my own time when I oughta be home with my feet up and the TV on."

"Why's that?"

"Because there's a reward," he said. "The insurance company's a bunch of cheap bastards, the reward's only ten percent, but what's ten percent of $350,000?"

"Thirty-five thousand dollars."

"Bookstore goes under, Bern, you can always become an accountant. You're gonna need some cash to get out from under this murder rap, right? Money for your lawyer, money for costs. The hell, everybody needs money, right? Otherwise you wouldn't have

157

to go out stealin' in the first place. So you come up with the paintin' and I haul it in for the reward and we split."

"How do we split?"

"Bern, was I ever greedy? Fifty-fifty's how we split an' that way everybody's happy. You wash my hand, I'll scratch your back, you know what I mean?"

"I think so."

"So we're talkin' seventeen-five apiece, and I'll tell you, Bern, you're not gonna beat that. All this publicity, a murder and all, you can't run out and find a buyer for it. And forget about workin' a deal where you sell it back to the insurance company, because these bastards set traps and all you'll wind up with is your tit in a wringer. Of course maybe you stole it to order, maybe you got a customer waitin', but can you take a chance with him? In the first place he could cross you, and in the second place you can take some of the pressure off your own self if the insurance company gets the picture back."

"You've got it all worked out."

"Well," he said, "a man's got to think for himself. Another thing is maybe you already fenced it, stole it to order and turned it over the same night." He shifted his weight from one foot to the other. "Say, what's she doin' in there, Bernie?"

"Answering a call of nature, I suppose."

"Yeah, well, I wish she'd shit or get off the pot. My back teeth are floatin'. What I was sayin', if you already offed the Moondrain, what you got to do is steal it back."

"From the person I sold it to?"

"Or from the person *he* sold it to, if it passed on down the line. I'm tellin' you, Bernie, this case'll quiet down a lot if the Moondrain gets recovered. That'll tend to separate the burglary aspect from the murder aspect, and maybe it'll get people lookin' elsewhere than yourself for the killer."

"It'll also put half of thirty-five thousand dollars in your pocket, Ray."

"And the other half in yours, and don't forget it. What the hell happened to Carolyn? Maybe I better go see if she fell in."

Whereupon my favorite dog groomer burst breathless into the room, hitching at the belt of her slacks with one hand, holding the other up with the palm facing toward us.

She said, "Bernie, there's been a disaster. Ray, don't go in there, don't even think about it. Bernie, what I did, I flushed a bloody tampon. I thought it'd be all right, and everything blocked up and backed up and there's shit all over the floor and it's still running. I tried to clean up but I only made it worse. Bernie, can you help me? I'm afraid it's gonna flood the whole store."

"I was just leavin'," Ray said, backing off. His face had a greenish tinge and he didn't look happy. "Bern, I'll be in touch, right?"

"You don't want to give us a hand?"

"Are you kiddin'?" he said. "Jesus!"

I was around the counter before he was out the door, and he wasn't taking his time, either. I went through toward the back room and ducked into the john, and there was nothing on the floor but red and black vinyl tiles in a checkerboard pattern. They were quite dry, and about as clean as they generally are.

There was a man sitting on my toilet.

He didn't look as though he belonged there. He was fully dressed, wearing gray sharkskin trousers with a gray glen-plaid suit jacket. His shirt was maroon and his shoes were a pair of scuffed old wingtips, somewhere between black and brown in hue. He had shaggy rust-brown hair and a red goatee, ill-trimmed and going to gray. His head was back and his jaw slack, showing tobacco-stained teeth that had never known an orthodontist's care. His eyes, too, were open, and they were of the sort described as guileless blue.

"Well, I'll be damned," I said.

"You didn't know he was in here?"

"Of course not."

"That's what I figured. You recognize him?"

"The artist," I said. "The one who paid a dime at the Hewlett Collection. I forget his name."

"Turner."

"No, that's another artist, but it's close. The guard knew his name, called him by name. Turnquist."

"That's it. Bernie, where are you going?"

"I want to make sure there's nobody in the store," I said, "and I want to turn the bolt, and I want to change the sign from *Open* to *Closed*."

"And then what?"

"I don't know yet."

"Oh," she said. "Bernie?"

"What?"

"He's dead, isn't he?"

"Oh, no question," I said. "They don't get much deader."

"That's what I thought. I think I'm gonna be sick."

"Well, if you have to. But can't you wait until I get him off the toilet?"

FIFTEEN

"YOU CAN RENT 'em for only fifty bucks a month," she said. "That's a pretty good deal, isn't it? Comes to less than two dollars a day. What else can you get for less than two dollars a day?"

"Breakfast," I said, "if you're a careful shopper."

"And a lousy tipper. The only thing is they got a one-month minimum. Even if we bring the thing back in an hour and a half, it's the same fifty bucks."

"We might not bring it back at all. How much of a deposit did you have to leave?"

"A hundred. Plus the first month's rental,

so I'm out a hundred and a half. But the hundred comes back when we return the thing. *If* we return the thing."

We paused at the corner of Sixth Avenue and Twelfth Street, waiting for the light to change. It changed and we headed across. At the opposite side Carolyn said, "Didn't they pass a law? Aren't there supposed to be access ramps at all corners?"

"That sounds familiar."

"Well, do you call this a ramp? Look at this curb, will you? You could hang-glide off of it."

"You push down on the handles," I said, "and I'll lift. Here we go."

"Shit."

"Easy does it."

"Shit with chocolate sauce. I mean we can manage it, even a steep curb, but what's a genuinely handicapped person out on his own supposed to do, will you tell me that?"

"You've been asking that question once a block."

"Well, my consciousness is being raised every time we have to shlep this damned thing up another curb. It's the kind of cause I could get worked up about. Show me a petition and I'll sign it. Show me a parade and I'll march. What's so funny?"

"I was picturing the parade."

"You've got a sick sense of humor, Bernie. Anyone ever tell you that? Help me push—I'm giving our friend here a bumpy ride."

Not that our friend was apt to complain. He

was the late Mr. Turnquist, of course, and the thing we were pushing, as you've probably figured out, was a wheelchair, leased from Pitterman Hospital and Surgical Supply on First Avenue between Fifteenth and Sixteenth Streets. Carolyn had gone there, rented the contraption, and brought it back in the trunk of a cab. I'd helped her get it into the bookstore, where we'd unfolded it and wrestled Turnquist into it.

By the time we left the store he looked natural enough sitting there, and a lot better than he'd looked on the throne in my john. There was a leather strap that fastened around his waist, and I'd added a couple of lengths of old lamp cord to secure his wrists to the chair's arms and his ankles to an appropriately positioned rail. A lap robe—an old blanket, really, slightly mildewed—covered him from the neck down. A pair of Foster Grants hid his staring blue eyes. A peaked tweed cap that had been hanging on a nail in my back room since March, waiting for its owner to reclaim it, now sat on Turnquist's head, doing its best to make him a shade less identifiable. And in that fashion we made our way westward, trying to figure out what the hell was happening, and getting distracted once a block when Carolyn started bitching about the curbs.

"What we're doing," she said. "Transporting a dead body. Is it a felony or a misdemeanor?"

"I don't remember. It's a no-no, that's for sure. The law takes a dim view of it."

"In the movies, you're not supposed to touch anything."

"I never touch anything in the movies. What you're supposed to do is report dead bodies immediately to the police. You could have done that. You could have come right out of the john and told Ray there was a corpse sitting on the pot. You wouldn't have even had to make a phone call."

She shrugged. "I figured he'd want an explanation."

"It's likely."

"I also figured we didn't have one."

"Right again."

"How'd he get there, Bernie?"

"I don't know. He felt fairly warm to the touch but I haven't touched a whole lot of dead people in my time and I don't know how long it takes them to cool off. He could have been in the store yesterday when I locked up. I closed the place in a hurry, remember, because I'd just been arrested and that kept me from concentrating fully upon my usual routine. He could have been browsing in the stacks, or he could have slipped into the back room and hidden out on purpose."

"Why would he do that?"

"Beats me. Then he could have been there and sometime in the course of the night or morning he could have gone to the john, sat down on it without dropping his pants, and died."

"Of a heart attack or something?"

"Or something," I agreed, and the wheelchair hit a bump in the sidewalk. Our passenger's head flopped forward, almost dislodging cap and sunglasses. Carolyn straightened things out.

"He'll sue us," she said. "Whiplash."

"Carolyn, the man's dead. Don't make jokes."

"I can't help it. It's a nervous reaction. You think he just died of natural causes?"

"This is New York. Murder's a natural cause in this city."

"You think he was murdered? Who could have murdered him?"

"I don't know."

"You think somebody else was in the store with him? How did they get out?"

"I don't know."

"Maybe he committed suicide."

"Why not? He was a Russian agent, he had a cyanide capsule in a hollow tooth, and he knew the jig was up, so he let himself into my store and bit down on the old bicuspid. It's natural enough that he'd want to die in the presence of first editions and fine bindings."

"Well, if it wasn't a heart attack or suicide—"

"Or herpes," I said. "I understand there's a lot of it going around."

"If it wasn't one of those things, and if somebody killed him, how did they do it? You think you locked two people in the store last night?"

"No."

"Then what?"

"He could have slipped in when I opened up this morning. I might not have noticed. Then, while I was picking up coffee and taking it to your place—"

"That rotten coffee."

"—he could have gone into the john and died. Or if there was someone with him that person could have killed him. Or if he came alone, and then someone else came along, he could have opened the door for that person, and then the person could have killed him."

"Or the murderer managed to get locked in the store either last night or this morning, and when Turnquist showed up the murderer let him in and murdered him. Could either one of them let the other in without a key?"

"No problem," I said. "I didn't do much of a job of locking up when I went for coffee. I left the bargain table outside and just pressed the button so the springlock would work. I don't even remember double-locking the door with the key." I frowned, remembering. "Except I must have, because it was bolted when I came back. I had to turn the key in the lock twice to turn both the bolt and the springlock. Shit."

"What's the matter?"

"Well, that screws it up," I said. "Say Turnquist let the killer in, which he could have done from inside just by turning the knob. Then the killer left Turnquist dead on the potty and went out, but how did he lock the door?"

"Don't you have extra keys around somewhere? Maybe he found them."

"You'd really have to look for them, and why would he bother? Especially when I didn't have the door double-locked in the first place."

"It doesn't make sense."

"Hardly anything does. Watch the curb."

"Shit."

"Watch that, too. People seem to have stopped picking up after their dogs. Walking's becoming an adventure again."

We managed another curb, crossed another street, scaled the curb at the far side. We kept heading west, and once we got across Abingdon Square, the traffic, both automotive and pedestrian, thinned out considerably. At the corner of Twelfth and Hudson we passed the Village Nursing Home, where an old gentleman in a similar chair gave Turnquist the thumbs-up sign. "Don't let these young people push you around," he counseled our passenger. "Learn to work the controls yourself." When he got no response, his eyes flicked to me and Carolyn. "The old boy a little bit past it?" he demanded.

"I'm afraid so."

"Well, at least you're not dumping the poor bastard in a home," he said, with not a little bitterness. "He ever comes around, you tell him I said he's damn lucky to have such decent children."

We walked on across Greenwich Street, took a left at Washington. A block and a half down, between Bank and Bethune, a warehouse was being transmuted into co-op living lofts.

The crew charged with performing this alchemy was gone for the day.

I braked the wheelchair.

Carolyn said, "Here?"

"As good a place as any. They angled a plank over the steps for the wheelbarrows. Make a good ramp for the chair."

"I thought we could keep on going down to the Morton Street Pier. Send him into the Hudson, chair and all."

"Carolyn—"

"It's an old tradition, burial at sea. Davy Jones's Locker. 'Full fathom five my father lies—' "

"Want to give me a hand?"

"Oh, sure. Nothing I'd rather do. 'Well, at least you're not dumping the poor bastard in a home.' Hell no, old timer. We're dumping the old bastard in a seemingly abandoned warehouse where he'll be cared for by the Green Hornet and Pluto."

"Kato."

"Whatever. Why do I feel like Burke and Hare?"

"They stole bodies and sold them. We're just moving one around."

"Terrific."

"I told you I'd do this myself, Carolyn."

"Oh, don't be ridiculous. I'm your hench-person, aren't I?"

"It looks that way."

"And we're in this together. It's my cat that got us in this mess. Bern, why can't we leave him here, chair and all? I honest to God don't care a rat's ass about the hundred dollars."

"It's not the money."

"What is it, the principle of the thing?"

"If we leave the chair," I said, "they'll trace it."

"To Pitterman Hospital and Surgical Supply? Big hairy deal. I paid in cash and gave a phony name."

"I don't know who Turnquist was or how he fits into this Mondrian business, but there has to be a connection. When the cops tie him to it they'll go to Pitterman and get the description of the person who rented the chair. Then they'll take the clerk downtown and stick you in front of him in a lineup, you and four of the Harlem Globetrotters, and who do you figure he'll point to?"

"I expect short jokes from Ray, Bernie. I don't expect them from you."

"I was just trying to make a point."

"You made it. I thought it would be more decent to leave him in the chair, that's all. Forget I said anything, okay?"

"Okay."

I got the wire off his wrists and ankles, unstrapped the belt from around his waist, and managed to stretch him out on his back on a reasonably uncluttered expanse of floor. I retrieved the cap and sunglasses and blanket.

Back on the street I said, "Hop on, Carolyn. I'll give you a ride."

"Huh?"

"Two people pushing an empty wheelchair are conspicuous. C'mon, get in the chair."

"You get in it."

"You weigh less than I do, and—"

"The hell with that noise. You're taller than I am and you're a man, so if one of us has to play Turnquist you're a natural choice for the role. Get in the chair, Bern, and put on the cap and the glasses." She tucked the blanket around me and the mildew smell wafted to my nostrils. With a sly grin, my henchperson released the handbrake. "Hang on," she said. "And fasten your seat belt. Short jokes, huh? We may hit a few air pockets along the way."

SIXTEEN

BACK AT THE STORE, I checked the premises for bodies, living or dead, before I did anything else. I didn't find any, nor did I happen on any clues as to how Turnquist had gotten into my store or how he'd happened to join his ancestors in that great atelier on high. Carolyn wheeled the chair into the back room and I helped her fold it. "I'll take it back in a cab," she said, "but first I want some coffee."

"I'll get it."

"Not from the felafel joint."

"Don't worry."

When I got back with two coffees she said the phone had rung in my absence. "I was gonna answer it," she said, "and then I didn't."

"Probably wise."

"This coffee's much better. You know what we oughta do? In either your place or my place we oughta have one of those machines, nice fresh coffee all day long. One of those electric drip things."

"Or even a hotplate and a Chemex pot."

"Yeah. Of course you'd be pouring coffee for customers all day long, and you'd never get rid of Kirschmann. He'd be a permanent guest. I really grossed him out, didn't I?"

"He couldn't get out of here fast enough."

"Well, that was the idea. I figured the more disgusting I made it, the faster he'd split. I was trying to wait him out, you know, figuring he might leave if I stayed out of the room long enough, but it looked as though he wasn't gonna cave without peeing, so—"

"I almost left myself. He's not the only one you grossed out."

"Oh, right. You didn't know I was faking it."

"Of course not. I didn't know there was a dead man in there."

"Maybe I went into too much detail."

"Don't worry about it," I said, and the phone rang.

I picked it up and Wally Hemphill said, "You're a hard man to get hold of, Bernie. I was thinking you'd jumped bail."

"I wouldn't do that. I don't know anybody in Costa Rica."

"Oh, a guy like you would make friends anywhere. Listen, what do you know about this Mondrian?"

"I know he was Dutch," I said. "Born in 1872 in Amberfoot or something like that. He began, you may recall, as a painter of naturalistic landscapes. As he found his own style he grew artistically and his work became increasingly abstract. By 1917—"

"What's this, a museum lecture? There's a painting missing from Onderdonk's apartment worth close to half a million dollars."

"I know."

"You get it?"

"No."

"It might be useful if you could come up with it. Give us a bargaining chip."

"Suppose I gave them Judge Crater," I said, "or a cure for cancer."

"You really haven't got the painting?"

"No."

"Who got it?"

"Probably the person who killed him."

"You didn't kill anybody and you didn't take anything."

"Right."

"You were just there to leave fingerprints."

"Evidently."

"Nuts. Where do you go from here, Bernie?"

"Around in circles," I said.

I got off the phone and went in back, with Carolyn trailing after me. There's a sort of cupboard next to the desk, filled with things I haven't gotten around to throwing out, and I keep a sweat shirt and some other running gear there. I opened it, took inventory, and removed my shirt.

"Hey," she said. "What are you doing?"

"Getting undressed," I said, unbelting my pants. "What's it look like?"

"Jesus," she said, turning her back on me. "If this is a subtle pass, I pass on it. In the first place I'm gay and in the second place we're best friends and in the third place—"

"I'm going for a run, Carolyn."

"Oh. With Wally?"

"Without Wally. A nice lope around Washington Square until my mind clears up. There's nothing in it now but false starts and loose ends. People keep coming out of the woodwork asking me for a painting I never even had my hands on. They all want me to have it. Kirschmann smells a reward and Wally smells a fat fee and I don't know what all the other people smell. Oil paint, probably. I'll run and work the kinks out of my mind and maybe all of this will start to make sense to me."

"And what about me? What'll I do while you're doing your Alberto Salazar impression?"

"You could take the wheelchair back."

"Yeah, I have to do that sooner or later, don't I? Bern? I wonder if any of the people who saw you in the wheelchair will recognize you jogging around Washington Square."

"Let's hope not."

"Listen," she said, "anybody says anything, just tell 'em you've been to Lourdes."

Washington Square Park is a rectangle, and the sidewalk around it measures just about five-eighths of a mile, which in turn is just about a kilometer. It's flat if you're walking, but when you run there's a slight slope evident, and if you run counterclockwise, as almost everybody does, you feel the incline as you run east along the southern border of the park. I felt it a lot on the first lap, with my legs still a little achey from the previous day's ordeal in Central Park, but after that it didn't bother me.

I was wearing blue nylon shorts and a ribbed yellow tank top and burgundy running shoes, and there was a moment when I found myself wondering whether Mondrian would have liked my outfit. Scarlet shoes would have suited him better, I decided. Or vermillion, like the galleries.

I took it very slow and easy. A lot of people passed me, but I didn't care if old ladies with aluminum walkers whizzed by me. I just put one wine-colored foot after the other, and somewhere around the fourth lap my mind started to float, and I suppose I ran three more laps after that but I wasn't keeping score.

I didn't think about Mondrian or his paintings or all the crazy people who wanted them. I didn't really think about anything, and after my close to four miles I picked up the plastic

174

bag of stuff I'd left with one of the chess-players at the park's southwest corner. I thanked him and trotted west to Arbor Court.

Carolyn wasn't home, so I used the tools I'd brought along to let myself into her building and then her apartment. The vestibule lock was candy but the others were not, and I wondered what curious villain had picked those locks without leaving a hint of his presence, and why he couldn't use the same talents to hook the Mondrian out of the Hewlett Collection all by his own self.

I got in, locked up, stripped and showered, the last-named act being the reason I'd come to Arbor Court. I dried off and put on the clothes I'd been wearing earlier and hung my sopping shorts and tank top over the shower curtain rod. Then I looked in the fridge for a beer, made a face when I failed to find one, and fixed some iced tea from a mix. It tasted like what you would expect.

I made a sandwich and ate it and made another sandwich and started eating it, and some clown outside slammed on his brakes and hit his horn, and Ubi hopped onto the window ledge to investigate. I watched him stick his head through the bars, the tips of his whiskers just brushing the bars on either side, and I thought of Archie's whiskers and found myself feeling uncommonly sorry for the poor cat. There were two people dead already and I was charged with one murder and might very well be charged with the other, and all I could think of was how forlorn Carolyn's cat must be.

I looked up a number, picked up the phone and dialed it. Denise Raphaelson answered on the third ring and I said, "This is Bernie, and we never had this conversation."

"Funny, I remember it as if it were yesterday."

"What do you know about an artist named Turnquist?"

"That's why you called? To find out what I know about an artist named Turnquist?"

"That's why. He's probably crowding sixty, reddish hair and goatee, bad teeth, gets all his clothes from the Goodwill. Sort of a surly manner."

"Where is he? I think I'll marry him."

Denise was a girlfriend of mine for a while, and then she rather abruptly became a girlfriend of Carolyn's, and that didn't last very long. She's a painter, with a loft on West Broadway called the Narrowback Gallery where she lives and works. I said, "Actually, it's a little late for that."

"What's the matter with him?"

"You don't want to know. Ever hear of him?"

"I don't think so. Turnquist. He got a first name?"

"Probably. Most people do, except for Trevanian. Maybe Turnquist's his first name and he doesn't have a last name. There are a lot of people like that. Hildegarde. Twiggy."

"Liberace."

"That's his last name."

"Oh, right."

"Does Turnquist ring a bell?"

"Doesn't even knock softly. What kind of painter is he?"

"A dead one."

"That's what I was afraid of. Well, he's in good company. Rembrandt, El Greco, Giotto, Bosch—all those guys are dead."

"We never had this conversation."

"What conversation?"

I hung up and looked up Turnquist in the Manhattan book, and there was only one listing, a Michael Turnquist in the East Sixties. Things are never that easy, and he certainly hadn't dressed to fit that address, but what the hell. I dialed the number and a man answered almost immediately.

I said, "Michael Turnquist?"

"Speaking."

"Sorry," I said. "I must have the wrong number."

The hell with it. I picked up the phone again and dialed 911. When a woman answered I said, "There's a dead body at a construction site on Washington Street," and gave the precise address. She started to ask me something but I didn't let her finish her sentence. "Sorry," I said, "but I'm one of those people who just don't want to get involved."

I was lost in something, possibly thought, when a key turned in one of the locks. The sound was repeated as someone opened the other two locks in turn, and I spent a couple of seconds trying to decide what I'd do if it wasn't Carolyn.

Suppose it was the Nazi, coming to swipe the other cat. I looked around for Ubi but didn't see him, and then the door swung inward and I turned to look at Carolyn and Elspeth Peters.

Except it wasn't Elspeth Peters, and all it took was a second glance to make that clear to me. But I could see why my henchperson had taken a second glance at the Peters woman, because the resemblance was pronounced.

I could also see why she'd taken more than a couple glances at this woman, who obviously had to be Alison the tax planner. She was at least as attractive as Elspeth Peters, and the airy quality of Ms. Peters that went so well with old-timey lady poets and secondhand books was replaced in Alison by an earthy intensity. Carolyn introduced us—"Alison, this is Bernie Rhodenbarr. Bernie, this is Alison Warren"— and Alison established her credentials as a political and economic lesbian with a firm no-nonsense handshake.

"I didn't expect you," Carolyn said.

"Well, I stopped in to use the shower."

"Right, you were running."

"Oh, you're a runner?" Alison said.

We got a little mileage out of that, so to speak, and Carolyn put some coffee on, and Alison sat down on the couch and Ubi turned up and sat in her lap. I went over to the stove, where Carolyn was fussing with the coffee.

"Isn't she nice?" she whispered.

"She's terrific," I whispered back. "Get rid of her."

"You've got to be kidding."

"Nope."

"Why, for Christ's sake?"

"We're going to the museum. The Hewlett."

"Now?"

"Now."

"Look, I just got her here. She's all settled in with a cat on her lap. The least I can do is give her a cup of coffee."

"Okay," I said, still whispering. "I'll split now. Get away as soon as you can and meet me in front of the Hewlett."

When I handed over my two singles and two quarters, the attendant at the Hewlett was nice enough to point out that the gallery would be closing in less than an hour. I told him that was all right and accepted my lapel pin in return. The whole exchange brought the late Mr. Turnquist to life for me, and I remembered the fierce animation with which he'd lectured to us about art. I suppose I'd depersonalized the man in order to drag his body across town and dump him, and I guess it had been necessary, but now I saw him again as a person—quirky and abrasive and vividly human—and I felt sorry he was dead and sorrier that I'd used him after death as a prop in a macabre farce.

The feeling was a dismal one and I shook it off as I made my way to the upstairs gallery where the Mondrian was on display. I entered with a perfunctory nod at the uniformed guard. I half expected to find a blank spot on the wall where *Composition with Color* had lately hung, or another painting altogether, but Mondrian was right where he belonged and I was glad to see him again.

Half an hour later a voice at my elbow said, "Well, it's good, Bernie, but I don't think it would fool many people. It's hard to make a pencil sketch look like an oil painting. What are you doing?"

"Sketching the painting," I said, without looking up from my notebook. "I'm guessing at the measurements."

"What are the initials for? Oh, the colors, right?"

"Right."

"What's the point?"

"I don't know."

"The guy downstairs didn't want to take my money. The place is gonna close any minute. What I did, I gave him a dollar. Are we gonna steal the painting, Bernie?"

"Yes."

"Now?"

"Of course not."

"Oh. When?"

"I don't know."

"I don't suppose you know how we're gonna do it, either."

"I'm working on it."

"By drawing in your notebook?"

"Shit," I said, and closed the notebook with a snap. "Let's get out of here."

"I'm sorry, Bern. I didn't mean to hassle you."

"It's okay. Let's get out of here."

We found a bar called Gloryosky's a couple of blocks up Madison. Soft lighting, deep carpet, chrome and black formica, and some Little Orphan Annie murals on the walls. About half the patrons were gulping their first après-work drinks while the rest looked as though they hadn't made it back from lunch. Everybody was thanking God that it was Friday.

"This is nice," Carolyn said as we settled into a booth. "Dim lights, gaiety, laughter, the clink of ice cubes and a Peggy Lee record on the jukebox. I could be happy here, Bernie."

"Cute waitress, too."

"I noticed. This joint has it all over the Bum Rap. It's a shame it's so far from the store." The waitress appeared and leaned forward impressively. Carolyn gave her a full-tilt smile and ordered a martini, very cold, very dry, and very soon. I asked for Coca-Cola and lemon. The waitress smiled and departed.

"Why?" Carolyn demanded.

"Pardon?"

"Why Coke with lemon?"

"It cuts some of the sugary taste."

"Why Coke in the first place?"

I shrugged. "Oh, I don't know. I guess I'm not in the mood for Perrier. Plus I figure I can use a little sugar rush and a caffeine hit."

"Bern, are you being willfully obtuse?"

"Huh? Oh. Why no booze?"

"Right."

I shrugged again. "No particular reason."

"You're gonna try breaking into the museum? That's crazy."

"I know, and I'm not going to try. But whatever I do I've got a complicated evening coming up and I guess I want to be at the top of my form. Such as it is."

"Myself, I figure I'm better with a couple of drinks."

"Maybe you are."

"Not to mention the fact that I couldn't survive another ten minutes without one. Ah, here we are," she said, as our drinks appeared. "You can tell him to start mixing up another of these," she told the waitress, "because I wouldn't want to get too far out in front of him."

"Another round."

"Just another martini," she said. "He's got to sip that. Didn't your mother ever tell you? Never gulp anything fizzy."

I squeezed the lemon into the Coke, stirred and sipped. "She's got a great laugh," Carolyn said. "I like a girl with a nice sense of humor."

"And a nice set of—"

"Those too. There's a lot to be said for curves, even if your buddy Mondrian didn't believe in them. Straight lines and primary colors. You think he was a genius?"

"Probably."

"Whatever genius is. As far as having something to hang on the wall, I'm a lot happier with my Chagall litho."

"That's funny."

"What is?"

"Before," I said. "Standing in front of the

painting, I was thinking how great it would look in my apartment."

"Where?"

"Over the couch. Sort of centered over the couch."

"Oh yeah?" She closed her eyes, trying to picture it. "The painting we just saw? Or the one you saw in Onderdonk's apartment?"

"Well, the one we just saw. But the other was the same idea and the same general proportions, so it would do, too."

"Over the couch."

"Right."

"You know, it might look kind of nice in your place," she said. "Once all this mess is cleared away, you know what you'll have to do?"

"Yeah," I said. "Something like one-to-ten."

"One-to-ten?"

"Years."

"Oh," she said, and dismissed the entire penal system with an airy wave of her hand. "I'm serious, Bern. Once everything's cleared up, you can sit down and paint yourself a Mondrian and hang it over the couch."

"Oh, come on."

"I mean it. Face it, Bern. What old Piet did back there doesn't look all that hard to do. Okay, he was a genius because he thought of it first, and his proportions and colors were brilliant and perfect and fit into some philosophical system, whatever it was, but so what? If all you're looking to do is make a copy for your own place, how hard could it be to follow his measurements and copy his colors and just paint it? I mean there's no drawing involved, there's no shading, there's no changes in texture. It's just a white canvas with black lines and patches of color. You wouldn't have to spend ten years at the Art Students League to do that, would you?"

"What a thought," I said. "It's probably harder than it looks."

"Everything's harder than it looks. Grooming a Shih Tzu's harder than it looks, but you don't have to be a genius. Where's that sketch you made? Couldn't you follow the dimensions and paint it on canvas?"

"I can paint a wall with a roller. That's about it."

"Why'd you make the sketch?"

"Because there's too many paintings," I said, "and unless they're side by side I couldn't tell them apart, Mondrian being Mondrian, and I thought a sketch might be useful for identification purposes. If I ever see any picture besides the one in the Hewlett. I couldn't do it."

"Couldn't do what?"

"Paint a fake Mondrian. I wouldn't know what to do. All the black bands are straight like a knife edge. How would you manage that?"

"I suppose you'd need a steady hand."

"There must be more to it than that. And I wouldn't know how to buy paints, let alone mix colors."

"You could learn."

"An artist could do it," I said.

"Sure. If you knew the technique, and—"

"It's a shame we didn't get to Turnquist before he died. He was an artist and he admired Mondrian."

"Well, he's not the only artist in New York City. If you want a Mondrian for over the couch and you don't want to try painting it yourself, I'm sure you could find someone to—"

"I'm not talking about a Mondrian for my apartment."

"You're not? Oh."

"Right."

"You mean—"

"Right."

"Where's the waitress, dammit? A person could die of thirst around here."

"She's coming."

"Good. I don't think it'll work, Bern. I was talking about making something that'd look good over your couch, not something that would fool experts. Besides, where would we find an artist we could trust?"

"Good point."

The waitress arrived, setting a fresh martini in front of Carolyn and having a look at my Coke, which was still half full. Or half empty, if you're a pessimist.

"That's perfect," Carolyn told her. "I bet you used to be a nurse, didn't you?"

"That's nothing," she said. "It's supposed to be a secret, but I just know you won't tell anyone. The bartender used to be a brain surgeon."

"He hasn't lost his touch. It's a good thing I've got Blue Cross."

The waitress did her exit-laughing number, taking Carolyn's eyes with her. "She's cute," said my partner in crime.

"A shame she's not an artist."

"Clever repartee, a great personality, and a nifty set of wheels. You figure she's gay?"

"Hope does spring eternal, doesn't it?"

"That's what they tell me."

"Gay or straight," I said, "what we really need is an artist."

The whole room seemed to go silent, as if someone had just mentioned E.F. Hutton. Except that other conversations were still going on. It's just that we stopped hearing them. Carolyn and I both froze, then turned our eyes slowly to meet one another's exophthalmic gazes. After a long moment we spoke as if in a single voice.

"Denise," we said.

SEVENTEEN

"HOLD THIS," Denise Raphaelson said. "You know, I can't remember the last time I stretched a canvas. Who bothers nowadays? You buy a stretched canvas and save yourself the aggravation. Of course I don't usually get customers who specify the size they want in centimeters."

"It's becoming a metric universe."

"Well, you know what I always say. Give 'em a gram and they'll take a kilo. This should be close, Bernie, and anybody who takes a yardstick to this beauty will already have six other ways to tell it's not the real thing. But the measurements'll be very close. Maybe it'll be a couple millimeters off. Remember that cigarette that advertised it was a silly millimeter longer?"

"I remember."

"I wonder whatever happened to it."

"Somebody probably smoked it."

Denise was smoking one of her own, or letting it burn unattended in a scallop shell she used as an ashtray. We were at her place and we were stretching a canvas. *We* meant Denise and me. Carolyn had not accompanied me.

Denise is long limbed and slender, with dark brown curly hair and fair skin lightly dusted with freckles. She is a painter, and she does well enough at it to support herself and her son Jared, with the occasional assistance of a child-support check from Jared's father. Her work is abstract, very vivid, very intense, very energetic. You might not like her canvases but you'd be hard put to ignore them.

And, come to think of it, you could say much the same of their creator. Denise and I had kept occasional company over a couple of years, sharing a fondness for ethnic food and thoughtful jazz and snappy repartee. Our one area of disagreement was Carolyn, whom she affected to despise. Then one day Denise and Carolyn commenced to have an affair. That didn't take too long to run its course, and once it was over Carolyn didn't see Denise anymore, and neither did I.

I could say I don't understand women, but what's so remarkable about that? Nobody does.

"This is gesso," Denise explained. "We want a smooth canvas so we put this on. Here, take the brush. That's right. A nice even coat. It's all in the wrist, Bernie."

"What does this do?"

"It dries. It's acrylic gesso so it'll dry in a hurry. Then you sand it."

"I sand it?"

"With sandpaper. Lightly. Then you do another coat of the gesso and sand it again, and a third coat and sand it again."

"And you on the opposite shore will be?"

"That's it. Ready to ride and spread the alarm through every something village and farm."

"Every Middlesex village and farm," I said, which was the way Longfellow had put it. *Middlesex* sort of hung in the air between us. "It comes from Middle Saxons," I said. "According to where they settled in England. Essex was the East Saxons, Sussex was the South Saxons, and—"

"Leave it alone."

"All right."

"'Every bisexual village and farm.' I suppose No Sex was the North Saxons, huh?"

"I thought we were going to leave it alone."

"It's like a scab, it's irresistible. I'm going to see if I can't find a book with the painting reproduced. *Composition with Color*, 1942. God knows how many paintings he did with that title. There's a minimalist I know on Harrison Street who calls everything he paints Composition #104. It's his favorite number. If he ever amounts to anything, the art historians are going to go batshit trying to straighten it all out."

I was sanding the third coat of gesso when she returned with a large book entitled *Mondrian and the Art of De Stijl*. She flipped it open to a page near the end, and there was the painting we'd seen in the Hewlett. "That's it," I said.

"How are the colors?"

"What do you mean? Aren't they in the right place? I thought you took my sketch along."

"Yes, and it's a wonderful sketch. Burglary's gain was the art world's loss. Books of reproductions are never perfect, Bernie. The inks never duplicate the paint a hundred percent. How do these colors compare to what you saw in the painting?"

"Oh," I said.

"Well?"

"I don't have that kind of an eye, Denise. Or that kind of a memory. I think this looks about right." I held the book at arm's length, tilted it to catch the light. "The background's darker than I remember it. It was whiter in—I want to say real life, but that's not what I mean. You know what I mean."

She nodded. "Mondrian used off-whites. He tinted his white with a little blue, a little red, a little yellow. I can probably make up something that looks sort of all right. I hope this isn't going to have to fool an expert."

"So do I."

"Let me see how you did with the gesso. That's not bad. I think what we want now is a coat or two of white, just to get that smooth canvas effect, and then a coat of tinted white, and then—I wish I could have like two weeks to work on this."

"So do I."

"I'm going to use acrylics, obviously. Liquid acrylics. He used oils but he didn't have some lunatic at his elbow who wanted the finished painting in a matter of hours. Acrylics dry fast but they're not oils and—"

"Denise?"

"What?"

"There's no point making ourselves crazy. We'll just give it our best shot. Okay?"

"Okay."

"I've got a few things to do, but I can come back after I do them."

"I can handle this myself, Bernie. I don't need help."

"Well, I was thinking while I was putting the gesso on the canvas. There are a few things I can be doing at the same time."

"Only one person can work on a canvas at a time."

"I know that. See how this sounds to you."

I told her what I had in mind. She listened and nodded, and when I finished she didn't say anything but stopped to light a cigarette. She smoked it almost to the filter before she spoke.

"Sounds elaborate," she said.

"I guess it is."

"Complicated. I think I see what you're getting at, but I've got the feeling I'm better off not knowing too much. Is that possible?"

"It's possible."

"I think I want music," she said, and lit another cigarette and switched on her radio, which was tuned to one of the FM jazz stations. I recognized the record they were playing, a solo piano recording of Randy Weston's.

"Brings back memories," I said.

"Doesn't it? Jared's over at a friend's house. He'll be home within the hour. He can help."

"Great."

"I love the Hewlett Collection. Of course Jared has a fierce resentment against the place."

"Why?"

"Because he's a kid. Kids aren't allowed, remember?"

"Oh, right. Not even accompanied by an adult?"

"Not even accompanied by the front four of the Pittsburgh Steelers. Nobody under sixteen, no exceptions, nohow."

191

"That does seem a little high-handed," I said. "How's a kid supposed to develop an appreciation for art in this town?"

"Oh, it's real tough, Bernie. Outside of the Met and the Modern and the Guggenheim and the Whitney and the Museum of Natural History and a couple of hundred private galleries, a young person in New York is completely bereft of cultural resources. It's really hell."

"If I didn't know better, I'd swear you were being sarcastic."

"Me? Not in a million years." She sucked on her cigarette. "I'll tell you, it's a pleasure to go in there and not have eight million kids bouncing off the walls. Or class groups, with some brain-damaged teacher explaining at eighty decibels what Matisse had in mind while thirty kids fidget around, bored out of their basketball sneakers. The Hewlett's a museum for grownups and I love it."

"But Jared doesn't."

"He will the day he turns sixteen. Meanwhile it has the lure of forbidden fruit. I think he must be convinced it's the world's storehouse of erotic art and that's why he's not allowed in it. What *I* like about the place, aside from the childless aspect and the quality of the collection, is the way the paintings are hung. Hanged? Hung?"

"Whatever."

"Hung," she said decisively. "Murderers are hanged, or they used to be. Paintings and male models are hung. There's plenty of space between the paintings at the Hewlett.

You can look at them one at a time." She looked meaningfully at me. "What I'm trying to say," she said, "is I have a special feeling for the place."

"I understand."

"Assure me once more that this is in a good cause."

"You'll be helping to ransom a cat and keep an antiquarian bookman out of jail."

"Screw the bookman. Which cat is it? The Siamese?"

"You mean Burmese. Archie."

"Right. The friendly one."

"They're both friendly. Archie's just more outgoing."

"Same difference."

Randy Weston had given way to Chick Corea, and now that record had also ended and a young man with an untrained voice was bringing us the news. The first item had to do with progress in some arms-limitations talks, which may have had global importance but which I must admit I didn't pay heed to, and then the little big mouth was telling us that an anonymous tip had led police to the body of a man identified as Edwin P. Turnquist in a West Village warehouse. Turnquist had been stabbed in the heart, probably with an icepick. He was an artist and a latter-day bohemian who'd hung out with the early Abstract Expressionists at the old Cedar Tavern, and who'd been living at the time of his death in an SRO rooming house in Chelsea.

That would have been plenty, but he wasn't

finished. Prime suspect in the case, he added, was one Bernard Rhodenbarr, a Manhattan bookseller with several arrests for burglary. Rhodenbarr was out on bail after having been charged with homicide in the death of Gordon Kyle Onderdonk just days ago at the fashionable and exclusive Charlemagne Apartments. Onderdonk was presumed to have been murdered in the course of a burglary, but Rhodenbarr's motive for the murder of Turnquist had not yet been disclosed by police sources. "Perhaps," the little twerp suggested, "Mr. Turnquist was a man who knew too much."

I went over and turned off the radio, and the ensuing silence stretched out like the sands of the Sahara. It was broken at length by the flick of a Bic as Denise kindled yet another cigarette. Through a cloud of smoke she said, "The name Turnquist rings a muted bell."

"I thought it might."

"What was his first name—Edwin? I still never heard of him. Except in that conversation we never had."

"Uh."

"You didn't kill him, did you, Bernie?"

"No."

"Or that other man? Onderdonk?"

"No."

"But you're in this up to your eyeballs, aren't you?"

"Up to my hairline."

"And the police are looking for you."

"So it would seem. It would be, uh, best if they didn't find me. I used up all my cash posting a bond the other day. Not that any judge would let me out on bail this time around."

"And if you're in a cell on Rikers Island, how can you right wrongs and catch killers and liberate pussycats?"

"Right."

"What do they call what I am? Accessory after the fact?"

I shook my head. "Unwitting accomplice. You never turned the radio on. If I get out of this, there won't be any charges, Denise."

"And if you don't?"

"Er."

"Forget I asked. How's Carolyn holding up?"

"Carolyn? She'll be okay."

"Funny the turns human lives take."

"Uh-huh."

She tapped the canvas. "The one in the Hewlett's not framed? Just a canvas on a stretcher?"

"Right. The design continues around the edge."

"Well, he painted that way sometimes. Not always but sometimes. This whole business is crazy, Bernie. You know that, don't you?"

"Yeah."

"All the same," she said, "it just might work."

EIGHTEEN

IT WAS SOMEWHERE around eleven when I left the Narrowback Gallery. Denise had offered me the hospitality of the couch but I was afraid to accept it. The police were looking for me and I didn't want to be anyplace they might think of looking. Carolyn was the only person who knew I'd gone to Denise's, and she wouldn't talk unless they lit matches underneath her fingernails, but suppose they did? And she might let it slip to a friend—Alison, for instance—and the friend might prove less closemouthed.

For that matter, the police might not need a tip. Ray knew Denise and I had kept company in the past, and if they went through the routine of checking all known associates of the suspect, the fat would be in the fire.

Meanwhile it was in the frying pan and I was on the street. In an hour or so the bulldog edition of the *Daily News* would also be on the street, and it would very likely have my picture in it. For the time being I was my usual anonymous self, but I didn't feel anonymous; walking through SoHo, I found myself seeking shadows and shrinking from the imagined stares of passersby. Or perhaps the stares weren't imagined. Spend enough time shrinking in shadows and people are apt to stare at you.

On Wooster Street I found a telephone booth. A real one, for a change, with a door that drew shut, not one of those new improved numbers that leaves you exposed to the elements. Such booths have become rare to the point that some citizen had failed to recognize this particular one for what it was, mistaking it instead for a public lavatory. I chose privacy over comfort and closed myself within.

When I did this, a little light went on—literally, not figuratively. I loosened a couple of screws in the overhead fixture, took down a sheet of translucent plastic, and unscrewed the bulb a few turns, then put the plastic back and tightened the screws. Now I was not in the spotlight, which was fine for me. I called Information, then dialed the number the operator gave me.

I got the precinct where Ray Kirschmann hangs his hat, except that he doesn't, given as he is to wearing it indoors. He wasn't there. I called Information again and reached him at his house in Sunnyside. His wife answered and put him on without asking my name. He said "Hello?" and I said, "Ray?" and he said, "Jesus. The man of the hour. You gotta stop killin' people, Bernie. It's a bad habit and who knows what it could lead to, you know what I mean?"

"I didn't kill Turnquist."

"Right, you never heard of him."

"I didn't say that."

"Good, because he had a slip of paper with your name and the address of your store in his pocket."

Could it be? Had I overlooked something that incriminating in my search of the dead man's pockets? I wondered about it, and then I remembered something and closed my eyes.

"Bernie? You there?"

I hadn't searched his pockets. I'd been so busy getting rid of him I hadn't taken five minutes to go through his clothes.

"Anyway," he went on, "we found one of your business cards in his room. And on top of that we got a phone tip shortly after the body was discovered. What we got, we got two phone tips, and I wouldn't be surprised if they were the same person. First one told us where the body was, second said that if we wanted to know who killed Turnquist we should ask a fellow named Rhodenbarr. So what the hell, I'm askin'. Who killed him, Bern?"

"Not me."

"Uh-huh. We let guys like you out on bail and what do you do but commit more crimes? I can see gettin' carried away with a big hulk like Onderdonk, havin' to hit him and hittin' too hard. But shovin' an icepick in a shrimp like Turnquist, that's a pretty low thing to do."

"I didn't do it."

"I suppose you didn't search his room, either."

"I don't even know where it is, Ray. One of

the reasons I called you was to get his address."

"He had ID in his pocket. You coulda got it off that."

Shit, I thought. Everything had been in Turnquist's pockets but my two hands.

"Anyway," he said, "why'd you want his address?"

"I thought I might—"

"Go search his room."

"Well, yes," I admitted. "To find the real killer."

"Somebody already turned his room inside out, Bernie. If it wasn't you, then it was somebody else."

"Well, it certainly wasn't me. You found my card there, didn't you? When I search dead men's rooms I don't make a point of leaving a calling card."

"You don't make a point of killin' people, either. Maybe the shock left you careless."

"You don't believe that yourself, Ray."

"No, I don't guess I do. But they got an APB out on you, Bernie, and your bail's revoked, and you better turn yourself in or you're in deep shit. Where are you now? I'll come get you, make sure you can surrender yourself with no hassles."

"You're forgetting the reward. How can I come up with the painting if I'm in a cell?"

"You think you got a shot at it?"

"I think so, yes."

There was a lengthy pause, as pride warred with greed while he weighed an impressive arrest against a highly hypothetical $17,500. "I don't like telephones," he said. "Maybe we should talk it over face to face."

I started to say something but a recording cut in to tell me my three minutes were up. It was still babbling when I broke the connection.

There wasn't a single acceptable movie on Forty-second Street. There are eight or ten theaters on the stretch between Sixth and Eighth Avenues and the ones that weren't showing porn featured epics like *The Texas Chain Saw Massacre* and *Eaten Alive by Lemmings*. Well, it figured. Get rid of sex and violence and how would you know Times Square was the Crossroads of the World?

I settled on a house near Eighth Avenue where a pair of kung fu movies were playing. I'd never seen one before, and all along I'd had the right idea. But it was dark inside, and half empty, and I couldn't think of a safer place to pass a few hours. If the cops were really working at it, they'd have circulated my picture to the hotels. The papers would be on the street any minute. A person could sleep on the subway, but transit cops tend to look at you, and even if they didn't I'd have felt safer curling up on the third rail.

I took a seat off to one side and just sat there looking at the screen. There wasn't much dialogue, just sound effects when people got their chests kicked in or fell through plate glass windows, and the audience was generally quiet except for murmurs of approval when someone came to a dramatically bad end, which happened rather often.

I sat there and watched for a while. At some point I dozed off and at another I woke up. The same movie may have been playing, or it might have been the other one. I let the on-screen violence hypnotize me, and before I knew it I was thinking about everything that had happened and how it had all started with a refined gentleman turning up at my shop and inviting me to appraise his library. What a civilized incident, I thought, with such a brutal aftermath.

Wait a minute.

I sat up straighter in my seat and blinked as a wild-eyed Oriental chap on the screen smashed a woman's face with his elbow. I scarcely noticed. Instead, in my mind I saw Gordon Onderdonk greeting me at the door of his apartment, unfastening the chain lock, drawing the door wide to admit me. And other images played one after another across the retina of the mind, while snatches of a dozen different conversations echoed in accompaniment.

For a few minutes there my mind raced along as though I'd just brewed up a whole potful of espresso and injected it straight into a vein. All of the events of the past few days suddenly fell into place. And, on the screen in front of me, agile young men made remarkable leaps and stunning pirouettes and kicked and slashed and chopped the living crap out of each other.

I dozed off again, and in due course I awoke again, and after sitting up and blinking a bit I remembered the mental connections I'd made. I thought them through and they still made as much sense as ever, and I marveled at the way everything had come to me.

It struck me, on my way up the aisle to the exit, that I might have dreamed the whole solution. But I couldn't really see that it made very much difference. Either way it fit. And either way I had a lot to do.

NINETEEN

I STOOD IN a doorway on West End Avenue and watched a couple of runners on their way to the park. When they'd cantered on by I leaned out a ways and fixed an eye on the entrance to my building. I kept it in view, and after a few minutes a familiar shape emerged. She walked to the curb, the ever-present cigarette bobbing in the corner of her mouth. At first she started to turn north, and I started to wince, and then she turned south and walked half a block and crossed the street and made her way to me.

She was Mrs. Hesch, my across-the-hall neighbor, an ever-available source of coffee and solace. "Mr. Rhodenbarr," she said now. "It's good you called me. I was worried. You wouldn't believe the things those *momsers* are saying about you."

"Just so you don't believe them, Mrs. Hesch."

"Me? God forbid. I know you, Mr. Rhodenbarr. What you do is your business—a man has to make a living. And when it comes to neighbors you can't be beat. You're a nice young man. You wouldn't kill anybody."

"Of course I wouldn't."

"So what can I do for you?"

I gave her my keys, explained which one went in which lock, and told her what I needed. She was back fifteen minutes later with a shopping bag and a word of caution. "There's a man in the lobby," she said. "Regular clothes, no uniform, but I think he's an Irisher and he looks like a cop."

"He's probably both of those things."

"And there's two men, also looking like cops, in that dark green car over there."

"I already spotted them."

"I got the suit you told me and a clean shirt, and I picked you out a nice tie to go with it. Also socks and underwear which you didn't mention but I figure what does it hurt? Also the other things which I don't have to know what they are, and how you use them to open locks I don't want to know, but it's clever where you keep them, behind the fake electric outlet.

You could fix me a place like that to keep things in?"

"First thing next week, if I can just stay out of jail."

"Because the burglaries lately have been something awful. You put on that good lock for me, but even so."

"I'll fix you up with a hidey hole first chance I get, Mrs. Hesch."

"Not that I got the Hope Diamond upstairs, but why take chances? You're all right now, Mr. Rhodenbarr?"

"I think so," I said.

I changed clothes in a coffee shop lavatory, tucked my burglar's tools into various pockets, and left my dirty clothes in the wastebasket. The British would have called it a dustbin, and who had told me so recently? Turnquist, and Turnquist was dead now, with an icepick in his heart.

I bought a disposable razor in a drugstore, made quick use of it in another coffee shop restroom, and promptly disposed of it. The same drugstore sold me a pair of sunglasses rather like the ones Turnquist had worn when we wheeled him across town. I'd worn them myself on the way back to the store, and they were there now on a shelf in my back room, and it struck me as curious that I'd bought two pairs of drugstore sunglasses in as many days. In the ordinary course of things, years would go by before I bought a pair of sunglasses.

The day was overcast and I wasn't sure the

sunglasses helped; they might hide my eyes, but at the same time they drew a certain amount of attention. I wore them for the time being and rode the subway downtown to Fourteenth Street. Between Fifth and Seventh Avenues there are schlock stores of every description, selling junk at cut-rate prices, their wares spilling out onto the sidewalk. One had a table piled high with clear-lensed eyeglasses. People who wanted to save an optician's fee could try on pair after pair until they found something that seemed to help.

I tried on pair after pair until I found a heavy horn-rimmed pair that didn't seem to distort things at all. Nonprescription glasses always look like stage props because of the way the light glints off them, but these glasses would disguise my appearance reasonably well without looking like a disguise. I bought them, and a few doors down the street I tried on hats until I found a dark gray fedora that looked and felt right.

I bought a knish and a Coke from a Sabrett vendor, tried to tell myself I was eating breakfast, made a couple of phone calls, and was at the corner of Third Avenue and Twenty-third Street when a rather battered Chevy pulled up. The way the man steals, you'd think he could afford a flashier automobile.

"I looked right at you an' didn't recognize you," he said as I got into the front seat next to him. "You oughta put on a suit more often. It looks nice. Of course you ruin the whole effect wearin' runnin' shoes with it."

"Lots of people wear running shoes with a suit these days, Ray."

"Lotsa guys eat peas with a knife but that don't make it right. The hat an' the glasses, you look like a tout at Aqueduct. What I oughta do, Bern, I oughta take you in. You'll be outta trouble and I'll wind up with a citation."

"Wouldn't you rather wind up with a reward?"

"You call it a reward and I call it two in the bush." He sighed the sigh of the long-suffering. "This is crazy, what you're askin'."

"I know."

"But I played along with you in the past, and I gotta admit it paid off more'n it didn't." He looked at the hat, the glasses, the running shoes, and he shook his head. "I wish you looked a little more like a cop," he said.

"This way I look like a cop wearing a disguise."

"Well, it's some disguise," he said. "It'd fool anybody."

He left the car in a no-parking zone and we walked up a flight of stairs and down a corridor. Periodically Ray pulled out his shield and showed it to somebody who passed us on through. Then we took an elevator down to the basement.

When you're a civilian and you show up to identify a body, you wait on the first floor and they bring up the late lamented on an elevator. When you're a cop they save time and let you go down to the basement, where they pull out a drawer and give you a peek. The attendant, a whey-faced little man who hadn't seen the sun since he posed for Charles Addams, pulled a card from a file, led us across a large and silent room, and opened a drawer for us.

I took one look and said, "This isn't the right one."

"Gotta be," the attendant said.

"Then why does the toe tag say *Velez, Concepción*?"

The attendant examined it himself and scratched his head. "I don't get it," he said. "This is 228-B and right here on the card it says"—he looked at us accusingly—"it says 328-B."

"So?"

"So," he said.

He led the way and pulled out another drawer, and this time the toe tag said *Onderdonk, Gordon K.* Ray and I stood looking in companionable silence. Then he asked me if I'd seen enough, and I said I had, and he spoke to the attendant and told him to close the drawer.

On the way upstairs I said, "Can you find out if he was drugged?"

"Drugged?"

"Seconal or something. Wouldn't it show in an autopsy?"

"Only if somebody went looking for it. You come across a guy with his head beaten in, you examine him and determine that's what killed him, hell, you don't go an' check to see if he also had diabetes."

"Have them check for drugs."

"Why?"

"A hunch."

"A hunch. I'd feel better about your hunches if you didn't look like a racetrack tout. Seconal, huh?"

"Any kind of sedative."

"I'll have 'em check. Where do we go from here, Bernie?"

"Separate ways," I said.

I called Carolyn and let her carry on for a few minutes until her panic played itself out. "I'm going to need your help," I said. "You're going to have to create a diversion."

"That's my specialty," she said. "What do you want me to do?"

I told her and went over it a couple of times, and she said it sounded like something she could handle. "It would be better if you had help," I said. "Would Alison help you?"

"She might. How much would I have to tell her?"

"As little as possible. If you have to, tell her I'm going to be trying to steal a painting from the museum."

"I can tell her that?"

"If you have to. In the meantime—I wonder. Maybe you should close the Poodle Factory and go over to her house. Where does she live, anyway?"

"Brooklyn Heights. Why should I go there, Bern?"

"So you won't be where the cops can hassle you. Is Alison with you now?"

"No."

"Where is she, at home?"

"She's at her office. Why?"

"No reason. You don't happen to know her address in Brooklyn Heights, do you?"

"I don't remember it, but I know the building. It's on Pineapple Street."

"But you don't know the number."

"What's the difference? Oh, I bet you're looking for a place to hole up, aren't you?"

"Good thinking."

"Well, her place is nice. I was there last night."

"So that's where you were. I tried you early this morning and I couldn't reach you. Wait a minute. You were at Alison's last night?"

"What's the matter with that? What are you, the Mother Superior, Bern?"

"No, I'm just surprised, that's all. You'd never been there before, had you?"

"No."

"And it's nice?"

"It's very nice. What's so surprising about that? Tax planners make a decent living. Their clients tend to have money or else they wouldn't have to worry about taxes."

"It seems to me everybody has to worry about taxes. You saw the whole apartment? The, uh, bedroom and everything?"

"What the hell is that supposed to mean?

209

There's no bedroom, what she's got is a giant studio. It's about eight hundred square feet but it's all one room. Why?"

"No reason."

"Is this a roundabout way of asking me if we slept together? Because that's none of your business."

"I know."

"So?"

"Well, you're right about it being none of my business," I said, "but you're my best friend and I don't want to see you get hurt."

"I'm not in love with her, Bern."

"Good."

"And yes, we slept together. I figured she was used to men hassling her and conning her and trying to exploit her, so I picked my strategy accordingly."

"What did you do?"

"I told her I'd only put the tip in."

"And now you're at the Poodle Factory."

"Right."

"And she's at her office."

"Right."

"And I'm wasting my time worrying about you."

"Listen," she said, "I'm touched. I really am."

I cabbed down to the Narrowback Gallery, wearing the sunglasses so that the driver wouldn't see anything recognizable in his rear-view mirror. When I got out I switched to my other glasses so I'd be less conspicuous. I was still wearing the hat.

Jared opened the door, took in the glasses and the hat, then looked down at what I was carrying. "That's pretty neat," he said. "You can carry anything in there and people figure it's an animal. What have you got in there, burglar tools?"

"Nope."

"I bet it's swag, then."

"Huh?"

"Swag. Loot. Plunder. Can I see?"

"Sure," I said, and opened the clasps and lifted the hinged top.

"It's empty," he said.

"Disappointing, huh?"

"Very." We moved on into the loft, where Denise was touching up a canvas. I examined what she'd done in my absence and told her I was impressed.

"You ought to be," she said. "We worked all night, both of us. I don't think we got an hour's sleep between us. What have you been doing in the meantime?"

"Staying out of jail."

"Well, keep on doing it. Because when all of this is history I expect a substantial reward. I won't settle for a good dinner and a night on the town."

"You won't have to."

"You can throw in dinner and a night out as a bonus, but if there's a pot of gold at the end of this rainbow, I want a share."

"You'll get it," I assured her. "When will all this stuff be ready?"

"Couple hours."

"Two hours, say?"

"Should be."

"Good," I said. And I called Jared over and explained what I had in mind for him. A variety of expressions played over his face.

"I don't know," he said.

"You could organize it, couldn't you? Get some of your friends together."

"Lionel would go for it," Denise suggested. "And what about Pegeen?"

"Maybe," he said. "I don't know. What would I get?"

"What do you want? Your pick of every science fiction book that comes through my store for the next—how long? The next year?"

"I don't know," he said. He sounded about as enthusiastic as if I'd offered him a life-time supply of cauliflower.

"Make sure you get a good deal," his mother told him. "Because you'll have a lot to handle. I wouldn't be surprised if there's a TV news crew. If you're the leader you'll be the one they interview."

"Really?"

"Stands to reason," she said.

He thought about it for a moment. I started to say something but Denise silenced me with a hand. "If somebody made a couple of phone calls," Jared said, "then they'd know to have camera crews there."

"Good idea."

"I'll get Lionel," he said. "And Jason Stone and Shaheen and Sean Glick and Adam.

Pegeen's at her father's for the weekend, but I'll get— I know who I'll get."

"All right."

"And we'll need signs," he said. "Bernie? What time?"

"Four-thirty."

"We'll never make the six o'clock news."

"You'll make the eleven o'clock."

"You're right. And not that many people watch the six o'clock on Saturday anyway."

He tore off down the stairs. "That was terrific," I told Denise.

"It was wonderful. Look, if you can't manipulate your own kid, what kind of a parent are you?" She moved in front of one of the canvases, frowned at it. "What do you think?"

"I think it looks perfect."

"Well, it doesn't look perfect," she said, "but it doesn't look bad, does it?"

TWENTY

IT WAS LUNCH hour when I hit the downtown financial district. The narrow streets were full of people. Stock clerks and office girls, those vital cogs in the wheel of free enterprise, passed skinny cigarettes from hand to hand and smoked their little capitalist brains out. Older men in three-piece suits shook their heads at all of this and dove into bars for sanctuary and solace.

I made a phone call. When no one answered I joined the take-out line at a luncheonette and emerged with two sandwiches and a container of coffee in a brown paper bag. I carried it into the lobby of a ten-story office building on Maiden Lane. I was still wearing the hat and the horn-rimmed glasses and carrying the pet carryall that Jared had found so disappointingly empty. I stopped on my way to the elevator to sign *Donald Brown* on the log sheet, entering my destination (*Rm. #702*) and my time of arrival (*12:18*). I took the elevator to the seventh floor and then walked up a flight, having prevaricated about everything but the time. I found the office I was looking for. The lock on the door was rather less challenging than Rubik's Cube. I set down the pet carrier but held the lunch bag in one hand while I opened the door with the other.

Inside the office I sat down at one of those metal desks with a fake wood-grain top and unpacked my lunch. I opened up one sandwich, removed the slices of pastrami and turkey, tore them into small pieces, and arranged them in a pile on the desk top. I ate the other sandwich and drank the coffee, looked up something in the Manhattan phone book, and dialed a number. A woman answered. The voice was familiar but I wanted to be absolutely certain,

214

so I asked to speak to Nathaniel. The voice told me that I had the wrong number.

I made a couple of other calls and talked to some people, and then I dialed 0 and said, "This is Police Officer Donald Brown, my shield number's 23094, and I need you to get an unlisted number for me." I told her the name and read off the number I was calling from. She called back less than a minute later and I wrote down the number she gave me. I said, "Thanks. Oh, and what's the address on that?" and she told me the address. I didn't have to write it down.

I dialed the number. A woman answered. I said, "This is Bernie. You wouldn't believe how I've missed you."

"I don't know what you're talking about," she said.

"Ah, darling," I said. "I can't eat, I can't sleep—"

The phone clicked in my ear.

I sighed and dialed another number. I went through channels and then a familiar voice came on the line. "Okay, give," it said. "How'd you know?"

"They found Seconal?"

"Chloral hydrate, the ever-popular Mickey Finn. How'd you take one look at a dead man with his head beaten in and figure drugs? Even on *Quincy* they gotta run tests and stick things in microscopes."

"I'm working up a new series. *Bernie Rhodenbarr, Psychic Pathologist.*"

We said a few more reasonably pleasant

things to one another. I hung up and made a couple more calls, rummaged in some desk drawers and pawed through a filing cabinet. I left the contents of drawers and cabinet as I'd found them. Then I dropped the lunch bag and wrappings in the wastebasket, along with the bread from the pastrami-and-turkey sandwich and the empty coffee container. I opened the case I'd brought along, and a few minutes later I closed it and fastened its clasps.

"Off we go," I said.

On the way out I checked my watch and entered *12:51* under time of departure.

The sun was out so I switched to sunglasses and caught a cab at the corner of Broadway and John Street. I gave the driver a West Village address. He was a recent arrival from Iran with uncertain English and a very vague sense of the geography of Manhattan, so I guided him and we both got lost. But we wound up on a familiar street and I paid him off and sent him on his way.

I entered a building I'd never been in before, carding my way past the locked vestibule door. I walked through the building to another locked door which led to a rear courtyard. The lock wasn't a problem, and I left part of a toothpick jammed up against the springbolt so it would be even less of a problem on the way back.

The courtyard held some garbage cans and a neglected garden. I crossed it and clambered over a concrete-block fence leading to another courtyard, where I peered into a window, then opened it, and then closed it. I retraced my steps, case in hand, scaling the block fence, retrieving my broken toothpick as I reentered the building, finally emerging on the street and walking a few blocks and catching another cab.

Back at the Narrowback Gallery, Jared let me in and eyed the case I was carrying. "You've still got it," he said.

"Right you are."

"*Now* is it filled with swag?"

"See for yourself."

"Still empty."

"Uh-huh."

"What are you going to do with it?"

"Nothing," I said.

"Nothing?"

"Nothing. You keep it. I'll tell you, I'm sick of carrying the damn thing around." I walked over to where his mother was eyeing a canvas. "Looks good," I said.

"You bet it does. We're lucky Mondrian didn't have acrylics to play with. He could have painted five hundred pictures a year."

"You mean he didn't?"

"Not quite."

I extended a finger, touched paint. "Dry," I said.

"And as ready as they'll ever be." She sighed and picked up a menacing-looking implement with a curved blade. I think it's a linoleum knife. I'm not made of linoleum, but

I'd certainly hate to irritate somebody who had one of them in his hand. Or her hand, for that matter.

"This goes against the grain," Denise said. "You're sure about this?"

"Positive."

"About an inch? Like about so?"

"That looks good."

"Well, here goes," she said, and she began cutting the canvas off the stretcher.

I watched the process. It was unsettling. I'd watched her paint the thing, and I'd painted part of it myself, affixing masking tape to the primed canvas, filling in the lines, peeling off the tape when the quick-drying paint had set. So I knew Mondrian had been no closer to the thing than, say, Rembrandt. Even so, I got a funny feeling in the pit of my stomach as the knife slashed through it as if it were, well, linoleum.

I turned away and went over to where Jared lay stretched out on the floor, writing *UNFAIR!* on a large square of cardboard with an El Marko marking pen. Several completed signs, neatly tacked to strips of wooden lath, leaned up against a metal table. "Good work," I told him.

"They should show up well," he said. "The media's been alerted."

"Great."

"Performance art," Denise was saying. "First you paint a picture and then you destroy it. Now all we need is Christo to wrap it in aluminum foil. Shall I wrap it up or will you eat it here?"

"Neither," I said, and began removing my clothes.

I got to the Hewlett Gallery a few minutes after three, walking a little stiffly in my suit. I was wearing the hat and the clear-lensed horn-rimmed glasses, the latter of which had begun giving me a headache an hour or so earlier. I handed over my suggested contribution of $2.50 without a murmur and went through the turnstile and up a flight of stairs to my favorite gallery.

I'd managed to work up a certain amount of anxiety over the possibility of the Mondrian's having been moved, or removed altogether for loan to the exhibit that was being organized, but *Composition with Color* was right where it was supposed to be. The first thing I thought was that it didn't look anything like what we'd thrown together in Denise's loft, that the proportions and colors were completely wrong, that we'd produced something on a par with a child's crayon copy of the *Mona Lisa*. I looked again and decided that legitimacy, like beauty, is largely in the eye of the beholder. The one on the wall looked right because it was there on the wall, with a little brass plaque by its side to attest to its noble origins.

I just studied it for a while. Then I wandered a bit.

Back on the ground floor, I walked through a room full of eighteenth-century French canvases, Boucher and Fragonard, idealized bucolic scenes of fauns and nymphs, shepherds and Bo-Peeps. One canvas showed a pair of barefoot rustics picnicking in a sylvan glade, and studying that canvas under a uniformed guard's watchful gaze were Carolyn and Alison.

"You'll notice," I murmured to them, "that both of those little innocents have Morton's Foot."

"What's that mean?"

"It means their second toes are longer than their big toes," I said, "and they'll need special orthotic implants if they're planning to run marathons."

"They don't look like runners to me," Carolyn said. "They look horny as toads, as a matter of fact, and the only kind of marathon they're likely to be in is—"

"Jared and his friends are in position outside," I cut in. "Give them five minutes to get started. Okay?"

"Okay."

In a stall in the men's room I took off my jacket and shirt, then put them on again and walked somewhat less stiffly to the gallery where the Mondrian was hanging. No one paid me any attention because there was a lot of noise and commotion out in front of the building and people were drifting toward the entrance to see what was going on.

The sound of rhythmic chanting rose to my ears. *"Two, four, six, eight! We need art to appreciate!"*

I stepped closer to the Mondrian. Time crawled and the kids went on chanting and I glanced for the thousandth time at my watch and started wondering what they were waiting for when suddenly all hell broke loose.

There was a loud noise like a clap of thunder, or a truck backfiring, or a bomb going off, or, actually, rather like a cherry bomb left over from the Fourth of July. And then, from another direction there was a great deal of smoke and cries of *Fire! Fire! Run for your lives!*

Smoke positively billowed. People bolted. And what did I do? I grabbed the Mondrian off the wall and ran into the men's room.

And caromed off a balding fat man who was just emerging from a stall. "Fire!" I shouted at him. "Run! Run for your life!"

"My word," he said, and away he went.

A few minutes later, so did I. I left the men's room and hastened down a flight of stairs and out the main entrance. Fire trucks had drawn up and police were everywhere and Jared and his troops brandished their signs, dodging cops and throwing themselves in front of portable TV cameras. Throughout it all, the Hewlett's security staff kept a tight rein on things, making sure no one walked off with a masterpiece.

I perspired beneath my hat, blinked behind my glasses, and walked right past all of it.

I caught the six o'clock news in a dark and dingy tavern on Third Avenue, and there was young Jared Raphaelson, angrily asserting Youth's right of access to great public art collections, then quickly disclaiming all responsibility for the terrorist assault on the Hewlett and the mysterious disappearance of Piet Mondrian's masterpiece, *Composition with Color*.

"We don't think the kids are directly involved," a police spokesman told the camera. "It's a little early to tell yet, but it looks as though some quick-witted thief took the opportunity to cut the painting from its frame. We found the frame itself, all broken and with shreds of canvas adhering to it, in the second-floor washroom. Now it looks as though the kids must be responsible for the fire, although they deny it. What happened was somebody tossed an explosive device called a cherry bomb of the type used to celebrate Independence Day, and it happened to go off in a wastebasket in which some tourist had evidently discarded a few rolls of film, and what would have been a big bang turned into a full-scale trash fire. The fire itself didn't cause any real damage. It put out a lot of smoke and shook people up some, but it didn't amount to anything except to provide cover to the thief."

Ah, well, I thought. Accidents will happen. And I kept a close eye on the screen, looking for a sign of the quick-witted opportunistic thief. But I didn't see him. Not on that channel, at any rate.

A museum official expressed chagrin at the loss of the painting. He talked about its artistic importance and with some reluctance estimated its value at a quarter of a million dollars. The announcer mentioned the recent robbery-cum-murder at the Charlemagne, in which another Mondrian was taken, and wondered whether press coverage of that theft might have led the present thief to pick Mondrian rather than some other masterpiece.

The museum official thought that was highly possible. "He might have taken a van Gogh or a Turner, even a Rembrandt," he said. "We have paintings worth ten or more times what the Mondrian might bring. That's why this strikes me as an impulsive, spur-of-the-moment act. He knew the Mondrian was valuable, he'd heard what the Onderdonk Mondrian was valued at, and when the opportunity presented itself he acted swiftly and decisively."

They cut for a commercial. In Carney's Bar and Grill, an impulsive, spur-of-the-moment guy in horn-rims and a fedora picked up his glass of beer and swiftly and decisively drank it down.

TWENTY-ONE

"WHAT YOU GOT in there?" the child demanded.
"Fission poles?"

Fission poles?

"Andrew, don't bother the man," said its
mother, and flashed me a brave smile. "He's
at that age," she said. "He's learned how to
talk, and he hasn't learned how to shut up."

"Man goin' fishin'," said Andrew.

Oh. *Fishin'* poles.

Andrew and Andrew's mother and I, along
with perhaps four other people, were sheltering
ourselves behind a transparent barrier designed
to protect bus passengers from the elements,
even as its construction had enriched several public officials a few scandals ago. I had
one arm around a cylindrical cardboard tube
which stood five feet tall and ran about four
inches in diameter. I forebore advising Andrew
that it did not contain fishing poles. It con-
tained—what? Bait?

Something like that.

Two buses came. They're like cops in bad
neighborhoods; they travel in pairs. Andrew
and his mother got on one of them, along
with our other companions in the shelter. I

224

remained behind, but there was nothing remarkable in this. A variety of buses travel south on Fifth Avenue, bound for a variety of destinations, so I merely seemed to be waiting for another bus.

I don't know what I was waiting for. Divine intervention, perhaps.

Across the street and a little to my left loomed the massive bulk of the Charlemagne, as fiercely impregnable as ever. I'd breached its portals three times, once at Onderdonk's invitation, twice bearing flowers, and in fairy tales the third time is the charm. But now I had to get in there a fourth time, and everyone who worked for the building knew me by now, and you couldn't get into the goddamned building even if nobody knew you from Adam.

There's always a way, I told myself. What little story had I made up for Andrea? Something about a helicopter to the roof? Well, that was fanciful, surely, but was it absolutely out of the question? There were private helicopter services. They'd take you up for a couple of hours of soaring over the city for a fee. For a considerably higher fee, one such bold entrepreneur would no doubt drop you off on a particular roof, especially if he weren't required to stand by and lift you off again.

There were problems, however. I didn't have the money to hire a limousine, let alone a helicopter, and I hadn't the faintest idea where to find an avaricious helicopter pilot, and I rather suspected they didn't do business at night anyway.

Hell.

The buildings that adjoined the Charlemagne were no help, either. All were significantly lower than their neighbor, by a minimum of four floors. It was theoretically possible to outfit oneself with Alpine climbing gear and proceed from the roof of one of those buildings, sinking pitons into the mortar between the Charlemagne's bricks, clambering hand over hand to the top of the Charlemagne's roof, and getting in that way. It was also theoretically possible to master the lost art of levitation and float halfway to heaven, and this struck me as a little easier than pretending the Charlemagne was the Matterhorn.

Besides, I had no reason to think I could crack the security of one of the neighboring buildings, either. They'd have security-conscious doormen and concierges of their own.

Flowers wouldn't work, not for Leona Tremaine, not for anyone else. Other things get delivered to buildings—liquor, ice, anchovy pizza—but I'd used the deliveryman number and I was sure I couldn't get by with it again. I thought of various disguises. I could be a blind man. I already had the dark glasses; all I'd need would be a white cane. Or I could be a priest or a doctor. Priests and doctors can get in anywhere. A stethoscope or a Roman collar will get you in places you can't even crack with a clipboard.

But not here. They'd phone upstairs, whoever I said I was, whoever I was presumably visiting.

A blue-and-white patrol car cruised slowly down the avenue. I turned a little to the side, putting my face in shadow. The car coasted through a red light and kept going.

I couldn't just stand there, could I? And I'd be more comfortable inside than out, sitting than standing. And, since there didn't seem to be any way I could work that night, there was no real reason to abstain from strong drink.

I crossed the street and went around the corner to Big Charlie's.

It was a much more opulent establishment than the name would have led you to expect. Deep carpet, recessed lighting, banquette tables in dark corners, a piano bar with well-padded and backed barstools. Waitresses in starched black-and-white uniforms and a bartender in a tuxedo. I was glad I was wearing a suit and I felt deeply ashamed of the sneakers and the fedora.

I doffed the latter and tucked the former beneath one of the banquettes. I ordered a single-malt Scotch with a splash of soda and a twist of lemon peel, and it came in a man-sized cut glass tumbler that looked and felt like Waterford. And perhaps it was. Stores sold a whole pint of whiskey for what this place charged for a drink, so Big Charlie ought to be able to spend a fair amount on glassware.

Not that I begrudged him a cent. I sipped and thought and sipped and thought, and a pianist with a touch like a masseuse and a voice like melted butter worked her way through Cole Porter, and I sent my mind around the corner to the Charlemagne and looked for a way in.

There's always a way in. Somewhere in the course of my second drink I thought of phoning in a bomb scare. Let 'em evacuate the building. Then I could just mingle with the crowd and wander back in. If I was wearing pajamas and a robe at the time of mingling, who'd think for a moment that I didn't belong there?

Now where was I going to get pajamas and a robe?

I found some interesting answers to that question, the most fanciful of which involved a daring burglary of Brooks Brothers, and I was just finishing my third drink when a woman came over to my table and said, "Well, which are you? Lost or stolen or strayed?"

"A. A. Milne," I remembered.

"Right!"

"Somebody's mother. James James Morrison Morrison—"

"Weatherby George Dupree," she finished for me. "Now how did I know that you would know? Perhaps it's because you look so soulful. And so lonely. It's said that loneliness cries out to loneliness. I don't know who said that, but I don't believe it was Milne."

"Probably not," and there was a silence, and I should have invited her to join me. I didn't.

No matter. She sat down beside me anyhow, a supremely confident woman. She was wearing a low-cut black dress and a string of pearls and she smelled of costly perfume and expensive whiskey, but then that last was the only kind Big Charlie sold.

"I'm Eve," she said. "Eve DeGrasse. And you are—"

I very nearly said Adam. "Donald Brown," I said.

"What's your sign, Donald?"

"Gemini. What's yours?"

"I have several," she said. She took my hand, turned it, traced the lines in my palm with a scarlet-tipped index finger. "'Yield' is one of them. 'Slippery When Wet' is another."

"Oh."

The waitress, unbidden, brought us both fresh drinks. I wondered how many it would take before this woman looked good to me. It wasn't that she was unattractive, exactly, but that she was a sufficient number of years older than I to be out of bounds. She was well built and well coiffed, and I suppose her face had been lifted and her tummy tucked, but she was old enough to be—well, not my mother, maybe, but perhaps my mother's younger sister. Not that my own mother actually *had* a younger sister, but—

"Do you live near here, Donald?"

"No."

"I didn't think so. You're from out of town, aren't you?"

"How did you know?"

"Sometimes one can sense these things." Her hand dropped to my thigh, gave a little squeeze. "You're all alone in the big city."

"That's right."

"Staying in some soulless hotel. Oh, a comfortable room, I'm sure of that, but lifeless and anonymous. And so lonely."

"So lonely," I echoed, and drank some of my Scotch. One or two more drinks, I thought, and it wouldn't much matter where I was or who I was with. If this woman had a bed, any sort of a bed, I could pass out in it until daybreak. I might not win any points for gallantry that way, but I'd at least be safe, and God knew I was in no condition to wander the streets of New York with half the NYPD looking for me.

"You don't have to stay in that hotel room," she purred.

"You live near here?"

"Indeed I do. I live at Big Charlie's."

"At Big Charlie's?"

"That's right."

"Here?" I said stupidly. "You live here in this saloon?"

"Not here, silly." She gave my leg another companionable squeeze. "I live at the real Big Charlie's. The big Big Charlie's. Oh, but you're from out of town, Donald. You don't know what I'm talking about, do you?"

"I'm afraid not."

"Charlemagne equals Charles the Great equals Big Charlie. That's how they named this place, because the owner's a couple of fags named Les and Maurie, and they could have called it More or Less, only they didn't. But you're from out of town so you don't know

230

there's an apartment building around the corner called the Charlemagne."

"The Charlemagne," I said.

"Right."

"An apartment house."

"Right."

"Around the corner. And you live there."

"Right you are, Donald Brown."

"Well," I said, setting my glass down unfinished. "Well, what are we waiting for?"

I recognized the doorman and the concierge and Eduardo, the kindly elevator operator. None of them recognized me. They didn't even take a second glance at me, perhaps because they didn't take a first glance at me, either. I could have been wearing a gorilla suit and they'd have been just as careful to avert their eyes. Ms. DeGrasse was, after all, a tenant, and I don't suppose I was the first young man she'd ever pulled out of Big Charlie's and brought on home, and the staff was no doubt well tipped to keep their eyes in their sockets where they belonged.

We rode the elevator clear to the fifteenth floor. I'd gulped air furiously as we walked from the bar to the building, but it takes more than a few lungfuls of New York's polluted atmosphere to counteract the effects of three and a half large whiskeys, and I felt a little woozy in the elevator. The light in there, unkind as it was to my companion, didn't help either. We walked to her door, and she had more trouble opening it with the key than I generally have without one, but I let her do the honors and she got it open.

Inside, she said, "Oh, Donald!" and swept me in her arms. She was almost my height, and there was quite a bit of her. She wasn't fat or blowsy or anything. There was just a lot of her, that's all.

I said, "You know what? I think we could both use a drink."

We used three. She drank hers and I dumped mine in an areca palm that looked as though it was going to die soon anyway.

Perhaps it was just intimidated by its surroundings. The apartment looked like a spread in *Architectural Digest,* with not much furniture and a lot of carpeted platforms and such. The only picture on the wall was a mural and it was all loops and swirls without a single right angle to be found in it. Mondrian would have hated it, and you'd have had to take the whole wall to steal it.

"Ah, Donald—"

I'd hoped she might dim out with all that whiskey, but it didn't seem to be affecting her at all. And I wasn't getting a whole lot more sober with the passage of time. I thought, *Oh, what the hell,* and I said, "Eve!" and we went into a clinch.

There was no bed in her bedroom, just another carpeted platform with a mattress on it. It did the job. And so, much to my surprise, did I.

It was odd. At first I just concentrated on not thinking about my mother's younger sister, which should have been a cinch in view of the fact that she'd never had one. Then I tried to build a fantasy incorporating our age differences, imagining myself as an eager youth of seventeen and Eve as a ripe, knowing woman of thirty-six. That didn't work too well because I imagined myself right back into a state of coltish clumsiness and embarrassment.

Finally I just gave up and forgot who either of us was, and that worked. I don't know if the whiskey helped or hindered, but one way or another I stopped thinking about what was going on and just let it happen, and damned if it didn't.

Go figure.

TWENTY-TWO

AFTERWARD, THE HARDEST part was staying awake long enough for her to fall asleep. I kept catching myself just as my mind was starting to drift, following some abstruse line of thought along one of those tangled paths that lead to Dreamland. Each time I yanked myself conscious, and each time it felt like a narrow escape.

When her breathing changed I stayed put for a minute or two, then slipped off the mattress and dropped from the sleeping platform to the floor. The carpet was deep and I padded silently across it, reclaimed my clothes, and put them on in the living room. I was almost to the door when I remembered my five-foot tube and went back for it. "I'll bet you're an architect," Eve had said, "and I'll bet you've got blueprints in there." I'd asked her how she'd guessed. "Those glasses," she said, "and that hat. And those sensible sensible shoes. Hell, Donald, you *look* like an architect."

I squinted through the judas, unlocked the door, cracked it and checked the hallway. Outside, I thought of using my picks to lock the door behind me and decided against it. Eve's lifestyle was such that she probably slept behind unlocked doors as a regular thing. For that matter, it wasn't inconceivable that departing guests often went through her purse on the way out, or that she considered such actions not theft but a quid pro quo. A fair exchange, they say, is no robbery.

I used the fire stairs to reach the eleventh floor. For a moment I couldn't remember which door led to the Appling apartment, and then I spied the telltale burglar alarm keyhole, the one to which no alarm system was attached. I had my ring of picks in hand and one slim piece of steel probing the innards of the Poulard lock when something stopped me.

And a good thing, too, because there were people inside that apartment. I must have heard something that made me put my ear to the door, and when I did that I heard what must have been the laugh track of a television situation comedy. I put my eye where my pick had been, and, surprise! Light showed through the keyhole.

The Applings were home. Even now, as I stood lemminglike on the brink of their apartment, Mr. A. might be paging idly through his plundered stamp collection. At any moment he might let out a great bellow, doubtless startling his wife and driving Mary Tyler Moore reruns clear out of her head. Whereupon he might reflexively dash to the door, yank it open, and find—what?

An empty hallway, because by the time I'd reached this stage in my thoughts I was already through the fire door and on the stairs again. I climbed three flights, which put me back on Fifteen where I'd left Eve DeGrasse, hesitated for a moment in front of the fire door, then climbed another flight of stairs and opened the door with my picks.

There was an argument going on behind a closed door, but it was another door than Onderdonk's. His had a piece of paper taped to it proclaiming that the premises within were ordered sealed by the New York Police Department. The seal was symbolic rather than literal; Onderdonk's lock provided the only tangible barrier to Onderdonk's apartment. It was a Segal drop-bolt, a good enough lock, but I'd already picked it open once and it held no secrets for me.

But I didn't open it at once. First I listened, ear to door, and then I put my eye to the keyhole and stooped lower to see if any light issued forth from beneath the door. Nothing, no light, no sound, nothing.

I let myself in.

Other than mine, there were no bodies, living or otherwise, in the Onderdonk apartment. I checked everywhere, even the kitchen cupboards, to establish as much. Then I let the tapwater run until it was hot enough to make instant coffee. The resultant beverage wouldn't have thrilled El Exigente, nor would it get me sober, but at least I'd be a wide-awake drunk instead of a falling-down one.

I drank it, shuddering, and then I got on the phone.

"Bernie, thank God. I was worried sick. I was afraid something happened. You're not calling from jail, are you?"

"No."

"Where are you?"

"Not in jail. I'm all right. You and Alison got out okay?"

"Sure, no problem. What a scene! I think we coulda grabbed the *Mona Lisa* on the way out, except it's in the Louvre. But I've gotta tell you the big news—the cat's back!"

"Archie?"

"Archie. We went and had a drink, and then we had another drink, and then we came home and Ubi rushed over to be petted, which isn't like him, and I was petting him and I looked up and there was Ubi on the other side of the room, so I looked down at the cat I was petting and damned if it wasn't old Archie Goodwin himself. Whoever broke in to take him broke in again to return him, and left the locks just the way I left them, same as the other time."

"Amazing. The Nazi kept her word."

"Kept her word?"

"I gave her the painting and she returned the cat."

"How'd you find her?"

"She found me. It's too complicated to explain right now. The important thing is he's back. How are his whiskers?"

"Gone on one side. His balance is sort of weirded out, like he's very unsure of himself when it comes to leaps and pounces. I can't make up my mind whether to trim 'em on the other side or just wait for 'em to grow back in."

"Well, take your time deciding. You don't have to do anything tonight."

"Right. Alison was amazed to see him. I think she was as amazed as I was."

"I can believe it."

"Bernie, what do you think you're doin', collectin' Moondrains? Because I understand they got a couple at the Guggenheim and I wondered if that's where you're gonna strike next."

"Always a pleasure to talk to you, Ray."

"The pleasure's mine. Are you crazy or

somethin'? And don't tell me it wasn't you because I saw you on television. That's about the dumbest lookin' hat I ever saw in my life. I think I recognized the hat more'n I recognized you."

"Makes a good disguise, doesn't it?"

"But you weren't carryin' anythin', Bern. What did you do with the Moondrain?"

"Folded it very small and tucked it inside my hat."

"What I figured. Where are you?"

"In the belly of the beast. Listen, I've got a job for you, Ray."

"I already got a job, remember? I'm a police officer."

"That's not a job, it's a license to steal. What's that line in *Casablanca*."

" 'Play it again, Sam.' "

"Actually he never says it exactly that way. It's 'Play it, Sam,' or 'Play the song, Sam,' or some variation like that, but he never says, 'Play it again, Sam.' "

"That's really fascinatin', Bern."

"But that wasn't the line I meant. 'Round up the usual suspects.' *That's* the line I meant. And that's what I want you to do."

"I don't get it."

"You will when I explain."

"Bernie, it's been a madhouse here. Things are just starting to settle down. How about that kid of mine, huh?"

"He's a trouper."

"His fathead of a father called up. How

238

could I allow such a thing, and he's thinking seriously of instituting a custody suit, unless of course I agree to a reduction in alimony and child support payments, blah blah blah. Jared says he'll live at the Hewlett before he lives with his old man. You think he's got a case?"

"I don't even think he thinks he's got a case, but I'm not a lawyer. How's Jared holding up under questioning?"

"His answers turn into political speeches. Don't worry. He hasn't mentioned you."

"What about his buddies?"

"You mean the other members of his cadre? They couldn't mention you if they wanted to. Jared's the only one who knows this afternoon's incident was anything other than a political action of the Young Panthers."

"Is that what they're calling themselves?"

"I think it's a media invention, but I also think it might stick. Jared's friend Shaheen Vladewicz suggested Panther Cubs, but his other friend Adam informed them that panthers don't have cubs, they have kittens, and Panther Kittens was rejected as insufficiently militant. Anyway, our secret's safe. I think Jared's beginning to believe he thought up the whole thing and you cashed in on it at the last minute."

"A quick-witted opportunist of a thief."

"Well, if the shoe fits. Incidentally, you left that case here. That cat carrier or whatever it is."

"Well, give it to someone with a cat. I won't be needing it. Carolyn got her cat back."

"No shit?"

"Only in the litter box."

"She really got the cat back?"

"So she tells me."

"And the Hewlett? Are they going to get their Mondrian back?"

"What Mondrian?"

"Bernie—"

"Don't worry, Denise. Everything's going to work out fine."

"Everything's going to work out fine."

"Gee, I hope you're right, Bernie. I don't know, though. I went out this morning figuring to do fifteen miles, and after ten miles I started to get this funny feeling on the inside of my right knee. Not a pain exactly but a feeling, a sensitivity, you know what I mean? Now what they say is you run *to* pain but not *through* pain, but what do you do about sensitivity? I figured as soon as it became pain I'd stop, but it just stayed sensitive and got a little *more* sensitive, and I did my fifteen miles and then did three miles on top of it, eighteen miles altogether, and I came home and took a shower and lay down, and now my knee's throbbing like a bastard."

"Can you walk on it?"

"I could probably run another eighteen miles on it. It's throbbing with sensitivity, not with pain. It's crazy."

"Well, it'll work out. Wally, there was an incident at a museum this afternoon—"

"Jesus Christ, I almost forgot. I don't even

240

know if I should be talking to you. Were you involved in that?"

"Of course not. But the leader of the kids' protest is the son of a friend of mine, and—"

"Oh, here we go."

"Wally, how'd you like to make a name for yourself representing the Young Panthers? I don't think anybody's going to bring charges against them, but there'll be reporters wanting interviews and there might even be a book or a movie in the thing, and Jared's going to need someone to look out for his interests. And his father's talking about a custody suit, so Jared's mother's going to need somebody looking out for her interests, and—"

"You got an interest in the mother?"

"We're just good friends. As a matter of fact, Wally, I think you might like the mother. Denise, her name is."

"Oh?"

"Got a pencil? Denise Raphaelson, 741-5374."

"And the kid's name is Jason?"

"Jared."

"Same difference. When should I call her?"

"In the morning."

"It's already morning, for Christ's sake. Do you know what time it is?"

"I don't call my lawyer to find out the time. I call my lawyer when there's something I want him to do for me."

"Is there something you want me to do for you?"

"Thought you'd never ask."

"Miss Petrosian? 'I sing of sorrow / I sing of weeping / I have no sorrow. / I only borrow—'"

"Who is this?"

"'I only borrow / From some tomorrow / Where it lies sleeping / Enough of sorrow / To sing of weeping.' It's Mary Carolyn Davies, Miss Petrosian. Your old favorite."

"I don't understand."

"What's to understand? It's a nice straight-forward poem, it seems to me. The poet's saying that she draws against a store of future miseries in order to write about a depth of emotion she hasn't yet experienced."

"Mr. Rhodenbarr?"

"The same. I have your painting, Miss Petrosian, and you have only to come and collect it."

"You have—"

"The Mondrian. It's yours for a thousand dollars. I know that's no money, a ridiculous sum, but I have to get out of town fast and I need every cent I can raise."

"I can't get to the bank until Monday and—"

"Bring what cash you can and a check for the balance. Get a pencil and write down the address and time. And don't be early or late, Miss Petrosian, or you can forget all about the painting."

"All right. Mr. Rhodenbarr? How did you find me?"

"You wrote down your name and number for me. Don't you remember?"

"But the number—"

"Turned out to be that of a Korean fruit store on Amsterdam Avenue. I was disappointed, Miss Petrosian, but not surprised."

"But—"

"But you're listed in the book, Miss Petrosian. The Manhattan phone book, the white pages. I can't be the first person to have called the fact to your attention."

"No, but—but I didn't give you my name."

"You said Elspeth Peters."

"Yes, but—"

"Well, with all due respect, Miss Petrosian, I wasn't fooled. The way you hesitated when you gave your name, and then the wrong number, well, it was a dead giveaway."

"But how on earth did you know my real name?"

"A bit of deduction. When amateurs select an alias, they almost always keep the same initials. And they very frequently choose as a last name some form of modified first name. Jackson, Richards, Johnson. Or Peters. I guessed that your real name began with a P, and that it very likely had the same root as Peters. Something about your features suggested further that you might be of Armenian descent. I pulled out the phone book, turned to the P-e-t's, and looked for an Armenian-sounding name with the initial E."

"But that's extraordinary."

"The extraordinary is only the ordinary, Miss Petrosian, with the addition of a little extra. That's not mine, by the way. A grade-school teacher of mine used to say that. Isabel Josephson was her name, and as far as I know it was not an alias."

"I'm only a quarter Armenian. And I'm said to take after my mother's side of the family."

"I'd say there's a distinct Armenian cast to your features. But perhaps I just had one of those psychic flashes people are subject to now and then. It hardly matters. You want that painting, don't you?"

"Of course I want it."

"Then write this down...."

"Mr. Danforth? My name is Rhodenbarr, Bernard Grimes Rhodenbarr. I apologize for the lateness of the call, but I think you'll excuse the intrusion when you've heard what I have to say. I have a couple of things to tell you, sir, and a question or two to ask you, and an invitation to extend. . . ."

Phone calls, phone calls, phone calls. By the time I was done my ears ached from taking their turns pressed against the receiver. If Gordon Onderdonk knew what I was doing with his message units, he'd turn over in his drawer.

When I was finished I made another cup of coffee and found a Milky Way bar in the freezer and a package of Ry-Krisp in a cupboard. It made a curious meal.

I ate it anyway, went back to the living room and killed a little time. It was late but not late enough. Finally it *was* late enough, and

244

I let myself out of Onderdonk's apartment, leaving the door unlocked. I walked all the way down to the fifth floor, smiling as I passed the sleeping Ms. DeGrasse on Fifteen, sighing as I passed the Applings on Eleven, shaking my head as I passed Leona Tremaine on Nine. I had a bad moment getting through the fire door lock on Five. I don't know why. It was the same simple proposition as all the other fire door locks, but perhaps my fingers were stiff from dialing the telephone. I unlocked the door, and I crossed the hallway to another door, and after a careful look and listen I opened the door.

I was as quiet as a mouse. There were people asleep within and I didn't want to wake them. And I had a great many things to do.

And, finally, they were all done. I slipped ever so quietly out of that fifth-floor apartment, locked the locks after me, and went up the stairs again to Sixteen.

You know, I think that was the worst part of it. Climbing stairs is hard work, and climbing ten flights of stairs (there was still, thank God, no thirteenth floor) was very hard work. The New York Road Runners Club has a race each year up eighty-six flights of stairs to the top of the Empire State Building, and some lean-limbed showoff wins it every time, and he's welcome to it. Ten flights of stairs was bad enough.

I let myself into Onderdonk's apartment once again, closed the door, locked it, and took a little time to catch my breath.

TWENTY-THREE

"OH, GREAT," I said. "Everybody's here."

And indeed everybody was. Ray Kirschmann had shown up first, flanked by a trio of fresh-faced young lads in blue. He talked to someone downstairs, and a couple of building employees came up to the Onderdonk apartment and set up folding chairs to supplement the Louis Quinze pieces that were already on hand. Then the three uniformed cops stuck around, one upstairs, the others waiting in the lobby to escort people up as they arrived, while Ray went out to pick up some of the other folks on the list.

While all this was going on, I stayed in the back bedroom with a book and a thermos of coffee. I was reading Defoe's *The History of Colonel Jack,* and the man lived seventy years without ever writing a dull sentence, but I had a little trouble keeping my mind on his narrative. Still, I bided my time. A man likes to make an entrance.

Which I ultimately did, saying, *Oh, great. Everybody's here.* It was comforting the way every head turned at my words and every eye followed me as I skirted the semicircular grouping of chairs and dropped into the leather wing chair facing them. I scanned the little sea of faces—well, call it a lake of faces. They looked back at me, or at least most of them did. A few turned their eyes to gaze over the fireplace, and after a moment so did I.

And why not? There was Mondrian's *Composition with Color*, placed precisely where it had been on my first visit to the Charlemagne, and positively glowing with its vivid primary colors and sturdy horizontal and vertical lines.

"Makes a powerful statement, doesn't it?" I leaned back, crossed my legs, made myself comfortable. "And of course it's why we're all here. A common interest in Mondrian's painting is what binds us all together."

I looked at them again, not as a group but as individuals. Ray Kirschmann was there, of course, sitting in the most comfortable chair and keeping one eye on me and another on the rest of the crowd. That sort of thing can leave a man walleyed, but he was doing a good job of it.

Not far from him, in a pair of folding chairs, were my partner in crime and her partner in lust. Carolyn was wearing her green blazer and a pair of gray flannel slacks, while Alison wore chinos and a striped Brooks Brothers shirt with the collar buttoned down and the sleeves rolled up. They made an attractive couple.

Not far from them, seated side by side on a six-foot sofa, were Mr. and Mrs. J. McLendon Barlow. He was a slender, dapper, almost elegant man with neatly combed iron gray hair and a military bearing; with his posture he could have been just as comfortable on one of the folding chairs and left the sofa for somebody who needed it. His wife, who could have passed for his daughter, was medium height and slender, a large-eyed creature who wore her long dark hair pinned up in what I think they call a chignon. I know they call something a chignon, and I think that's what it is. Was. Whatever.

Behind and to the right of the Barlows was a chunkily built man with the sort of face Mondrian might have painted if he'd ever gotten into portrait work. It was all right angles. He was jowly and droopy-eyed, and he had a moustache that was graying and tightly curled hair as black as India ink, and his name was Mordecai Danforth. The man sitting next to him looked about eighteen at first glance, but if you looked closer you could double the figure. He was very pale, wore rimless spectacles and a dark suit with an inch-wide black silk tie, and his name was Lloyd Lewes.

A few feet to Lewes's right, Elspeth Petrosian sat with her hands folded in her lap, her lips set in a thin line, her head cocked, her expression one of patient fury. She was neatly dressed in Faded Glory jeans and a matching blouse, and was wearing Earth Shoes, with the heel lower than the toe. Those were all the rage a few years back, with ads suggesting that if everybody wore them we could wipe out famine and pestilence, but you don't see them much any-more. You still see a lot of famine and pesti-lence, though.

To the right and to the rear of Elspeth, in another of the folding chairs, was a young man whose dark suit looked as though he only wore it on Sundays. Which was fine, because that's what day it was. He had moist brown eyes and a slightly cleft chin, and his name was Eduardo Melendez.

On Eduardo's left was another young man, also in a suit, but with a pair of New Balance 730s on his feet instead of the plain black oxfords Eduardo favored. I could see the top of one shoe and the sole of the other, because he was sitting on an upholstered chair with his right leg up on one of the folding chairs. He was Wally Hemphill, of course, and I guessed that his knee had finally made it from sensi-tivity to pain.

Denise Raphaelson was sitting a couple of yards from Wally. There were paint smears on her dungarees and her plaid shirt was starting to go in the elbow, but she looked all right to me. She evidently looked not bad to Wally, too, and the feeling seemed to be mutual, judging from the glances they kept stealing at one another. Well, why not?

Four more men filled out the audience. One had a round face and a high forehead and looked like a small-town banker in a television commercial, eager to lend you money so that you could fix up your home and make it an asset to the community you lived in. His name was

Barnett Reeves. The second was bearded and booted and scruffy, and he looked like someone who'd approach the banker and ask for a college loan. And be turned down. His name was Richard Jacobi. The third was a bloodless man in a suit as gray as his own complexion. He had, as far as I could tell, no lips, no eyebrows, and no eyelashes, and he looked like the real-life banker, the one who approved mortgages in the hope of eventual foreclosure. His name was Orville Widener. The fourth man was a cop, and he wore a cop's uniform, with a holstered pistol and a baton and a memo book and handcuffs and all that great butch gear cops get to carry. His name was Francis Rockland, and I happened to know that he was missing a toe, but offhand I couldn't tell you which one.

I looked at them and they looked at me, and Ray Kirschmann, who I sometimes think exists just to take the edge off moments of high drama, said, "Quit stallin', Bernie."

So I quit stalling.

I said, "I'd say I suppose you're wondering why I summoned you all here, but you're not. You know why I summoned you here. And, now that you're here, I'll—"

"Get to the point," Ray suggested.

"I'll get to the point," I agreed. "The point is that a man named Piet Mondrian painted a picture, and four decades later a couple of men got killed. A man named Gordon Onderdonk was murdered in this very apartment, and

250

another man named Edwin Turnquist was murdered in a bookstore in the Village. *My* bookstore in the Village, as it happens, and along with Mondrian I seem to be the common denominator in this story. I left this apartment minutes before Onderdonk was killed, and I walked into my own store minutes after Turnquist was killed, and the police suspected me of having committed both murders."

"Perhaps they had good reason," Elspeth Petrosian suggested.

"They had every reason in the world," I said, "but I had an edge. I knew I hadn't killed anybody. Beyond that, I knew I'd been framed. I'd been led to this apartment on the pretext that its owner wanted his library appraised. I spent a couple of hours examining his library, came up with a figure and accepted a fee for my work. I walked out with my fingerprints all over the place, and why not? I hadn't done anything wrong. I didn't care if I left my fingerprints on the coffee table or my name with the concierge. But it was crystal clear to me that I'd been invited here for the sole purpose of establishing my presence here, so that I could take the rap for burglary and homicide, the theft of a painting and the brutal slaying of its rightful owner."

I took a breath. "I could see that much," I went on, "but it didn't make sense. Because I'd been framed not by the murderer but by the victim, and where's the sense in that? Why would Onderdonk wander into my shop with a cock-and-bull story, lure me up here, get me to leave my prints on every flat surface that would take them, and then duck into the other room to get his head beaten in?"

"Maybe the murderer capitalized on an opportunity," Denise said. "The way some quick-witted thief seized a chance to steal a painting yesterday afternoon."

"I thought of that," I said, "but I still couldn't figure Onderdonk's angle. He'd had me up here to frame me for something, and what could it be if it wasn't his murder? The theft of the painting?

"Well, that seemed possible. Suppose he decided to fake a burglary in order to stick it to his insurance company. Why not add verisimilitude by having the fingerprints of a reformed burglar where investigators could readily find them? It didn't really make sense, because I could justify my presence, so framing me would only amount to an unnecessary complication, but lots of people do dumb things, especially amateurs dabbling at crime. So he could have done that, and then his accomplice in the deal could have double-crossed him, murdered him, and left the reformed burglar to carry the can for both the burglary and the murder."

"Reformed burglar," Ray grunted. "I could let that go once, but that's twice you said it. Reformed!"

I ignored him. "But I still couldn't make sense out of it," I said. "Why would the murderer tie Onderdonk up and stuff him in a closet? Why not just kill him and leave him where he fell? And why cut the Mondrian canvas from its stretcher? Thieves do that in museums when they have to make every second count, but this killer figured to have all the time in the world. He could remove the staples and take the painting from the stretcher without damaging it. For that matter, he could wrap it in brown paper and carry it out with the stretcher intact."

"You said he was an amateur," Mordecai Danforth said, "and that amateurs do illogical things."

"I said dumb things, but that's close enough. Still, how many dumb things can the same person do? I kept getting stuck on the same contradiction. Gordon Onderdonk went to a lot of trouble to frame me, and what he got for his troubles was killed. Well, I was missing something, but you know what they say—it's hard to see the picture when you're standing inside the frame. I was inside the frame and I couldn't see the picture, but I began to get little flashes of it, and then it became obvious. The man who framed me and the murder victim were two different people."

Carolyn said, "Slow down, Bern. The guy who got you over here and the guy who got his head bashed in—"

"Were not the same guy."

"Don't tell me that's not Onderdonk down there in the morgue," Ray Kirschmann said. "We got a positive ID from three different people. That's him, Gordon Kyle Onderdonk, that's the guy."

"Right. But somebody else came into my shop, introduced himself as Onderdonk, invited me up here, opened the door for me, paid me two hundred dollars for looking at some books, and then beat the real Onderdonk's brains out as soon as I walked out the door."

"Onderdonk himself was here all the time?" This from Barnett Reeves, the jolly banker.

"Right," I said. "In the closet, all trussed up like a chicken and with enough chloral hydrate in his bloodstream to keep him quiet as an oiled hinge. That's why he was out of sight, so I wouldn't step on him if I took a wrong turn on my way to the bathroom. The murderer didn't want to risk killing Onderdonk until he had the frame perfectly fitted around me. That way, too, he could make sure the time of death coincided nicely with my departure from the building. Medical examiners can't time things to the minute—it's never that precise—but he couldn't go wrong timing things as perfectly as possible."

"You're just supposing all this, aren't you?" Lloyd Lewes piped up. His voice was reedy and tentative, a good match for his pale face and his narrow tie. "You're just creating a theory to embrace some inconsistencies. Or do you have additional facts?"

"I have two fairly substantial facts," I said, "but they don't prove much to anyone but me. Fact number one is that I've been to the morgue, and the body in Drawer 328-B"—now how on earth did I remember that number?— "isn't the man who wandered into my bookstore one otherwise fine day. Fact number two is that the man who called himself Gordon Onderdonk is here right now, in this room."

I'll tell you, when everybody in a room draws a breath at the same moment, you get one hell of a hush.

Orville Widener broke the silence. "You have no proof for that," he said. "We have just your word."

"That's right, that's what I just told you. For my part, I suppose I should have guessed early on that the man I met wasn't Gordon Onderdonk. There were clues almost from the beginning. The man who let me into this apartment—I can't call him Onderdonk anymore so let's call him the murderer—he just opened the door an inch or two before he let me in. He kept the chainlock on until the elevator operator had been told it was okay. He called me by name, no doubt for the operator's benefit, but he fumbled with the lock until the elevator had left the floor."

"Is true," Eduardo Melendez said. "Mr. Onderdonk, he alla time comes into the hall to meet a guest. This time I doan see him. I think notheen of it at the time, but is true."

"I thought nothing of it myself," I said, "except that I wondered why a man security-conscious enough to keep a door on a chainlock when an announced and invited guest was coming up wouldn't have more than one Segal dropbolt lock on his door. I should have done some wondering later on, when

255

the murderer left me to wait for the elevator alone, dashing back into his apartment to answer a phone that I never heard ringing." I hadn't questioned that action, of course, because it had been a response to a fervent prayer, allowing me to dash down the stairs instead of getting shunted back onto the elevator. But I didn't have to tell them that.

"There was another thing I kept overlooking," I went on quickly. "Ray, you kept referring to Onderdonk as a big hulk of a man, and you made it sound as though clouting him over the head was on a par with felling an ox with a single blow. But the man who called himself Onderdonk wasn't anybody's idea of a hulk. If anything he was on the slight side. That should have registered, but I guess I wasn't paying attention. Remember, the first time I ever even heard the name Onderdonk was when the killer came into my bookshop and introduced himself to me. I assumed he was telling the truth, and I took a long time to start questioning that assumption."

Richard Jacobi scratched his bearded chin. "Don't keep us in suspense," he demanded. "If one of us killed Onderdonk, why don't you tell us who it is?"

"Because there's a more interesting question to answer first."

"What's that?"

"Why did the killer cut *Composition with Color* out of its frame."

"Ah, the painting," said Mordecai Danforth. "I like the idea of discussing the painting, especially in view of the fact that it seems to have been miraculously restored. There it reposes on the wall, a perfect example of Mondrian's mature style. You'd never know some foul fiend cut it from its stretcher."

"You wouldn't, would you?"

"Tell us," said Danforth. "Why did the killer cut the painting?"

"So everyone would know it had been stolen."

"I don't follow you."

Neither, from the looks on their faces, did most of his fellows. "The killer didn't just want to steal the painting," I explained. "He wanted the world to know it was gone. If he just took it, well, who would realize it was missing? Onderdonk lived alone. I suppose he must have had a will, and his worldly goods must go to somebody, but—"

"His heir's a second cousin in Calgary, Alberta," Orville Widener cut in. "And now we're coming to my part of the field. My company underwrote Onderdonk's insurance and we're on the hook for $350,000. I gather the painting was stolen so that we'd have to pay, but what we ask in a situation like that is *Qui bono?* I'm sure you know what that means."

"Cooey Bono," Carolyn said. "That was Sonny's first wife, before he was married to Cher. Right?"

Widener ignored her, which I thought showed character. "To whose good?" he said, translating the Latin himself. "In other words, who benefits? The policy's payable to Onder-donk, and in the event of his death it becomes part of his estate, and his estate goes to some-body in western Canada." His eyes narrowed, then turned toward Richard Jacobi. "Or is that Canadian relative actually among those present?"

"He's in Canada," Wally Hemphill said, "because I spoke to him at an hour that was equally uncivilized in either time zone. He's empowered me to look out for his interests in this matter."

"Indeed," said Widener.

It was my turn. "The cousin never left Calgary," I said. "The painting was stolen not for the insurance, considerable though it may be. The painting was stolen for the same reason its owner was murdered. Both acts were committed to conceal a crime."

"And what crime was that?"

"Well, it's a long story," I said, "and I think we should make ourselves comfortable and have a cup of coffee. Now how many of you want cream and sugar? And how many just cream? And how many just sugar? And the rest of you want it all the way black? Fine."

I don't think they really wanted coffee, but what I wanted was a breathing spell. When Carolyn and Alison had served the nasty stuff all around the room, I sipped some of mine, made a face, and started in.

"Once upon a time," I said, "a man named Haig Petrosian had a painting in his dining room. It would later be called *Composition with Color,* but Petrosian probably didn't call it anything but 'My friend Piet's picture,' or words to that effect. Whatever he called it, it disappeared around the time of his death. Maybe a family member spirited it away. Maybe a servant made off with it, perhaps acting on the belief that the old man wanted her to have it."

"Perhaps Haig Petrosian's son William stole it," Elspeth Petrosian said, with a sharp glance to her right and another sharp glance at me.

"Perhaps," I said agreeably. "Whoever took it, it wound up in the possession of a man who found a wonderful way to make money. He bought paintings and gave them away."

Carolyn said, "That's a way to make money?"

"It is the way this fellow did it. He would buy a painting by an important artist, a genuine painting, and he would lend it to a show or two in order to establish its provenance and his history as its owner. Then a talented if eccentric artist would be engaged to produce a copy of the painting. The owner would let himself be persuaded to donate the painting to a museum, but in the course of things it would be the copy that wound up getting donated. Farther on down the line, he'd donate the painting to another institution in another part of the country, and once again it would be a copy that changed hands. Occasionally he might vary the pitch by selling the painting to a collector, picking someone who wouldn't be likely to show it. In the course of a decade, he could sell or donate the same painting five or six times, and if he stuck to abstract artists like Mondrian and had his wacky painter vary the precise design a bit from one canvas to the next, he could get away with it forever.

"And the richer you are to start with, the more profitable it is. Donate a painting appraised at a quarter of a million dollars and you can save yourself over a hundred thousand dollars in taxes. Do that a couple of times and you've more than paid for the painting, and you've still got the original painting yourself. There's only one problem."

"What's that?" Alison asked.

"Getting caught. Our killer found out that Mr. Danforth was putting together a retrospective exhibit of Piet Mondrian's works, which in and of itself was no cause for alarm. After all, his fake paintings had survived such exposure in the past. But it seemed that Mr. Danforth was aware that there were far more Mondrians in circulation than Mondrian ever painted. What is it they used to say about Rembrandt? He painted two hundred portraits, of which three hundred are in Europe and five hundred in America."

"Mondrian's not been counterfeited on that grand a scale," Danforth said, "but in the past few years there have been some disconcerting rumors. I decided to combine the retrospective with an exhaustive move to authenticate or denounce every Mondrian I could root out."

"And toward that end you enlisted the aid of Mr. Lewes."

"That's right," Danforth said, and Lewes nodded.

"Our killer learned as much," I said, "and he was scared. He knew Onderdonk intended to put his painting in the show, and he wasn't able to talk him out of it. He couldn't let on that the painting was a fake, not after he'd sold it to Onderdonk himself, and perhaps Onderdonk began to suspect him. That's supposition. What was clear was that Onderdonk had to die and the painting had to disappear, and it had to be a matter of record that the damned thing disappeared. All he had to do was frame me for the theft and murder and he was home free. It didn't matter if the charges stuck. If I went up for the job, fine. If not, that was fine, too. The cops wouldn't look for someone with a private motive for Onderdonk's death. They'd just decide I was guilty even if they couldn't make the charges stick, and they'd let the case go by the boards."

"And we'd pay the cousin in Calgary $350,000 for a fake painting," Orville Widener said.

"Which wouldn't affect the killer one way or the other. His interest was self-preservation, and that's a pretty good *Qui bono* six days out of seven."

Ray said, "Who did it?"

"Huh?"

"Who sold the fake paintings and killed Onderdonk? Who did it?"

"Well, there's really only one person it could be," I said, and turned toward the little sofa. "It's you, isn't it, Mr. Barlow?"

We had another one of those hushes. Then J. McLendon Barlow, who'd been sitting up very straight all along, seemed to sit up even straighter.

"Of course that's nonsense," he said.

"Somehow I thought you might deny it."

"Palpable nonsense. You and I have never met before today, Mr. Rhodenbarr. I never sold a painting to Gordon Onderdonk. He was a good friend and I deeply regret his tragic death, but I never sold him a painting. I defy you to prove that I did."

"Ah," I said.

"Nor did I ever visit your shop, or represent myself to you or to anyone else as Gordon Onderdonk. I can understand your confusion, since it is a matter of record that I did in fact donate a painting of Mondrian's to the Hewlett Gallery. I'd hardly be inclined to deny it; there's a plaque on the gallery wall attesting to the fact."

"Unfortunately," I murmured, "the painting seems to have disappeared from the Hewlett."

"It's clear that you arranged its disappearance in preparing this farce. I certainly had nothing to do with it, and can provide evidence of my whereabouts at all times yesterday. Furthermore, it's to my disadvantage that the painting has disappeared, since it was unquestionably genuine."

I shook my head. "I'm afraid not," I said.

"One moment." Barnett Reeves, my jolly banker, looked as though I'd offered a dead rat as collateral. "I'm the curator of the Hewlett, and I'm quite certain our painting is genuine."

I nodded at the fireplace. "That's your painting," I said. "How positive are you?"

"That's not the Hewlett Mondrian."

"Yes it is."

"Don't be a fool. Ours was cut from its stretcher by some damned vandal. That painting's intact. It may well be a fake, but it certainly never hung on our walls."

"But it did," I said. "The man who stole it yesterday, and I'd as soon let him remain anonymous, was by no means a vandal. He wouldn't dream of slashing your painting, genuine or false. He went to the Hewlett carrying a bit of broken stretcher with the outside inch of canvas of a homemade fake Mondrian. He dismantled the stretcher on our specimen, opening the staples and hiding the canvas under his clothing. He hung the pieces of stretcher down his trouser legs. And he left evidence behind to make you assume he'd cut the painting from its mounting."

"And that painting over the fireplace—"

"Is your painting, Mr. Reeves. With the stretcher reassembled and the canvas reattached to it. Mr. Lewes, would you care to examine it?"

Lewes was on his way before I'd finished my sentence. He whipped out a magnifying glass, took a look, and drew back his head almost at once.

"Why, this is painted with acrylics!" he said, as if he'd found a mouse turd on his plate. "Mondrian never used acrylics. Mondrian used oils."

"Of course he did," said Reeves. "I told you that wasn't ours."

"Mr. Reeves? Examine the painting."

He walked over, looked at it. "Acrylics," he agreed. "And not ours. What did I tell you? Now—"

"Take it off the wall and look at it, Mr. Reeves."

He did so, and it was painful to watch the play of expression across the man's face. He looked like a banker who'd foreclosed on what turned out to be swampland. "My God," he said.

"Exactly."

"Our stretcher," he said. "Our stamp incused in the wood. That painting was hanging in the Hewlett where thousands of eyes looked at it every day and nobody ever noticed it was a fucking acrylic copy." He turned, glared furiously at Barlow. "You damned cad," he said. "You filthy murdering bounder. You fucking counterfeit."

"It's a trick," Barlow protested. "This burglar pulls fake rabbits out of fake hats and you fools are impressed. What's the matter with you, Reeves? Can't you see you're being flimflammed?"

"I was flimflammed by you," Reeves said, glowering. "You son of a bitch."

Reeves took a step toward Barlow, and Ray Kirschmann was suddenly on his feet, with a hand on the curator's forearm. "Easy," he said.

"When this is all over," Barlow said, "I'll bring charges against you, Rhodenbarr. I think any court would call this criminal libel."

"That's really a frightening prospect," I said, "to someone who's currently wanted for two murders. But I'll keep it in mind. You won't be pressing any charges, though, Mr. Barlow. You'll be upstate pressing license plates."

"You've got no evidence of anything."

"You had easy access to this apartment. You and your wife live on the fifth floor. You didn't have the problem of getting in and out of a high-security building."

"A lot of people live here. That doesn't make any of us murderers."

"It doesn't," I agreed, "but it makes it easy to search your apartment." I nodded at Ray, and he in turn nodded at Officer Rockland, who went to the door and opened it. In marched a pair of uniformed officers carrying yet another Mondrian. It looked for all the world just like the one Lloyd Lewes had just damned as an acrylic fake.

"The genuine article," I said. "It almost glows when it's in the same room with a copy, doesn't it? You might have carved up the painting you palmed off on Onderdonk, but you took good care of this one, didn't you? It's the real thing, the painting Piet Mondrian gave to his friend Haig Petrosian."

"And we had a warrant," Ray said, "in case you were wondering. Where'd you boys find this?"

"In a closet," one said, "in the apartment you said on the fifth floor."

Lloyd Lewes was already holding his glass to the canvas. "Well, this is more like it," he said. "It's not acrylic. It's oil paint. And it certainly looks to be genuine. Quite a different thing from that, that specimen over there."

"Now there's been some mistake," Barlow said. "Listen to me. There's been some mistake."

"We also found this," the cop said. "In the medicine cabinet. No label, but I tasted it, and if it ain't chloral hydrate it's a better fake than the painting."

"Now that's impossible," Barlow said. "That's impossible." And I thought he was going to explain why it was impossible, that he'd flushed all the extra chloral hydrate down the john, but he caught himself in time. Listen, you can't have everything.

"You have the right to remain silent," Ray Kirschmann told him, but I'm not going to go through all that again. Miranda-Escobedo's a good or a bad thing, depending on whether or not you're a cop, but who wants to put it down word for word all the time?

TWENTY-FOUR

AFTER A FEW urgent words to his wife, something about which lawyer to call and where to reach him, two of the uniformed police officers led J. McLendon Barlow off in handcuffs. Francis Rockland stayed behind, and so did Ray Kirschmann.

There was a respectful silence, broken at length by Carolyn Kaiser. "Barlow must have killed Turnquist," she said, "because Turnquist was the artist he used, and Turnquist could expose him. Right?"

I shook my head. "Turnquist was the artist, all right, and Barlow might have killed him sooner or later if he felt he had to. But he certainly wouldn't have come down to my bookstore to do it. Remember, I'd met Barlow as Onderdonk, and all I had to do was catch sight of him walking around hale and hearty and the whole scheme would collapse. It's my guess that Barlow never even left his apartment after the murder. He wanted to stay out of sight until I was behind bars where I couldn't get a look at him. Isn't that right, Mrs. Barlow?"

All eyes turned to the woman who now sat alone on the couch. She cocked her head, started to say something, then simply nodded.

"Edwin P. Turnquist was an artist," I said, "and a fervent admirer of Mondrian's. He never considered himself a forger. God knows how Barlow got hold of him. Turnquist talked to total strangers in museums and galleries, and perhaps that's how they first made one another's acquaintance. At any rate, Barlow latched on to Turnquist because he could use him. He got the man to copy paintings, and Turnquist derived great satisfaction from looking at his own work in respected museums. He was a frequent visitor to the Hewlett, Mr. Reeves. All the attendants knew him."

"Ah," said Reeves.

"He only paid a dime."

"And quite proper," Reeves said. "We don't care what you pay, but you must pay something. That's our policy."

"That and exclusion of the young. But no matter. When Barlow began to panic about your forthcoming retrospective exhibition, Mr. Danforth, he paid a call on Edwin Turnquist. I suppose he urged him to keep out of sight. The substance of their conversation is immaterial. More to the point, Turnquist realized that all along Barlow had not merely been playing a joke on the art world. He'd been making great sums of money at it, and Turnquist's idealism was outraged. He'd been satisfied with the subsistence wages he made as Barlow's forger. Art for art's sake was fine with him, but that Barlow should profit from the game was not."

I looked at the bearded man with the lank brown hair. "That's where you came into it, isn't it, Mr. Jacobi?"

"I never really came into it."

"You were Turnquist's friend."

"Well, I knew him."

"You had rooms on the same floor in the same Chelsea rooming house."

"Yeah. I knew him to talk to."

"You teamed up with Turnquist. One or the other of you followed Barlow to my shop. After that, and just hours before I came up here to appraise the books, you came to my shop alone and tried to sell me a book you'd stolen from the public library. You wanted me to buy it knowing it was a stolen book, and you figured I would because you thought I was an outlet for faked or stolen art. You thought that would give you some kind of an opening, some kind of hold on me, but when I wouldn't bite you didn't know what to do next."

"You make it sound pretty sinister," Jacobi said. "Eddie and I didn't know how you fit into the whole thing and I wanted to dope it out. I thought if I sold you the butterfly book you'd let something slip. But you didn't."

"And you didn't pursue it."

"I figured you were too honest. Any book dealer who'd turn down a deal like that wouldn't be into receiving stolen works of art."

"But Friday morning you evidently changed your mind. You and Edwin Turnquist came to my shop together. By then I'd been arrested for Onderdonk's murder and released on bail, and you figured I was tied in somehow. Turnquist, meanwhile, wanted to let me know what Barlow was up to. He probably guessed I'd been framed and wanted to help me clear myself."

I took a sip of coffee. "I opened the store and then went two doors down the street to visit a friend of mine. Maybe you two got there after I'd left. Maybe you were the bums I saw lurking in a doorway, and maybe you purposely dawdled across the street until you saw me leave. In either event, the two of you let yourselves in. I just left the door on the spring lock, and that wouldn't present any great problem for a man who can spirit large illustrated books out of libraries."

"Hell, I'm not a real book thief," Jacobi protested. "That was just to get your interest."

I let that pass for the time being. "Once inside," I said, "you turned the bolt so no one else would walk in and interrupt you. You led your good friend Turnquist to the back of the store where nobody could see you, and you stuck an icepick in his heart and left him sitting on the toilet."

"Why would I do that?"

"Because there was money to be made and he was screwing it up. He had a batch of forged canvases he'd painted in his spare time and he was planning to destroy them. You figured they were worth money, and you were probably right. For another, he had the goods on Barlow. Once I was safely behind bars, you could put the screws on Barlow and bleed him forever. If Turnquist talked, to me or to anybody else, he was taking away your meal ticket. You made up your mind to kill him, and you knew that if you killed him in my store I'd very likely get tagged with his murder, and that would get me out of the picture. Which would make it that much easier for you to turn up the heat under Barlow."

"So I killed him right there in your store."

"That's right."

"And then walked out?"

"Not right away, because you were still there when I came back. The door was bolted when I came back and I'd left it on the spring lock, and if it was bolted that meant you were still inside. I guess you must have hidden in the stacks or in the back room, and after I opened up you slipped out. That had me confused for a while, because I had a visitor shortly after I opened up"—I glanced significantly at Elspeth Petrosian—"and I never even noticed her come in. At first I suspected she'd been the one hiding in the back room and that she had murdered Turnquist, but I couldn't make sense out of that. You probably left just as she was walking in, or else you slipped out during my conversation with her. It was a lengthy and intense conversation, and I'm sure you could have departed without either of us having noticed."

He got to his feet, and Ray Kirschmann stood up immediately. Francis Rockland was already standing; he'd moved to within arm's reach of Jacobi.

"You can't prove any of this," Jacobi said.

"Your room was searched," Ray told him pleasantly. "You got enough city-owned books in there to start a branch library."

"So? That's petty theft."

"It's about eight hundred counts of petty theft. Tack all those short sentences together, you got yourself a pretty good-sized paragraph."

"Kleptomania," Jacobi said. "I have a compulsion to steal library books. It's harmless, and I eventually return them. It hardly qualifies me as a murderer."

"There were some pictures in there too," Ray said. "Fakes, I suppose, but you couldn't prove it by me. Mr. Lewes here's the expert, but all I can tell is they're paintin's without frames, and what do you bet they turn out to be the work of your buddy Turnquist?"

"He gave them to me. They were a gift of friendship, and I'd like to see you prove otherwise."

"We got a guy goin' door-to-door at your roomin' house, and what do you bet we turn up somebody who saw you carryin' those canvases from his room to yours? And that woulda been after he was killed an' before the body was discovered, and let's hear you explain that one away. Plus we got a note in his room, Turnquist's room, with Bernie's name and address, same as the note we found on the body. You want to bet they turn out to be your handwritin' and not his?"

"What does that prove? So I wrote down a name and address for him."

"You also phoned in a tip. You said if we wanted to know who killed Turnquist we should ask Bernie Rhodenbarr."

"Maybe somebody called you. It wasn't me."

"Suppose I told you that all incomin' calls are recorded? And suppose I told you that voice-print identification is as good as fingerprints?"

Jacobi was silent.

"We found somethin' else in your room," Ray said. "Show him, Francis."

Rockland reached into a pocket and produced an icepick. Richard Jacobi stared at it—hell, so did everybody else in the room—and I thought he was going to fall over in a faint. "You planted that," he said.

"Suppose I told you there were blood traces on it? And suppose I told you the blood type's the same as Turnquist's?"

"I must have left it in the bookshop," Jacobi blurted. "But that's impossible. I threw it in a Dempsey dumpster. Unless I'm wrong and I dropped it in the store, but no, no, I remember I had it in my hand on the way out."

"So you could stab me if I challenged you," I put in.

"You never even knew I was there. And you didn't follow me. Nobody followed me. Nobody even knew I left, and I went around the corner with the icepick hidden under my jacket and I went up Broadway and dumped it in the first dumpster I came to, and you couldn't possibly have gotten it out of there."

He drew himself triumphantly to his full height. "So it's a bluff," he told Ray. "If there's any blood on that thing it's not Eddie's. Somebody planted that icepick and it wasn't the murder weapon in the first place."

"I guess it was just another icepick that happened to be in your room," Ray said. "But now that you've told us where to look for the other one, I don't think we'll have a whole lot of trouble finding it. Should be easier than a needle in a haystack, anyway. What else do you want to tell us?"

"I don't have to tell you anything," Jacobi said.

"Now you're absolutely right about that," Ray said. "As a matter of fact, you have the right to remain silent, and you have the right to—"

Di dah di dah di dah.

After Rockland had led him away, Ray Kirschmann said, "Now we come to the best part." He went into the kitchen and returned with my five-foot cylindrical tube, uncapped it and drew out a rolled canvas. He unrolled it, and damned if it didn't look familiar.

Barnett Reeves asked what it was.

"A paintin'," Ray told him. "Another of the Moondrains, except it's a fake. Turnquist painted it for Barlow and Barlow sold it to Onderdonk and stole it back after he killed him. It's a perfect match for the broken frame and bits of canvas we found with Onderdonk's body in the bedroom closet."

"I can't believe it," Mrs. Barlow said. "Do you mean to say my husband carried that thing off and didn't have the brains to destroy it?"

"He probably didn't have the opportunity, ma'am. What was he gonna do, drop it down the incinerator? Suppose it was recovered? He put it where he thought it would be safe and intended to destroy it at leisure. But acting on my own initiative I discovered it through the use of established police investigative techniques."

Oh, God.

"Anyway," he went on, presenting it to Orville Widener, "here it is."

Widener looked as though his dog had just brought home carrion. "What's this?" he said. "Why are you giving it to me?"

"I just told you what it is," Ray said, "and I'm givin' it to you on account of the reward."

"What reward?"

"The thirty-five grand reward your company's gonna shell out for the paintin' they insured. I'm handin' you the paintin' in front of witnesses and I'm claimin' the reward."

"You must be out of your mind," Widener snapped. "You think we're going to pay that kind of money for a worthless fraud?"

"It's a fraud, okay, but it's a long ways from worthless. You can pay me the thirty-five grand and say thank you while you do it, because otherwise you'd be ponyin' up ten times as much to the cousin in Calgary."

"That's nonsense," Widener said. "We

don't have to pay anything to anybody. The painting's a fake."

"Doesn't matter," Wally Hemphill said, one hand on his wounded knee. "Onderdonk paid the premiums and you people took them. The fact that it was a fake and was overinsured doesn't alter your responsibility. The insured acted in good faith—he certainly believed it to be authentic and he had paid a price for it commensurate with the coverage he took out on it. You have to restore the insured painting to my client in Calgary or else reimburse him for a loss in the amount of $350,000."

"I'll see what our own legal people have to say about that."

"They'll say just what I just got through telling you," Wally said, "and I don't know what you're in a huff about. You're getting off cheap. If it weren't for Detective Kirschmann here, you'd pay the full insured value."

"Then Detective Kirschmann's costing your client money, isn't he, counselor?"

"I don't think so," Wally said, "because we need the fake in order to substantiate our suit against Barlow. Barlow's got money, and he got some of it from my client's deceased uncle, and I intend to bring suit to recover the price paid for the spurious Mondrian. And I'm also representing Detective Kirschmann, so don't think you can weasel out of paying him his reward."

"We're a reputable company. I resent your use of the word 'weasel.'"

"Oh, please," Wally said. "You people invented the word."

Barnett Reeves cleared his throat. "I have a question," he said. "What about the real painting?"

"Huh?" somebody said. Probably several people, actually.

"The real painting," Reeves said, pointing to the canvas that Lloyd Lewes had authenticated several revelations ago. "If there's no objection, I should like to take that back to the Hewlett Gallery, where it belongs."

"Now wait a minute," Widener said. "If my people are coming up with $35,000—"

"That's for that thing," Reeves said. "I want my painting."

"And you'll get yours," I said, gesturing toward the acrylic hanging over the fireplace. "That's the painting that was on display in your gallery, Mr. Reeves, and that's the painting you'll take back with you."

"We never should have had it in the first place. Mr. Barlow donated a genuine Mondrian—"

"Nope," I said. "He donated a fake, and he didn't even cheat you by doing it. Because it never cost you people a penny. He defrauded the Internal Revenue Service, and they'll probably have words with him on the subject, but he didn't defraud you beyond making a horse's ass out of you, and what's the big deal about that? A bunch of school kids made a horse's ass out of you just yesterday afternoon. You've got no claim on the painting."

"Then who does?"

"I do," Mrs. Barlow said. "The police officers took it from my apartment, but that doesn't mean my husband and I relinquish title to it."

"You don't have title," Reeves said. "You gave title to the museum."

"Not true," Wally said. "My client in Calgary should get the painting. It should have passed to Onderdonk, and so it now passes in fact to Onderdonk's heirs."

"That's all nonsense," Elspeth Petrosian cried. "That thief Barlow never had clear title to it in the first place. The painting belongs to me. It was promised to me by my grandfather, Haig Petrosian, and someone stole it before his wishes could be carried out. I don't care what Barlow paid for it or who he did or didn't sell it to. He never dealt with a rightful owner in the first place. That's my painting."

"I'd love to include it in the retrospective," Mordecai Danforth said, "while all of this is being sorted out, but I suppose that's out of the question."

Ray Kirschmann went over and put a hand on the painting. "Right now this paintin's evidence," he said, "and I'm impoundin' it. The rest of you got your claims and notions and you can fight it out, but the paintin' goes downtown while you drag each other through the courts, and once the lawyers get started it could go on for a good long while." To Reeves he said, "If I was you, I'd take that other one downtown and hang it back where it was.

By the time the papers write this up, half the city's gonna want to look at it, fake or no. You can waste time worryin' about lookin' like a horse's ass, but that'd just make you more of a horse's ass, because whatever you look like they're gonna be lined up around the block to look at this thing, and what's so bad about that?"

TWENTY-FIVE

"THIS IS A nice place," Carolyn said, "and they make a hell of a drink, even if they do charge twice as much as they should for it. Big Charlie's, huh? I like it."

"I thought you would."

"I like the girl playing piano, too. I wonder if she's gay."

"Oh, God."

"What's wrong with wondering?" She took a sip, set down her glass. "You left some things out," she said. "Explaining everything and making all the bits and pieces fit together, you left a few things out."

"Well, it was confusing enough as it was. I didn't want to make it impossible for people to follow."

"Uh-huh. You're a considerate guy. You left out the bit about the cat."

"Oh, come on," I said. "Two men had been murdered and a couple of paintings had been stolen. I couldn't waste people's time talking about a kidnapped cat. Anyway, he'd been ransomed and returned, so what was the point?"

"Uh-huh. Alison was Haig Petrosian's other granddaughter, wasn't she? The other one at the dining room table on Riverside Drive. She's Elspeth's cousin, and her father was Elspeth's Uncle Billy."

"Well, the resemblance was striking. Remember how you stared at Elspeth in my shop? The funny thing is at first I thought Andrea was the missing cousin, because she and Elspeth both have this habit of cocking their heads to the side, but that was just coincidence. The minute I saw Alison I knew she was the cousin and not Andrea."

"Andrea Barlow."

"Right."

"You left her out, too, didn't you? You didn't mention running into her in Onderdonk's apartment, let alone rolling around on the rug with her."

"Well, certain things ought to stay private," I said. "One thing she told me was true enough. She had been having an affair with Onderdonk, and as it happens her husband knew about it, which probably added to the zest with which he killed the man. Then he must have gloated over the man's death, and Andrea had visions of a police search of the premises uncovering some pictures Onderdonk had taken of the two of them with a time-release Polaroid. She went back for them, found them or didn't find them, who the hell knows, and then I walked in on her. No wonder she was terrified. She must have already found Onderdonk's body in the closet, so she knew it wasn't him, but who could it be? Either the police, in which case she had some fancy explaining to do, or her murderous husband coming to kill her and leave her there with her dead lover. Either way she was in deep trouble."

"And she was so relieved it was you that she was overcome with passion."

"Either that or she figured it made sense to screw her way to safety," I said, "but I'm inclined to give her the benefit of the doubt. But why mention all of that to the police?"

"Especially since you'd like to verb her again."

"Well—"

"And why not? She's got a nifty pair of nouns. I think I need another one of these, and don't you just love the little getups the waitresses wear? Let's order another round, and then you can tell me what really happened with the paintings."

"Oh, the paintings."

"Yeah, the paintings. This one's from here and that one's from there and this one's cut out of the frame and that one isn't and who can keep it all straight? I know some of what you said was true and I know some of it wasn't, and I want the whole story. But first I want another of these."

Who could deny her anything? She got what she wanted, first the drink and then the explanation.

"The painting Ray gave back to Orville Widener, the insurance guy, was one that Denise and I painted," I said. "Naturally Barlow destroyed the canvas he took from the Onderdonk apartment. All he had to do was slash it to ribbons and put it down the incinerator, and I'm sure he did just that. The canvas I gave to Ray, which he in turn gave to Widener, was the portion I cut out of the frame that I left at the Hewlett. And it doesn't matter if it doesn't match the piece of frame that was left in the closet with Onderdonk's corpse, because that frame will get conveniently lost. Ray'll see to that."

"What about the painting Reeves took back with him? Was that the one you took from the Hewlett? Did they have an acrylic fake on display all along?"

"Of course not. Turnquist was an artist and he wasn't in a hurry. He didn't use acrylics. He used oil paints, same as Mondrian, and the painting in the Hewlett was one of his."

"But what Reeves took back with him—"

"Was a second fake that Denise and I did, tacked to the stretcher from the Hewlett. Remember, it was the incused mark on the stretcher that convinced him. I'd already unstapled the canvas and taken the frame apart to get the painting out of the museum.

When I put it back together, I just tacked the acrylic fake to the Hewlett frame."

"And Reeves thinks that's what he had all along."

"So it would appear, and what's the difference? A fake is a fake is a fake is a fake."

"I didn't know Denise painted more than one fake."

"Actually she painted three of them. One got cut up, with the frame and some fragments left at the Hewlett and the rest of it returned to Orville Widener. The other went back to the Hewlett with Reeves."

"And the third?"

"Is hanging on a wall in the Narrowback Gallery, and it's a little different from the others in that the signature monogram is DR instead of PM. She's pretty proud of it, although I had a hand in it myself, and so did Jared."

"She painted three fakes and Turnquist painted two. You said Barlow destroyed one of the Turnquist fakes. What happened to the other one? The one you lifted out of the Hewlett."

"Ah," I said. "It's been impounded."

"Jesus, Bern. That was the *real* real one that was impounded, the one Mondrian himself painted, remember? Everybody's claiming it and there'll be court cases for years and—oh."

I guess I must have smiled.

"Bern, you didn't."

"Well, why not? You heard what Lloyd Lewes said. He looked at the canvas the two cops brought in and said it was an oil painting and it looked right. Why shouldn't it look right? After all, it sat in the Hewlett for years and nobody suspected a thing. Now it can sit in a locked closet at Number One Police Plaza for a few more years and nobody'll suspect a thing there, either. I took it along with me when I let myself into the Barlow apartment last night, stapled it to a stretcher and left it where the cops would find it."

"And the real Mondrian?"

"It was in the Barlow apartment when I got there, of course. I took it off its stretcher and stapled Turnquist's fake in its place. I had to have a stretcher for the Turnquist canvas, remember."

"Because you used the stretcher it was on in the Hewlett for one of Denise's fakes."

"Right."

"You know what the trouble is, Bern? There's too many Mondrians. It sounds like a Nero Wolfe novel, doesn't it? *Too Many Cooks, Too Many Clients, Too Many Detectives, Too Many Women.* And *Too Many Mondrians.*"

"Right."

"Denise painted three acrylic fakes, Turnquist painted two oil fakes, and Mondrian painted one. Except his was a real one, and are you gonna keep me in suspense forever, Bern? What happens to the real one?"

"It's going to go to the rightful owner."

"Elspeth Petrosian? Or Alison? She's got as much real claim on it as her cousin."

"Speaking of Alison—"

"Yeah," she said heavily. "Speaking of Alison.

When you figured they were cousins, that was how you knew Elspeth Peters was Armenian. And you looked through the phone book and—"

"Not quite. I looked through papers in Alison's office and found out her maiden name. That's a little simpler than reading the phone book."

"Is that where you got the cat?" She put a hand on mine. "I couldn't help figuring it out, Bernie. She took my cat, didn't she? And that's why she used the Nazi voice when she talked with me, because I would have recognized her real voice. She talked normally with you because she'd never met you. And she was nervous when we got to my place and you were there, because she thought you might recognize her voice from over the phone. Did you?"

"Not really. I was too busy recognizing the resemblance between her and her cousin Elspeth."

"She wasn't really that bad," Carolyn said thoughtfully. "She didn't hurt Archie, except for cutting his whiskers, and that's a far cry from mutilating him. And the closer she and I got, the more reassuring the Nazi became over the phone, until there was a point where I pretty much stopped worrying about the cat. You know something? When we got back to the apartment and the cat was there, I think she was as relieved as I was."

"I wouldn't be surprised."

She sipped her drink. "Bern? How'd she get past my locks?"

"She didn't."

"Huh?"

"Your cats liked her, remember? Especially Archie. She went through another building into the courtyard and coaxed him through the bars of the window. A person couldn't get in, but a cat could get out. That's one reason there were no traces of her visit inside the apartment. She never went inside the apartment except when she was with you. She didn't have to. The cat walked right out into her arms."

"When did you dope that out?"

"When I saw Ubi measuring the distance between the bars with his whiskers. They fit, which meant his head would fit, which meant his whole body would fit, and I knew that's how it was done. Which meant it had to be done by somebody the cat liked, and you told me early on how much the cat liked Alison."

"Yeah, animals are great judges of character. Bernie, were you gonna tell me all this?"

"Well—"

"Either you were or you weren't."

"Well, I wasn't sure. You seemed to be having a good time with Alison and I figured I'd let the relationship run its course before I said anything."

"I think it's run its course." She knocked back the rest of her drink and sighed philosophically. "Listen, I got my cat back," she said, "and I had a little excitement, and Alison was a big help at the Hewlett. I don't know if I could have managed the firecracker and the fire and everything without her. And I got laid, so why should I hold a grudge?"

"That's about how I felt about Andrea."

"Plus I might want to see her again."

"That's exactly how I felt about Andrea."

"Right. So I came out of it okay."

"Don't forget the reward."

"Huh?"

"From the insurance company. The $35,000. Ray's getting half of what's left after Wally takes his fee, and the rest gets cut up between you and Denise."

"Why?"

"Because you both worked for it. Denise labored like Michelangelo on the Sistine Chapel, and you risked arrest at the Hewlett, and for that you get rewarded."

"What about you, Bern?"

"I've got Appling's stamps, remember? And his wife's ruby earrings, except I don't think they're rubies. I think they're spinels. And it's funny, I almost feel bad about keeping them, but how could I put them back? If there's one thing I'm sure of it's that I'm never going to break into the Charlemagne again."

"I forgot about the stamps."

"Well, I'm going to sell them," I said, "and then we can all forget about them."

"Good idea." Her fingers drummed the tabletop. "You stole those stamps before any of this happened," she said. "Well, almost. While you were breaking into Appling's apartment, Barlow was murdering Onderdonk. That gives me a chill to think about."

"Me too, when you put it that way."

"But most of what happened came after

you took the stamps, and you didn't get anything for that part of it. You just spent a lot of money and had to post bond."

"I'll get the bond back. I'll have paid a fee to the bondsman, but that's no big deal. Wally won't charge me anything, not with all the business I threw his way. And I had a few incidental expenses, from cab rides to the icepick I planted in Jacobi's room."

"And the chloral hydrate you planted in Onderdonk's apartment."

"That wasn't chloral hydrate. That was talcum powder."

"The cop said it tasted like chloral hydrate."

"And Ray said there was a voiceprint record of Jacobi's telephone tip, and that there was blood on the icepick. This may come as a shock, Carolyn, but cops have been known to tell lies."

"It's a shock, all right. Anyway, you had expenses, and all you get is your freedom."

"So?"

"So don't you want part of the reward? Thirty-five thousand less Wally's fee'll be what? Thirty thousand?"

"Call it that. I don't know if he'll dare grab off that much, but lawyers are hard to figure."

"Thirty grand less half to Ray leaves fifteen, and if we cut that three ways it's five apiece, and that's plenty. Why don't you take a third, Bern?"

I shook my head. "I got the stamps," I said, "and *that's* plenty. And I got something else, too."

"What? A shot at Andrea and a shot at Eve DeGrasse? Big deal."

"Something else."

"What?"

"I'll give you a hint," I said. "It's all right angles and primary colors, and I'm going to hang it over my couch. I think that's the best place for it."

"Bernie!"

"I told you," I said. "The Mondrian's with its rightful owner. And who do you know who's got a better right to it?"

And I'll tell you something. It looks gorgeous there.

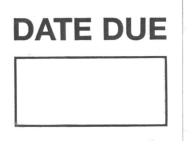

DATE DUE